better than perfect

Books by
MELISSA KANTOR

Maybe One Day

Confessions of a Not It Girl

If I Have a Wicked Stepmother,
Where's My Prince?

The Breakup Bible

Girlfriend Material

The Darlings Are Forever

The Darlings in Love

MELISSA KANTOR

better than perfect

An Imprint of HarperCollinsPublishers

HarperTeen is an imprint of HarperCollins Publishers.

Library of Congress Control Number: 2014945601
ISBN 978-0-06-227923-1 (trade bdg.)
ISBN 978-0-06-237822-4 (int. ed.)

Typography by Andrea Vandergrift
15 16 17 18 19 CG/RRDH 10 9 8 7 6 5 4 3 2 1
❖
First Edition

For Jennifer Klonsky

Tell me, what is it you plan to do
with your one wild and precious life?

—Mary Oliver, "The Summer Day"

1

"I'm going to miss you."

Jason's arms were around me so tightly I could barely breathe, but lack of oxygen wasn't the reason I didn't say anything. If I tried to talk I was definitely going to embarrass myself by bawling, so I just nodded.

He kissed the top of my head. "Don't think of it as being stuck at home. Think of it as a chance to study so you can kick my ass on the SATs."

"Sure, but will my perfect score come between us?" I asked, my cheek still pressed against his chest. Jason had scored a 2380 on his SATs, just shy of a perfect 2400. Those twenty points were a sore spot with him, and if I ever wanted to get him riled up, all I had to do was get a sad look on my face, sigh, and ask what it was like to have gotten *so close* to perfection.

"I'm man enough to handle it," he assured me.

Neither of us said anything about why I'd gotten a crap score on my June SATs, which I'd taken a week after my father broke the news to my mother that he was leaving her, just like neither of us said anything about the reason I wasn't going on a family vacation this year.

Neither of us said anything about how it's hard to go on a family vacation when you don't have a family anymore.

Since there was nothing to say, I stood on tiptoe and kissed him lightly on the lips.

"I'm going to need way more than that to get me through the next two weeks," he said. His hands on my hips were warmer than the August afternoon, and we kissed again, harder. Jason and I had been kissing since eighth grade, when he came up to me at Max Pinto's spin-the-bottle party and asked me if I'd done the English homework.

Which is how nerds fall in love.

I heard the click of the front door, and then Jason's mom called, "Okay, you two. Jason, it's time."

Given how often it happened, I probably shouldn't have gotten embarrassed whenever Jason's parents caught us kissing, but I did. In some ways I was more daring than Jason—I was the one who'd tried to get him to sneak a bottle of wine from his parents' wine fridge yesterday so we could drink it on our last night together—but when it came to PDA in front of his parents, he was the one who didn't care. I slipped out of

Jason's arms and turned to face his mom, my cheeks flushed.

"Sorry, Grace," I said as Jason wrapped his arm around me and pulled me close. We fit together perfectly. There had been about six months freshman year when I was a little taller than he was, but now he was exactly the right height for me to slide under his shoulder.

"Hey, Mom. I was just telling Juliet that you changed your mind about the international phone plan and she can text me as much as she wants."

Grace laughed and ran her fingers through her hair, which was dyed the same dirty blond that Jason's hair was naturally. "Try it and spend the rest of the year paying me back," she said. Apparently it cost a ton to do international texting, and even though the Robinsons had plenty of money, they weren't the type of parents to give Jason and his sister whatever they wanted whenever they wanted it. While he was in France, Jason and I were going to have to email, which his mom insisted was very romantic and old-fashioned.

"Remember," Grace added, "absence makes the heart grow fonder." She glanced at the thin gold watch on her wrist. "And . . . we've gotta go. We'll miss you, Juliet." After my dad moved out, Grace had asked me if I wanted her to ask my parents if I could join the Robinsons on their vacation, but I'd told her I couldn't miss the end of my internship at Children United. I'd competed against kids from all over the world to get accepted, and my English teacher who'd written my recommendation for the summer was also writing my recommendation for college. I told Grace that if he found out I'd ditched the program, he might not write my rec in the fall. My reason was a lie, but it was plausible enough that she just smiled and told me how impressed she was by my living up to my responsibilities.

Living up to your responsibilities was a big deal to Jason's mom.

I was embarrassed by how my throat got tight when she said she'd miss me, and I forced myself to give her a cheerful wave and a jaunty "bon voyage."

She waved back. Jason's mother was always beautifully dressed, and today she wore a simple but flattering red linen dress and a pair of red-and-white strappy sandals. The whole ensemble was *très Français.* "Let's go, Jason," she said again.

As soon as she shut the door, Jason put his arms around me. I leaned against him, trying not to see the next two weeks as a black hole I was getting sucked down into.

"You're gonna be okay," he said quietly.

Lost in my own thoughts, I wasn't quite listening to him, which seemed to happen to me a lot lately. "It's all so weird. Like, who am I now?"

Jason stepped away from me and took my shoulders in his hands. "J, that's crazy. You're still you."

"I don't know, J," I said. My eyes hit Jason right at his collarbone, and I didn't lift them to his face. I tried to find the words to explain what I was feeling. "You know that thing where you look at your hand and suddenly you're like, 'It's so weird that that's my hand.'"

"Stop." Jason's voice was commanding. Confident. It was his debating voice, the one that had won our team the regional championship last spring. He let go of my shoulders and lifted my chin. His dark gray eyes stared into mine as he enumerated points on his fingers. "One: you're a third-generation legacy. Two: you've got a 4.0 average. Three: you're one of ten Children United interns *in the whole world*. Four: you're going to spend every second while I'm away studying for your SATs, on which you will get a *near*-perfect score." I hip-checked him on that. "Next year, when we're at Harvard, this will all seem like a bad dream." When he said *Harvard*, he tapped me lightly on the nose. That was our plan: to get into Harvard early action.

Jason was our lead debater, but I was no slouch. I thought of countering his points one by one. *First: half the kids applying to Harvard are legacies. Second: there are thousands of applicants with 4.0 averages. Third: my internship has consisted of reading useless reports, summarizing them for no one, and sitting in on endless lectures delivered to nearly empty rooms. Fourth: every time I try to sit down and study for the SATs, the words just swim around on the page.*

But I didn't want our last few seconds together to consist of my whining. Instead, all I said was, "Hey! Don't jinx Harvard." I was superstitious about our acceptance, which was why, while he was wearing a white T-shirt that spelled out

HARVARD in red letters, I'd made him remove the Harvard bumper sticker that he'd put on my Amazon wish list.

The front door opened again, and Grace stuck her head out. "Jason! In the car! Now!"

You didn't mess with Grace when she said *Now!* like that. Jason opened his arms, and I slipped into them, hugging him back as tightly as he was hugging me, hoping some of his optimism about senior year—which was only two and a half weeks away—would enter my body by osmosis.

The jerk of the garage door rising was followed by the car honking as Mark backed the Lexus into the driveway. Isabella, Jason's little sister, rolled down her window and shouted, "Bye, Juliet! Bye! We'll miss you."

"Bye, Bella," I called back. I'd always wished I had a little sister; Jason and I had been together since Bella was six, so sometimes it felt almost like I had one.

His dad gave me a little salute. "Take care of yourself, Juliet," he said. Mark Robinson was always saying dad things. *Take care of yourself. Drive carefully. Do you kids need any money?* His saying that made me think of my own dad and how my mother said he was having a midlife crisis. My dad, on the other hand, said it was more complicated than that, that they'd both been unhappy for a long time. My older brother said I shouldn't even bother trying to figure out what was going on with them, that I had to focus on school because if my grades dropped first semester of senior year, I was screwed with colleges.

Apparently everybody understood and accepted what was going on with my family except me.

Jason gave me one last squeeze, and then he linked his pinky with mine. "J power," he said, gently squeezing.

I smiled and squeezed his pinky back. "J power," I echoed. Then he let go and headed toward the car. I stood on Jason's perfect lawn in front of Jason's perfect house and watched the car carrying his perfect family back down the driveway, and then—with Mark honking the horn good-bye—I watched it drive down the block, turn the corner, and disappear.

Pulling up into my own driveway ten minutes later, I had to admit that my house looked just as perfect as Jason's. The gardeners and the pool guy still showed up right on schedule, so it wasn't like in the movies where you know the family inside is falling apart because the grass is waist high and weeds are growing everywhere.

But as soon as I got out of the car, I could tell my mother was having a Bad Day. Exhibit A: it was a beautiful August afternoon, yet all the shades in the house were drawn. Ever since my dad had moved out, my mother had Good Days and Bad Days. On Good Days, she met friends for tennis, went for lunch, shopped. Maybe had a committee meeting.

On Bad Days, the shades stayed down. And so did she.

Bad Days were the real reason I hadn't gone to France with Jason's family.

"Mom?" I pushed open the front door. My whole life, my house had had the same smell—I'd always assumed it was some combination of my mom's perfume and this lavender-scented powder she had the housekeeper sprinkle on the rugs before she vacuumed. But now the house smelled ever so slightly different, and I'd started to wonder if what it had smelled like before hadn't been plain old happiness.

"Mom?" I called again.

I heard a faint response from the direction of my parents' bedroom. Or I guess I should say my mother's bedroom, since my dad had a new bedroom in his new apartment in Manhattan.

I walked up the stairs, passing the pale squares that lined the walls in place of the family photos that used to hang there. My mother had always been astonishingly organized. The minute there was the hint of a chill in the air, I came home to find my T-shirts replaced with sweaters, my shorts replaced with jeans, my sundresses in plastic bags at the back of my closet. So it wasn't exactly shocking that she spent the weekend after my father left removing evidence of our happy family from the walls. The surprising thing was that she hadn't already had the walls repainted and hung with replacement art.

I walked down the hallway to my mom's bedroom, my eyes on her door, forcing myself not to look at the gallery of blank squares that lined the hall. My mom's room smelled even worse than the rest of the house, as if the air in there were thicker somehow, or maybe just unhappier. The shades were pulled so low there was barely enough light to make out her shape on the bed.

"Mom?" I asked into the darkness. And then I said it again, more sharply this time. "Mom?"

There was a rustling of sheets, and one of my mother's arms stretched up over her head. "Hi, honey," she yawned.

"Mom, I thought you were getting up when I left." I tried to make my voice light, as if I were joking, not mad. Then I crossed the room, snapped up the shade, and opened the window.

"What time is it?" she asked.

I looked at her bedside clock. "Almost four."

"Sorry." She covered her mouth and yawned again. "My back was killing me, so I took a muscle relaxant. It must have really knocked me out. Have you been home long?"

Since June, I'd watched my mom—who used to know my schedule better than I did—try to fudge her way through conversations about my life. I'd first realized what she was doing when I came home after taking my SATs and she asked me how my morning had gone, clearly having no idea where I'd been. Over the summer she'd gotten cagier. She asked open-ended questions or offered up general statements that made it seem as if she was respecting my privacy when really she had no idea how I was spending my time.

"I was at Sofia's. We spent the day shooting smack and

hacking into people's bank accounts for cash."

"Ha-ha," said my mom, and then she added, "How could you be a hacker? You can't even remember the alarm code." At least she was trying to be funny. I gave her a smile. A for effort.

She shook her head and sat up against her pillows, reaching for a small bottle of pills on her bedside table. My mom had always taken medication—she had insomnia, so she sometimes took something to help her sleep. And whenever she had to do a presentation for this charity she was on the board of, she took something called a beta blocker so she wouldn't (as she put it) "sweat through my dress and then pass out." And her back bothered her sometimes, so she had a prescription for the muscle relaxant she'd apparently taken earlier.

There had been bottles of pills in her bathroom for as long as I could remember. But now her nightstand sported a veritable pharmacy: She had drugs that were supposed to help her sleep and drugs that were supposed to help her wake up. There were drugs she was supposed to take to not feel anxious and drugs she was supposed to take to not feel sad. But no matter how many pills she took, there were still days like this one, where no matter what time I came home, she was in bed.

"So where were you really?" she asked after swallowing a small blue pill.

"Mom, you know where I was. I was saying good-bye to Jason. They're leaving for France." I glanced at the clock again. They weren't even at the airport yet. I could throw some clothes in a bag, hop in my car, buy a plane ticket, and be holding Jason's hand on the runway before the sun set.

My mom rubbed her forehead. "I'm sorry, honey. I'm just so . . . fuzzy." And then she squeezed her eyes tightly as her voice broke. "I'm sorry we're not going on vacation this year." A tear slid out from between her lids, and she bit her lip. "I'm so sorry about everything."

This happened on Bad Days. On Good Days, I'd come home and my mother would be full of plans for the future: She was going to go back to work. She was going to redo the house. We were going to go on a cruise at Christmas. Some of the things she talked about doing really sounded fun, and I'd eat dinner imagining my mother returning to her job as a consultant, which she'd done before I was born, or picturing her and Oliver and me on a flight to Seattle, where we'd board a ship bound for Alaska. Other times, her ideas were tedious, like when she'd show me a dozen swatches of blue fabric and ask which one I thought would be best for the couch.

Still, anything was better than this. Bad Days just sucked.

"Mom, it's okay." I crossed over to the bed, sat down, and put my arm over her shoulders. She patted my hand and sniffled while I looked around the room. Even with the shades and the window up, it felt like a prison. I pictured Oliver, who'd stayed up at Yale for the summer and who'd texted me yesterday that he was going camping with friends for the week. I wondered if my dad had canceled the reservation we'd

de for the house in Maine that we rented every summer
if he was planning to go without us, to walk the familiar
floors of the house by himself. I imagined Jason getting out
of the car in the airport's long-term parking lot, the sound of
jet engines revving, assured he'd be thirty thousand feet up
in the air soon.

How come everyone had a get-out-of-jail-free card
except me?

I got to my feet. "Why don't I make us a salad?" I said. "I'll
put lots of fruit in the way you like it."

"I don't know if there's much in the fridge," said my mom.
She looked at me apologetically, and I noticed how much gray
there was in the roots of her hair. My parents had been a very
good-looking couple. I'm not just saying that because they're
my parents. My mom's hair was long and blond. (It had been
naturally blond when she was younger, and as she got older
and it got darker, she highlighted it.) She and my dad were in
great shape, and they both wore expensive, designer clothes.
My mom always liked it when I told her that one of my friends
had said she was well-dressed or beautiful, which happened
pretty regularly.

Right now, though, with her strangely bisected hair and
her wrinkled T-shirt and yoga pants, my mom wasn't going to
be getting compliments from my friends anytime soon. She
just looked tired. Tired and a little bit old.

"If there's nothing in the fridge, we can order." I didn't want

12

to look at her thinking about how old and tired she seemed, so I turned and went to the door. "I think you should take a shower and get dressed."

Because on Bad Days, I sounded like the mom.

"You're right, honey," she said. I heard her pull a tissue from the box on her bedside table and blow her nose. "Kathy called before."

I turned around. "Really? That's great. What'd she say?" Aunt Kathy was my mom's younger sister, and one of my favorite people in the world. She and her husband lived outside Portland, Oregon, and I guess they were what you'd call hippies. They didn't grow pot or homeschool their kids or anything, but they didn't care about stuff like money or fancy cars. Kathy taught preschool and her husband was a doctor on an Indian reservation. My mom and my grandparents had all gone to Harvard (well, my grandmother had gone to Radcliffe), but my aunt had gone to Oregon State. I sometimes wondered if she felt bad about that—whenever we were at my grandparents', there was always a *lot* of Harvard talk—but I'd never asked her.

"Well . . ." My mom furrowed her brow, then quoted her sister: "She said, 'I don't like the way you sound. I'm coming out to New York next week.'"

"Seriously? She's coming to visit?" I felt a sense of relief so intense it startled me. "That's awesome."

My mom laughed, then made a funny choking sound. She

buried her nose in her tissue, but not before I saw her face crumple.

"Mom, it's gonna be okay," I promised her. I could hear the irritation in my voice, and I wondered if she heard it too.

"I know," she squeaked. "I know, honey." She took some tissues out of the dispenser, one after the other in rapid succession, then blew her nose. "I'll be okay. Just let me shower and I'll come down."

"I'll see what we have to eat," I said. I waited to close the door behind me until she flipped the covers off her legs and got out of bed.

There was a blank rectangle on the wall immediately to the right of my parents' bedroom door; I didn't need to see the photo that had hung there to remember it. It was of my father, taken the day he and Oliver came home from their first father-son camping trip. My dad had a three-day growth of beard, and he was standing by the door of our old Subaru, a backpack in one hand, a fishing rod in the other. He looked like a man who could handle anything. He looked like a man who could *fix* anything.

I want my dad, I thought to myself. *I want my dad to fix this.*

But I knew he wasn't going to be able to. After all, his leaving was the reason everything was broken in the first place.

2

"Not like the religion," Sofia said, slapping my foot with the flash card she was holding. "Catholic *lowercase c*. We've done this one already."

"Okay, okay, okay," I said, biting my lip. Sofia was lying on her bed and I was lying on the floor with my legs hooked over the bed and basically draped across Sofia's lap. Sofia's room was tiny, which meant that when we were in it, we were always more or less on top of each other.

"You keep saying okay, but you're not saying what the definition is," Sofia said. She leaned on her elbow and looked down at me, her black curly hair tumbling over the edge of the bed. I'd always envied Sofia her hair, but she said it was more trouble than it was worth; all during swim season (and most of the off-season), she just shoved it into a ponytail.

"Patience is a virtue," I reminded her.

She rolled away onto her back. "You know what I think of when I hear stalling like that? I think of all the people who are applying to Harvard early action."

"Do I do this to you about Stanford?" Sofia was obsessed with going to California, which she believed was her spiritual home. Her mom's family was from there, so if she got in, her mom was going to move west with her, which Sofia was actually happy about. I couldn't imagine my mom moving to Cambridge with me if I got into Harvard. Of course, I couldn't imagine what was going to happen to her when I left, either.

It was one of the many, many things I tried not to think about lately.

"You are competing with *hundreds* of girls who want to go to Harvard," Sofia reminded me.

"Thank you *so* much, Sofia Taylor."

"*Thousands* of them!"

"What is your *point*?" I swung my feet off the bed and sat up, irritated.

Sofia sat up also and pointed at me with the index card. "My point is they can probably all define *catholic*. So why can't you?"

Like a bolt of lightning, the definition came to me. "Including a wide variety."

Sofia held up her palm. "High five, baby. That's the last of them."

I slapped her hand lightly, then lay back down. Sofia was also retaking the SAT, but she only wanted to get her score up by a little bit. Even though we were supposedly both studying, our study sessions had turned into her spending hours trying to drill vocabulary words into me.

"Do you want to stay for dinner?" she asked. "My mom says she misses you." Sofia's mom was a nurse on a maternity ward. She'd started working the night shift when we were sophomores because she said she got to see Sofia more if she worked from midnight to eight a.m. Usually they had dinner together before her mom went to work.

"Let me call my mom," I said. My mother and Jason's mother said they liked Sofia's mother, but sometimes I got the sense they didn't totally approve of her. She'd had Sofia on her own, and they lived in a pretty small apartment, and she worked, while both of our moms stayed home. Whenever Sofia and I had a sleepover, we almost always stayed at my house. My mom had never said I *couldn't* sleep at Sofia's. Instead, she'd say, "I think I'd prefer if you two slept here." Now she could use as an excuse the fact that Sofia's mother worked at night, but she'd "preferred" our sleeping at my house even when Sofia's mother was home.

I was a little nervous about leaving my mom alone, but staying at Sofia's for dinner wasn't exactly the same as going to France for two weeks with Jason's family. I dialed, but it went right to voice mail, and there was no answer on the home number.

17

When I'd left the house in the morning, my mom had been about to go play tennis with her friend Laura. She'd been wearing her whites and she'd seemed to be fine. But between then and now, had a Good Day become a Bad Day?

Suddenly I was mad. Why shouldn't I have a fun dinner with Sofia and her mom? Why should I have to worry about the quality of my mom's day?

I texted her. *having dinner @ sofia's. home later.* I hesitated, then added *call if u need me* before hitting send.

"Oh my God, Beth, this is amazing." In front of me was a plate with chicken and apricots, tomato salad, and corn on the cob. As I bit into the corn, I realized it was the first home-cooked meal I'd had all summer—even on Good Days my mom picked up dinner at La Scala or the Garden of Eating. The irony of my mom's judging Sofia's mother's mothering was fully revealed to me.

"It is good," agreed Beth, taking a bite herself. She was wearing her nurse's uniform: white pants and a bright pink short-sleeved top with blue teddy bears on it. Her gray hair was cut short, almost like a swim cap. Unlike my mom, Beth had never colored her hair, and she didn't seem to worry about how she looked or what she weighed or wore. She always commented on how nice my mom looked, and once Sofia had told me that her mom had said that my parents were *glamorous*. But it never seemed like Sofia's mom was jealous of how pretty my mom was or how happy my parents were. Which was probably smart given what my mom looked like lately and the way my parents' marriage had turned out.

Beth grinned, pleased with her cooking, and took a bite. "Sofia, the tomato salad is perfect."

"Thanks, Mom." Sofia made her face the picture of exaggerated puzzlement. "I wonder who taught me to make it."

"Hmmm," said Beth. Her smile widened, and she patted Sofia lightly on the cheek. "I wonder."

Sofia always used to say she was jealous of my family, but even before my parents separated, I was sometimes jealous of her. There was something so casual and easy about how she and her mom were together. My mom and I used to go out for dinner just the two of us sometimes, but it was always a Dinner. My mom would read about some new restaurant in Manhattan or near our house and she'd make a reservation and we'd get all dressed up, and once we were there, she'd order some seasonal cocktail and then she'd look around and say something like, "Here we are!" and it was like what she was really excited about was the *idea* of our being there. If Sofia's mom took us for dinner, it was usually to the Chinese restaurant in downtown Milltown, but somehow it was always more fun.

As if she could read my mind, Beth asked, "How's your mom doing?"

I didn't want to lie, but I knew my mom would be

embarrassed if Beth knew about her Bad Days. "She's been playing a lot of tennis, but her back was bothering her the other day, so she might have to slow down a little."

Beth didn't point out that she hadn't asked about my mother's tennis game. "Maybe we could have her over."

"Thanks," I said. "I know she'd appreciate that." I didn't know if she'd appreciate it, actually. My mom liked to host— she and my father were always throwing dinner parties, and when she went out with friends, she liked to pick up the check. I wondered how she'd feel about having dinner at Sofia's, if she'd be comfortable letting Beth cook for her. She'd bring an expensive bottle of wine, and she'd ask Beth if she liked it and tell her all the things she was supposed to be tasting in it—oak and cherry and undertones of, I didn't know, wheat or yeast or black beans or something. The whole thing sounded completely awful, but hopefully Beth wouldn't follow up on the invitation.

3

I ended up staying over at Sofia's. The movie we watched didn't end until after ten, and the last thing I felt like doing was driving home. I texted my mom that I wanted to stay, and to my surprise, she texted right back saying that was fine and telling me to have a good night.

Apparently, I'd been wrong about it being a Bad Day.

In the morning, Sofia and I took our practice SAT, and then we went to Bookers for coffee. While we were waiting for our lattes, my dad texted to ask how the test went, and I told him I thought I'd done better on the math section than I'd been doing, and he said that was great and he'd see me Wednesday for dinner. My parents had both been really worried when I got such bad SAT scores in June, like it had never occurred to them that their splitting up might have ramifications besides my dad's needing to inform everyone of his change of address. Suddenly my father had started calling me all the time and asking how I was feeling (which he'd never done when he was living at home and his work schedule meant we sometimes went days without seeing each other). He'd always asked about my practice SATs, though, so it wasn't like that was new. What was new was that now when he asked if they'd gone up, he'd tell me how proud he was of me and how impressed he was that I was working so hard. I think he was scared that if he didn't encourage me, I'd bomb the test and he'd have to tell all his friends how his son went to Yale and his daughter went to community college.

Sofia had to go to work at three. She was the assistant to the under–pastry chef at the Milltown Country Club. Jason and his family were members, and before we'd gotten too busy on weekends with extracurricular stuff, I'd gone a bunch of times as his guest, but I'd never played on the golf course, which overlooked the Long Island Sound and was what the club was famous for. Still, I'd always loved how you just signed for things you ordered. When I was younger, I'd begged my parents to join even though neither of them played golf and we belonged to a club with tennis courts and a pool that was closer to our house. Now that I was older and doing things like working with Children United (albeit ineffectively) for the right of girls in rural Pakistan to go to school, I wasn't so sure I'd groove on the club. Plus Sofia said that when you were an employee, you found out what a fascist state the place really was.

When I pulled into the driveway, I saw that the shades were down in my mother's bedroom. We were having another Bad Day.

"Mom!" I walked through the first floor, calling for her, but she didn't answer. I felt myself growing irritated. What had happened to the mother who made me go to school in fourth grade when Sarah Williams and Lucy Broder had kicked me out of the popular clique and I'd tried to convince my parents I was sick so I wouldn't have to face any of my now-ex-friends? *Hiding doesn't help anything,* my mom had said, snapping up my shades and getting clothes out of my drawers. *Your problems will still be there when you come out, so you might as well face them and get it over with.*

All I'd wanted was one lousy mental-health day, and she'd forced me to get dressed, eat breakfast, and go to school.

Meanwhile, here she was taking a mental-health *season.* What did she think, that if she stayed in bed long enough my father would realize he'd made a terrible mistake and move back home?

I got to the top of the stairs and flipped on the lights. When I saw that her door was closed, I got even more annoyed. My mom had a beautiful house, plenty of money. Food on the table. Two degrees from Harvard—where she'd gone as an undergraduate *and* for business school. All over the world were women who would kill to be in her position. My phone buzzed with an email. Since it was almost four o'clock in New York, I knew it was from Jason. Every night, at ten o'clock his time, right after his family went to dinner, he sent me an email. I wanted to open it immediately, but I forced myself to wait.

Reading it would be my reward for getting my mother out of bed.

"Mom!" I pushed open the door. It took a minute for my eyes to adjust to the darkness, and when they did, I saw that her bed was unmade and empty. "Mom?" I looked around the room—the door to the bathroom was closed. Could she possibly be taking a bath? My mother loved baths, which she called the greatest luxury of the civilized world. Personally, I couldn't think of anything more boring than taking a bath. Sometimes I even got bored in the shower. But if it cheered her up, who was I to complain?

"We went to Bookers, and I got cherry tomatoes at the farmers' market," I called through the bathroom door. "Sofia's mom told me how to make this awesome tomato salad I had at their house." As I talked, I straightened up my mother's night table, glad that there were fewer pill bottles there than I remembered seeing yesterday. I hated how many pills she'd been taking lately. As I crossed to the bathroom door, I picked up her robe from the floor.

"Mom?" I knocked at the door. "Does that sound good to you? Tomato salad?"

There still wasn't an answer. My mom had a radio in the bathroom, and sometimes she listened to music while she took a bath, but I couldn't hear any music playing. I knocked again. "Mom!" I shouted.

The only sound on the other side of the door was silence, and suddenly I felt uneasy. "Mom?" I snapped my knuckle against the wooden door. For no good reason, my heart started beating very fast, and I felt light-headed, as if there weren't enough oxygen in the room. "Mom!" There was still no answer, and I knocked harder, hard enough that my knuckle stung. I dropped the robe onto the floor and put my hand on the knob. To my relief, it turned easily in my hand, and as I pushed the door open, I thought of how stupid I'd been to be so scared and how my mom was probably out of the house and had left the bathroom door closed and here I'd been yelling at her and freaking myself out when she wasn't even there.

And then the door was open and I was looking at her body lying on the floor in a T-shirt and underwear, her hand and arm smeared with blood, blue pills scattered like drops of rain across the white tile floor.

4

The emergency waiting room was freezing cold. I shivered in my tank top and jean shorts, totally underdressed for the over-air-conditioned hospital. All around me, people slouched in their plastic chairs; it was impossible to tell who was really ill and who was just sick with waiting. The ambulance driver had told me to go to the desk and fill out paperwork, but I hadn't been able to answer any of the questions on the form. Even looking at the blank line under *date of birth* left me confused. March twenty-second. I wrote in the numbers: 3. 22. But what was the year? My mother was how old? She was forty-eight. Wait. She was forty-nine. No. Forty-eight. My father was forty-nine. My mother was forty-eight. So what year was she born? I tried to subtract forty-eight from the current year, but I kept losing track of the numbers. *Carry the one*, I thought to myself, and then the one would disappear and all I could see were the paramedics pumping my mother's chest and shooting her full of something and sitting in the ambulance next to her still, still body and the woman asking me who to call, who to call and me just staring at her and thinking, *No one. There's no one to call.* Because my brother was camping and was I seriously going to call my father and my mother would never forgive me if any of her friends saw her now and my grandparents were too old to be able to help. Finally I told her to call my aunt in Oregon because my aunt was someone who always knew what to do.

"Juliet Newman?" My head shot up. A woman with long, braided hair extensions was surveying the room. "Juliet Newman?"

"Here!" I shouted a little too loudly. A few heads turned in my direction, but most people were too caught up in their own troubles to worry about mine. I made my way down the aisle to the woman.

"Hello, Juliet. I'm Jordyn Phillips. I'm the social worker. I was just with your mother." She put her hand on my arm gently.

My mother was dead. That was the only reason she was holding my arm the way she was: because my mother had died. If I hadn't slept at Sofia's, my mother would be alive, but now she was dead. The floor dropped out from under me, and I could feel myself falling, falling down into the center of the earth. I stared at the woman, my mouth hanging open.

"She's resting comfortably," said Ms. Phillips.

My mother was alive. She was alive and resting comfortably. I stumbled in my relief, and Ms. Phillips gripped my arm to steady me.

"Juliet!" I snapped my head around and saw my father racing across the waiting area.

We'd talked and texted, but I'd only seen my dad once since he'd moved out. In July, I'd had a Wednesday off from Children United, and I'd met him at his office. We'd gotten sandwiches and taken them to a shady spot between two buildings with a waterfall and some benches. My dad called it a park, which seemed like a stretch. As we'd opened our sandwiches and settled onto the bench, I'd tried to remember the last time it had just been the two of us, and the only memory I could come up with was the previous summer, when he and I had done an ice run right before my parents' big Fourth of July party. Sometimes when I pictured my dad, I pictured his signature on his email.

It was a broiling day, and my sundress stuck to the backs of my legs. My dad was wearing a tie, but even though he was sweating, he didn't complain about the heat. He'd grown up without a lot of money and without a lot of the things that my brother and I took for granted, like central air conditioning and sleepaway camp and not having to have jobs after school.

It drove him crazy when we left lights on if we weren't in a room or turned the temperature in the house down to below seventy in the summer.

My dad asked about my internship and my classes for the fall, but all I really wanted to talk to him about was what was going on with him and my mom. Halfway through my sandwich, I asked him if it was true that he'd gotten tired of being married, which was what my mother said.

"Juliet," he'd said, wiping some mayo off the tip of his finger, "does that really sound like me? Do I strike you as a quitter?"

"No," I'd answered. Rather than look him in the eye, I watched him open the paper bag on his lap and push his napkin into it. "But it's not like being married is the same as working."

My dad crunched the bag into a ball. "In some ways it is, Juliet. You have to work hard to get through the bad times. But you need someone to meet you halfway."

I snapped my head up to look at him. "So you're saying it's Mom's fault? She wouldn't meet you halfway?"

"I'm not blaming your mother," he said patiently. "This is nobody's fault. I know that's hard to believe, but it's the only answer I have for you." It was what he always said when I asked him to explain what was going on, but this time I stared at him, not saying anything, a terrifying idea suddenly overwhelming me. Was there some awful secret that my parents were keeping from me?

I kept staring. Like my mother, my father was very good-looking. His hair had some gray in it, but it was still thick, unlike most of my friends' fathers'. He wore vaguely hipster glasses and, like my mother, he spent money on expensive clothes.

Had he been having an affair?

My dad was still talking. ". . . and I'm sorry, Juliet. What matters is that your mom and I both still love you and Oliver very much. We're still your parents even though we're not together anymore."

He was waiting for me to say something, but the possibility that he'd been unfaithful to my mother was too awful for me to speak it. Instead, I cleared my throat, then forced myself to joke, "Did you get that from a book or something?"

"What gave it away?" My dad grinned at me and reached over to tousle my hair. "Come on. If we walk a couple of blocks, we can get an ice cream cone for less than four dollars."

At the end of lunch, my dad had promised we'd see a lot of each other, more than we had when he was living at the house. We'd agreed to have dinner once a week—either he'd come out to Long Island or I'd stay in Manhattan and meet him after work.

The first week, he'd canceled because of a work dinner. The second week, he'd had to be out of town until Wednesday night, and he'd asked if I could do Thursday, but I'd said I had my SAT tutor. The third week, the same thing had happened, except he'd asked if we could do Tuesday night.

"I. Have. My. SAT. Tutor," I'd said, slowly and carefully, like maybe he wasn't a native English speaker.

"I know you have an SAT tutor. I'm sorry, but I thought it was Thursday night, not Tuesday night. Last week it was Thursday. So shoot me."

"No, Dad. Last week it was Tuesday *and* Thursday. And the week before that. And the week before that. In fact, I've been meeting my SAT tutor Tuesday and Thursday nights for the past *six months*. So shoot *me*. Or, wait. You're probably too busy to do that, either."

He ignored my sarcasm. "What about Saturday night?"

"Dad, I want to see my *friends* on Saturday night. It's the one night everyone doesn't have to be home early."

We'd agreed to have dinner this coming Wednesday. But now, here he was.

As soon as my dad was next to me, he reached for my hand. Unlike my mom, my dad didn't look physically different from how he'd looked before. His hair was the same, and he was wearing a blue shirt and a pair of khakis. He'd probably been at work. He and my mom had sometimes fought about how much he worked. "Are you all right?" he asked.

"Seriously?" I asked, pulling my hand from his.

"I'm sorry." He shook his head. "I meant . . . well, you know what I meant."

I didn't, actually, but before I could ask him, the social

worker extended her hand and said, "I'm Jordyn Phillips." I wasn't sure if she was intentionally interrupting my father and me or if she hadn't picked up on the tension between us.

He shook her hand. "My sister-in-law called me and said my wife is here."

My father used to refer to my mother as his wife all the time. *I believe my wife made a reservation. . . . I'm looking for my wife. . . . Have you met my wife?* But now his saying my mother was his wife felt dishonest, even though I knew that technically they were still married.

I said nothing about their separation, not even when Ms. Phillips said, "Mr. Newman, your wife is resting comfortably. Why don't we go somewhere we can talk in private?" I followed my dad and Ms. Phillips out of the waiting area and down a hallway lit with bright fluorescent lights.

We hadn't gone very far when she opened a gray door. Inside was a small room with a table and two plastic yellow chairs. The room was even more depressing than the waiting room. Were all hospitals so relentlessly awful?

My father didn't sit down, so neither did I. Ms. Phillips also stood.

"Mr. Newman, your wife may have made a suicide attempt."

Even though I was the one who'd found her, even though it wasn't like I'd thought she'd just lain down on the floor to have a nap, I made a funny noise with the back of my throat when

Ms. Phillips said that. She and my father turned to look at me.

"Honey, maybe you should wait outside," said my dad. His voice was soft, concerned, and I didn't know what to do with that. By way of answering him, I just shook my head. Once again, he reached for my hand, and this time I let him take it.

Ms. Phillips opened a folder she'd been carrying and started talking, glancing at it as she spoke. "Your daughter found your wife unconscious on the floor of her bathroom at approximately four o'clock this afternoon. There were several bottles of pills on her night table and in the bathroom with her. Given the dates the prescriptions were filled, it's difficult to know how many pills she actually took today. Because she had Ambien and Valium in her possession, both of which suppress respiration and which, taken in excess, can be fatal, we pumped her stomach and gave her a dose of ipecac, which is an emetic."

"What about the blood?" I asked.

My father turned to me. "What? What blood?"

She checked the folder again, then looked up at me. "There is no evidence that your mother had any self-inflicted wounds, though the bottom of one of her feet had a fairly deep cut on it that looked as if it might have been the result of her stepping on a piece of glass. The paramedics said there was water and a broken glass on the floor of the bathroom."

Even in the midst of my confusion, I felt a wave of relief so powerful my knees buckled. "So you're saying she *didn't* try to kill herself?"

But Ms. Phillips was looking at my father. "Do you know anything about your wife's medication? We're trying to figure out if she might have accidentally taken more than she was prescribed or if this was an intentional overdose."

"I'm not living at home right now," said my father. Ms. Phillips nodded and made a note on her paper. "But she has sometimes . . . abused prescription medication in the past. And she's not always careful about mixing drugs and alcohol."

"*What?* That's not true." I turned to Ms. Phillips. "It's not true," I said again.

"Juliet," said my father firmly, "I'm sorry, but it *is* true."

I kept talking to Ms. Phillips. "She's been depressed off and on all summer because my father *left*." I spoke quickly, as if I might not have the chance to finish before my father cut me off.

"I see," said Ms. Phillips, and when she wrote something down, I felt like I'd convinced her to believe me and not my dad.

"Juliet, you are mixing apples and oranges," said my father. "I'm sorry. I want to respect your mother's privacy, but this is something the people who are treating her have to know."

I stared at my father, seething, as Ms. Phillips finished writing. Then she flipped the folder closed. "The attending psychiatrist has suggested your wife be admitted to the hospital's psychiatric unit so we can evaluate her. He'll be out to speak to you soon, but I'd like to get us started on the paperwork so we can transfer her as soon as she's ready. If you could come with me, I'll get the insurance information I need." She nodded toward the door.

My father rubbed the side of his face as if he had a headache, then realized Ms. Phillips couldn't get past him. "Sorry," he said, and he opened the door and held it politely for Ms. Phillips and me to pass through.

In the hallway, Ms. Phillips started to head back the way we had come, but I said, "Wait." She turned around.

"I want to see her."

My father and Ms. Phillips were both looking at me. My father spoke first. "Juliet, I'm not sure that's such a good idea."

I kept my eyes on Ms. Phillips. I knew if I looked at my dad, I'd lose my courage. "I want to see her."

"I understand," said Ms. Phillips. She put her hand on my arm again, and I had the crazy urge to ask if she would let me go home with her.

I followed Ms. Phillips back into the waiting area, through an enormous set of double doors, and down a wide corridor. There were empty stretchers and gurneys up against the walls, and I wondered if one of them was the one my mom had come in on.

I'd assumed Ms. Phillips was taking me to a hospital room,

but she led me through another, smaller set of double doors, which opened up onto a space bigger than the waiting room. There was a central island with doctors and nurses in it, and all around the outer wall were beds, some of which were curtained off. A symphony of rhythmic beeps filled the space. An older man was on a bed directly in front of me with two elderly women, one on either side of him. One of the women was crying; the other was rocking slightly. I wondered what was wrong with him, and then one of the women turned slightly and saw me watching them. I looked away, embarrassed to have been caught spying.

Ms. Phillips led me around to the right of the island. When we got to an area where the curtains were closed, she stopped walking.

"She's in here," said Ms. Phillips. "Why don't I come in with you?"

It wasn't until she offered to stay with me that I realized how scared I was to see my mother alone, which was almost worse than anything else that had happened that day.

"She'll probably be asleep," said Ms. Phillips. "But if she isn't, we'll just stay a minute and then come on out. Her throat's probably sore from when they pumped her stomach, so it will be hard for her to talk."

I stepped through the curtain behind Ms. Phillips, picturing as I did what it meant to pump somebody's stomach. My own stomach clenched in sympathy.

My mother was lying on the bed, propped up slightly on two pillows. They must have taken off her T-shirt, because she was in a hospital gown under some blankets. There was a hairnet over her hair, but a few strands had come out, and they were spread out over the pillow like my mom had put her finger in an electrical outlet. She was asleep, and I watched her chest rise up and down slowly. By the fourth breath I realized I was breathing with her, almost as if she couldn't do it on her own.

Almost as if I was afraid she didn't want to do it on her own.

I wasn't sure how much time had passed when Ms. Phillips put her hand on my shoulder. "We should go, honey."

I nodded, my throat too thick to try to talk. My mom's arms lay along her sides, and on the wrist nearest me I saw a hospital bracelet and a ring of dark blue fabric, almost like a ribbon but thicker and closed with what looked like Velcro. I looked at the other wrist, and there was one there also.

"What are those?" I asked, pointing at the blue fabric and clearing my throat. But even before Ms. Phillips answered me, I knew exactly what they were. They were restraints. My mother was literally tied to her bed.

Ms. Phillips put her hand on mine and gave it a little squeeze. "Those are so she won't hurt herself, honey."

"Are they . . ." I took a breath, but taking deep breaths wasn't enough to stop myself from crying anymore. "Are they going to leave them on?" I imagined what it would be like to wake up and find your hands tied to the bed, attempting to jerk them free and finding they were too tightly bound for you to get out of them. I imagined my mother screaming for someone to come get her, how with her wild hair and tied-up wrists she'd seem crazy to whoever answered her call.

But of course maybe she was crazy. That was the whole reason she was lying here in the first place.

"We should go," Ms. Phillips said again, and this time I let her lead me out of the curtained area, back through the big room, and down the hall. It was a relief to have her guide my steps. I didn't know where I was going, and I was crying too hard to see even if I did.

Ms. Phillips waited while I washed my face in the bathroom, then walked me through the second set of double doors. She pointed out my dad, who was at the opposite end of the room talking through a wall of Plexiglas to the man at the desk. I wanted to give Ms. Phillips a hug, but she reached out her hand, and so I shook it.

"Good luck, Juliet," she said. "I know this is very hard. But we'll figure out exactly what happened, and then your mom's going to get whatever help she needs." I thanked her, said good-bye, and headed over to my dad.

He was giving the man all of the information I'd been unable to provide, and I stood a few feet away from him and listened while he talked. My mom's date of birth. Her social security number. Her primary care physician.

What else did my father know about my mother that I didn't?

When he'd finished, he came to where I was standing. "Hi," he said. He looked tired. Maybe not as tired as my mother, but way more tired than he had an hour ago.

"Why did you say that stuff about Mom?" I asked, my arms folded across my chest.

"Juliet, I know there are things we need to talk about, but"—he glanced around the crowded emergency room—"this might not be the best place to have this discussion."

"I'd say it's the perfect place!"

"Please don't make a scene, Juliet."

I'd already opened my mouth to say something, but when my dad said that, I shut it. Both of my parents hated scenes of any kind. If we were out in public and my brother or I started complaining about something or making a fuss, one of them would say, *You're making a scene*, and we were pretty much guaranteed to keep quiet.

My father put his hand on my shoulder. "I want you to come home with me," he said.

I stared at him. "Do you mean my home or your home?"

He looked surprised, like he'd just assumed I'd know what he meant but also like now that I'd asked, he really wasn't sure. "Well, why don't we go back to the house? I mean back to your"—he stumbled over the word, but only slightly—"house. And tomorrow, once we know more, you can come with me to Manhattan. And we can take it from there."

I shook my head.

"Juliet."

I was still shaking my head, faster now and more violently. "No," I said.

"Juliet, I know this has been a horrible ordeal. But we need to be practical."

"Mom wouldn't want you staying in the house," I said, which seemed as practical as anything I might say.

"She won't know I stayed there."

"I'm not lying to her," I said, and then I started to cry. "Why did you *say* that about her?" I put my hand over my eyes.

He put his other hand on my other shoulder. "Sweetheart."

"Stop *touching* me," I snapped, and I jerked away from him. A few heads turned our way.

His hands hung in the air briefly before he dropped them to his sides. "You've had a terrible day. I know that. And I'm sorry we haven't had a chance to talk about . . . everything. It's my fault. I know that. But right now I am trying to think of what's best for you." He kept his voice calm the whole time he was talking.

I'd always liked having a handsome father, but tonight his edgy glasses and crisp, perfectly fitted oxford just irritated me.

"I'm not going with you, Dad," I said, still shaking my head.

Snot and tears were dripping down my face, but I didn't care. "I'm not." I took a step away from him and toward the exit.

"Juliet, we need to talk."

"I can't talk to you," I said, walking backward toward the exit. "I'm going to Sofia's." I turned around and started walking faster.

"Juliet!" he called.

He didn't run after me, though. I'd known he wouldn't.

It would have meant making a scene.

5

Standing in the parking lot, amazed that so much had happened and yet it was still light out, I realized I didn't have my car. It reminded me of being an underclassman, when Sofia and I would go to Roosevelt Field Mall or the Miracle Mile and then have to call one of our mothers to come get us. Well, it wasn't like my mother could come get me now. I crossed the street and walked into a pub with MCMANUS'S written across the front in loopy green neon. Inside, everything was either dark wood or green. It was the kind of bar Sofia and I had discovered we could usually get served in even without fake IDs. Standing next to the hostess's podium, I couldn't imagine how walking into a bar, ordering a glass of wine, and getting it handed to me had ever made me happy and giggly or how it ever would again.

I was seventeen years old and my mother might have just tried to kill herself. How would *anything* ever make me happy again?

The hostess asked if she could help me in a way that made me think she'd asked more than once. I snapped to attention and asked if she had the number of a cab company.

"Island Taxi's right around the corner, hon. You're probably better off just going over there rather than calling." I must have looked like a crazy person, because she offered to get somebody to take me, but I thanked her and said I was okay. She didn't seem convinced, and she watched me as I headed to the door. I thought maybe there was blood on my tank top, but when I got onto the sidewalk and checked, I didn't see any.

The cab dropped me off in front of my house. I paid the man and got out, then stood on the lawn trying to force myself to go inside. I was usually pretty self-disciplined—in swim meets, if the stakes were high enough, I could push myself past the point where my lungs felt like they were going to explode, and even though public speaking terrified me, I was one of the best debaters on the team. But standing on my front lawn, which was damp from the early evening sprinkling it automatically got every other day, I knew there was no way I could take my key out of my bag, put it in the front door of my house, and walk through it.

Because what was I supposed to do once I got inside my house—clean my mother's blood off the bathroom floor?

I took my phone out of my bag even though I wasn't thinking about calling anyone. Jason's email was still unopened. I'd gotten it only a few hours earlier, but thinking back to that moment in my hallway when I'd decided to open it after waking my mom was like remembering something that had happened to someone else. Still, I automatically clicked on it and started reading.

> J, I love you and miss you more than I can say. But right now I am digesting an unbelievable meal and I have to admit that it is making the pain of your absence easier to bear . . .

I hit reply without bothering to finish reading what he wrote.

> Dear Jason, I have something very bad to tell you. Last night or early this morning, my mother might have tried to . . .

But then I stopped typing. Had she or hadn't she? I deleted *might have tried to* and instead wrote *swallowed some pills*. The words looked bizarre. And anyway, my mother had been swallowing some pills all summer. What she'd done last night was swallow too many pills. But how many? One too many? Two

44

too many? A bottle too many?

And how was I supposed to put what I'd just seen in an email anyway? I tried to imagine Jason, his stomach full of some insanely delectable meal, sitting on the terrace at the villa the Robinsons had rented and getting an email from me in which I said my mother might or might not have tried to kill herself. There was just no way. I had to call him.

But he didn't have service on his cell phone in Europe. Neither did Grace. Mark had service on his work cell phone, but I didn't have that number. My mom's phone might have it, though. I reached into my bag for my keys, but once I had them in my hand, I couldn't bring myself to put them in the front door. Opening the door would mean going into the house. Going into the house would mean going upstairs to get my mother's phone. Getting my mother's phone would mean going into her room and seeing . . . everything.

And anyway, Jason had been sitting on the terrace after dinner hours ago. By now his family was sound asleep. You didn't call people up in the middle of the night in the middle of their vacation and tell them your mother had taken too many pills. You just didn't *do* something like that.

I put the keys back in my bag and walked across the lawn to the driveway and got into my car. I put my hands on the steering wheel and turned it gently from side to side, like I used to do when I was a little kid and my parents would let me pretend to drive. I wanted to be someplace—anyplace—that wasn't my house, and I turned the ignition and backed out of the driveway, not even sure where I was going, just desperate to keep moving.

Deciding to find Sofia at the club happened when I'd already been driving in the opposite direction for almost twenty minutes. There was nobody behind me and nobody coming toward me, so I made an illegal U-turn so sharp my tires squealed in protest and headed toward the Milltown Country Club.

It was hot in the car, so I rolled the windows up and put the air conditioner on, but that only increased the sensation I had of being trapped, so I lowered the windows and left the air conditioner on. I cranked the volume up on the radio, but I couldn't find a song I could stand listening to, and I turned the music off. Then it was too quiet in the car, and I turned it back on and plugged my phone in, glancing down at the screen and searching for something to listen to, then looking back up at the road, then back at my phone. I was skimming through a bunch of random titles when I flew past the sign for the Milltown Country Club. Keeping one hand on my phone, I made a hard left into the driveway.

I didn't see the driver of the van that had been coming from the opposite direction and that was *also* making a turn into the Milltown Country Club's driveway. There was the sound of honking and of rubber screaming against pavement as he spun his van far over to the side of the driveway, narrowly missing one of the enormous oak trees that lined the drive. My stomach hit my throat as I slammed on my brakes and braced my arms against the steering wheel. But instead of the crunch of glass and metal, there was only the sound of a guy cursing his brains out.

I leaped out of my car. "I'm so sorry," I said. My voice and my hands were shaking. "That was all my fault. I'm really sorry."

"*Jesus*, woman!" said the driver. He had his head against the back of the seat, so I couldn't see him until I got up to the side of the van and put my head near the window. He was a little older than I was—maybe in college. He was also odd looking; it was almost as if his face was made up of different people's faces—nose from one person, lips from another. His eyes were very blue.

"I'm really sorry," I said again, squinting into the dark van. "I wasn't paying attention."

"Clearly," he said.

"Are you okay?" asked a girl from the passenger seat in lightly accented British English. Like the driver, she had bright blue eyes and black hair, but where he was weird looking and bloated, she was beautiful, her blunt-cut bob accenting sharp cheekbones and a delicate chin.

"I'm okay," I said, because it wasn't like I was going to tell a complete stranger that almost killing myself and two other people was hardly the worst thing that had happened to me all day. "Are *you* okay?" I asked her. "I'm really sorry."

"You've got to stop saying that," said the driver. "It's getting on my nerves."

"For Christ's sake, Sean, she's trying to be polite," said a male voice from inside the van. It had an accent like the girl's. Hearing another person in the van revealed the magnitude of the accident I'd almost just had. That was *three people* I'd come close to killing. My legs started to shake.

"Are you sure you're all right?" asked the girl. "You look a little done in."

The side door of the van opened, and a boy got out. He must have been in eighth or ninth grade, and he was holding an electric guitar.

"Hi," he said. "You okay?" He had the same eyes as the driver and the passenger, and the same black hair. I'd nearly taken out an entire family with my shitty driving.

"I'm okay," I said. "And again . . . I'm really sorry. And I'm sorry for saying sorry!" I added before the guy in the driver's seat could object.

I went back to my car. It was lucky no one had tried to enter the club driveway in the past five minutes, since I was stopped directly in the middle of it. There were black skid marks leading up to where I'd stopped and more leading to the van's tires. Just looking at how close they came before veering apart made my stomach rise up.

"Drive carefully, would you?" the driver called out to me, and even though it was a harsh thing to say and he said it harshly, there was something in his voice that might have been concern. He watched me get into my car before pulling back

48

onto the driveway ahead of my car.

Sitting in the driver's seat, I could feel my whole body twitching. I would gladly have curled up in a little ball in the backseat and lain there, shaking uncontrollably, until Sofia got off work and drove me home. But I was parked in the middle of the road. And Sofia didn't even know I was coming to see her. She didn't know anything.

At the thought of what I had to tell her, I started shaking harder.

I wasn't the kind of person who sat in her car shaking too hard to drive it, and the fact that that was exactly what I was doing started to make me angry. "Get ahold of yourself, Juliet." I said it firmly, the way my mom had talked to me when I'd wanted to stay in bed all day. "Get. It. Together. Now."

A few yards up the driveway, the van stopped, and I had the terrible feeling they'd discovered that something was wrong with their car after all. I gripped my hands into fists and tried to get control of my shaking. "Stop it now, Juliet. This is no big deal. If there's some kind of problem, all you need is your license and registration." The sound of my own voice made me feel better. I leaned forward to get the registration out of the glove compartment just as I heard the door of the van slide open. When I sat up, I saw that a guy in a white T-shirt and cargo shorts was jogging toward me. I wondered how many more people were in the van. It was turning out to be some kind of fucking clown car.

The guy bent down and put his head through the passenger-side window of my car. Sofia complained that because I had Jason, I never noticed how hot other guys were, but this guy was objectively hot. He had the same blue eyes as the other people in the van and the same black hair. His shoulders were broad under his T-shirt. If Sofia had been sitting next to me, she would have texted me *He's hawt.*

He gave me a slightly nervous smile. "My sister thought you might need a hand driving." Like the girl and the younger boy, he had a British accent. "She said she's always shaken up after a near miss like that. Which should tell you something about her driving. Do you want me to drive you up to the parking lot?"

"No, I'm fine," I said. My voice was clipped; I sounded like my mom when she talked to a pushy waiter.

Neither of us said anything for a minute. All you could hear was the quiet, except for a sound almost like a moth hitting a screen. When I turned to face the front of the car, I saw that my hand, which was holding the car registration, was shaking so much that the card was flapping against the steering wheel. I could tell that the boy was seeing it also.

"It's no trouble for me to drive you," he said finally.

"Yeah," I said after another long pause during which I studied the black skid marks on the asphalt. "Maybe that wouldn't be such a bad idea."

My legs were rubbery, so rubbery I wondered if I could

stand up, so I slid over to the passenger seat. The guy waited until I was settled, then walked around the car, opened the door, and got in. He slid the seat back, closed the door, and started the car up the hill. Neither of us said a word.

"I'm Declan, by the way."

"I'm Juliet," I said. I looked out the window. As we crested the hill, the two rows of trees ended and a wide lawn opened up in front of us, topped by the enormous clubhouse. A green-and-white awning swayed gently over the wide porch. There was the tinkle of piano music that I knew was coming from the lounge just on the other side of the veranda. Politics aside, there was something comforting about being at the Milltown Country Club, and I wanted to wrap it around me like a cashmere sweater.

In front of us, the van wound around to the side of the building, a route I'd never taken before. The guy driving my car—I'd forgotten his name already—followed it for a few yards, then suddenly slammed the brakes. I jerked forward. "Sorry," he said. "We're the band for tonight, so I was going to the service entrance. But there must be a members' parking lot."

"No, I'm not a member," I said. I purposely didn't add *but my boyfriend is.* When Jason and I started going out, I referred to him as my boyfriend about every five seconds. But freshman year, another couple in our group of friends got together, and I had to listen to Bethany say *my boyfriend* ten thousand times a day. Ever since then, I tried never to say those words. "I'm going to see my friend," I explained. "She works here. So, I mean, the service entrance is fine."

"Great," he said, driving again. "Maybe you and your friend will come to the show."

I shook my head. "I don't think so." I was going to tell Sofia what had happened and then . . . well, I didn't know what then. But I certainly wasn't going to sit through a concert.

The driveway ran between two rows of hedges along the lowest level of the back of the building, a part of the club I'd never seen. I was rubbing my hands against my thighs as if they were sweaty, which they weren't, and I imagined that the guy was glancing my way and wondering how he'd gotten stuck driving a mentally unstable girl the five hundred yards she was too shaky to drive. When the driveway opened up into the parking lot, he swung my car into a spot next to the van.

"Here you go," he said, turning off the car and handing me my keys.

I took the keys from him, opened the door, and headed for the building, relieved that my legs were holding me up. I'd walked a few feet from the car before I realized I hadn't even thanked him for the ride.

He was just closing the door of my car behind him when I got back. "Thanks," I said, embarrassed by my rudeness.

"No problem," he said, and he seemed to mean it.

"I really appreciate your driving me," I added.

"It's no big deal," he said.

There was a loud bang from the far side of the van, and the girl from the passenger seat said to someone I couldn't see, "Do you have to be such a complete wanker?" In reply, a voice I was sure was the driver's answered, "Blow me." Both of them sounded pretty annoyed, but my driver didn't bother investigating.

"Look, I don't know you, but are you sure you're okay?" he asked.

"I'm fine," I said. Immediately, to my complete and utter humiliation, my eyes started to well up.

He took a step toward me. "Jesus," he whispered. He patted the pockets of his cargo shorts, and on the third try extracted a couple of napkins. "They're clean," he assured me, pressing them into my hand.

"I'm really . . ." I blew my nose. "I'm really okay." Since I was still crying, I probably wasn't making the most convincing case for my okayness.

"Can I help you find your friend?" he asked.

I balled up the napkins and stuffed them in my pocket. "I'm just . . . I've had a really hard day. I'm sorry that . . . I'm really okay."

He studied my face, not rudely but curiously. "Well, okay then," he said finally. "I hope everything's . . . okay for you."

"Yeah," I said again. "Thanks." I suddenly remembered his name. "Thanks, Declan."

He gave me a two-fingered salute. "Anytime."

Feeling like a total ass for losing it in front of Declan, I headed toward the main house, which rose up over the parking lot like a mountain. There was a sign above the glass-and-wooden door I'd been walking toward that read EMPLOYEES ONLY. I opened it and went inside, where I found myself in a long, low-ceilinged corridor lit by fluorescent lights. It was nothing like the wide, carpeted hallways with their rococo moldings and wall sconces holding faux candles that I knew from upstairs at the club. I passed metal carts piled high with dirty coffee cups, used plates, and crumpled napkins, following the sound of loudly banging pots and pans, and then, pushing through another glass-and-wooden door, I found myself in the enormous kitchen.

There were at least a dozen people running around, all wearing hairnets and black aprons with elaborate white script *M*s on them. At first I didn't think Sofia was there, but then I spotted her over in a relatively quiet corner, standing in front of an enormous tray of pastry puffs that she was methodically filling with cream from a pastry bag.

I crossed the kitchen, half expecting someone to stop me, but everyone was too intent on whatever they were doing to care about who I was. Sofia jumped and spun around when I tapped her on the shoulder.

"Juliet!" She popped out one of her earbuds. "What are you doing here?"

Having started bawling when Declan asked me if I was okay, I was surprised that I delivered my news to Sofia without a single tear.

"My mom's in the hospital," I said. "She . . . she swallowed some pills."

"Oh my God," Sofia whispered. She put down the bag of cream she'd been holding and wrapped her arms around me.

I hugged her back for a long minute, then stepped away. "I'm okay," I said, even though she hadn't asked. Suddenly I didn't want sympathy and I didn't want to be hugged. "They're not sure what happened. They won't know until . . . I don't know when, actually." As I realized I had no idea how they were going to figure out what had happened with my mom, I gave a weird laugh, almost like a bark. Were they just going to ask her? *Mrs. Newman, you were found passed out on the floor of your bathroom. Did you mean to take too many pills, or was it an accident?*

Sofia watched me with an odd look on her face, waiting for me to explain, but all I said was, "I just . . . I don't want to go home."

"No, of course not." She started to untie her apron. "We'll go to my house."

"Let's go, Taylor," said a thin guy with a beard carrying another tray of cream puffs. "This is no time to socialize."

"Frank, I have to go," said Sofia, pulling off her hairnet. "I have an emergency."

"You're not going anywhere, Taylor," said the guy, carefully placing the tray down. "We've got two hundred people for dinner. Two seatings. You're here until midnight."

He sounded harsh, but it didn't seem to frighten Sofia. "Frank, I'm serious. I have to go."

Frank pushed the tray of pastry shells farther back on the table and turned to face us. Now I could see why she wasn't scared of him. He was a big guy and he had a beard, but he probably wasn't much older than we were.

"Look, Taylor, I want to help you and, you know"—he glanced at me—"your friend. But I can't let you go. Seriously. Mitch will have my ass."

"Frank—" Sofia started.

But I interrupted her. "Sofia, it's okay. Really. I'll just . . . I'll wait for you."

"Juliet, that's like"—she checked a clock on the wall—"five hours."

"It's fine," I said.

"Do you want to go home and wait for me? I'll give you my keys. My mom will be there." She turned to get her bag.

"No!" I grabbed her arm, my voice sharper than I'd meant it to be. I didn't want to sit with Sofia's mother. Suddenly, all I wanted was to be by myself.

"Juliet, what are you going to do until midnight?" she asked, so anxious I almost thought *she* was about to start crying.

Sofia's being upset only made me more calm. "I'll be fine."

"Do you want to just stay here? They'll never notice you. There's like a thousand members here tonight. You could say you're a guest of the Robinsons."

"Taylor," snapped Frank, "we've got to get this tray finished. Let's go."

Sofia ignored him. "Seriously. Just stay here."

"Sure," I said, but I couldn't really imagine saying I was a guest of Jason's family when I wasn't. Grace and Mark weren't chill about things like that. If I called and told them where I was, they'd probably let me have whatever I wanted. But they wouldn't like it if I started signing their names for stuff without asking.

"Just go to the library and take a book or something, okay? I'll call you as soon as I can." She hugged me again. "It's going to be okay," she whispered in my ear.

I hugged her back, then recrossed the kitchen, walked back down the long, empty corridor, and stepped outside into the sticky summer evening. Even though my phone was in my pocket, I'd missed three calls, one from my aunt Kathy and two from my dad. They'd both texted me, too. My aunt's text said she was taking the red-eye and she'd be at my house in the morning. My dad had just written: *Where are you?*

I didn't want to text my dad back. Why should I have to tell him where I was? He was a smart guy; let him figure it out himself.

I texted my aunt and told her I'd meet her at the house. Then I looked up at the darkening sky. I pictured Jason asleep in the villa his parents had rented, pictured waking him up to tell him about my mom. He'd be shocked, like Sofia had been. And then he'd say, just like she had, *It's going to be okay, J. Everything's going to be okay.*

But was it? How could everything be okay after what had happened?

There was a garbage can right next to me, and I had the crazy fantasy of tossing my phone into it so I wouldn't have to deal with any more calls or texts from people. After that, I could just get in my car and drive away. I'd find a job in a diner somewhere, waiting tables. I'd been planning on applying early to Harvard. Surely I could get a job waitressing.

I stood there, holding my phone and looking at the garbage can for a while, and then I chickened out. If I ran away, they'd find me. And once they found me, I'd have to come back. And when I came back, everyone would know I was the crazy girl who'd run away to work at a diner.

Instead of running away from home, I texted my dad. I told him I was okay. I told him I was with Sofia. I told him I would meet Kathy at the house in the morning. I asked him to stop texting me.

Because I was a good girl. And good girls didn't throw away their phones or leave home or make their parents worry about them for no reason.

. . .

I'd left my bag in the car, and now that I had several hours to kill, I headed back to retrieve it. When I got to my car, Declan, the girl from the passenger seat, the guy who'd been driving, and the kid who'd gotten out of the van earlier were talking to an older guy in a blue button-down and a pair of khakis. He was writing something on a clipboard, and as I approached, he ripped off a piece of paper and handed it to the girl.

"Display that prominently on your dashboard so security can see it," he said, and she nodded.

"What's with this one?" he asked, gesturing at my car with his elbow.

The girl opened her mouth to respond, but before she could say she had no idea whose car it was, I said, "That's mine." My voice had an edge to it.

The man swung around in my direction. He was simultaneously pale and sunburned, like an egg someone had roasted. "And who exactly are you?"

In an instant, it was clear that the man embodied the Milltown Country Club fascist state Sofia had spoken of.

"I'm Juliet," I said.

"Should this mean something to me?" he asked, sarcastically. He held his clipboard out to me. "If I look, will I find your name on this list? Or should I be asking you to leave now?"

My desire to tell him to go fuck himself was kept under control by the fact that if he asked me to leave, I'd have no place to go. I glared at him, furious and scared and silent.

It was Declan who answered him. "She's with us."

The girl, the driver, and the other boy turned to Declan, but none of them said anything to contradict him.

"She's with you?" asked the roasted-egg man, his voice dripping doubt as he looked from the four black-haired, blue-eyed people who'd gotten out of the aging van to me, blond and brown-eyed and standing in front of my spanking new Honda, my parents' birthday gift to me just four months ago.

"Tambourine," said Declan. He shook the tambourine I hadn't seen he was holding.

A car drove into the parking lot and pulled into a spot all the way at the other end. I could almost smell the egg man's desire to go and bully the new arrival vying with his desire to stay here and bully us. The sound of the other car's door slamming shut decided him. He glanced at my license plate, jotted something down on the piece of paper on his clipboard, tore it off, and handed it to me.

"Place this prominently on your dashboard."

I took the paper from him and nodded.

He glared at us. "And don't let me catch any of you wandering around the grounds, or I'll throw the whole bunch of you out. This is a private club, and you're here to perform, not enjoy yourselves." With that, he turned and marched across the lot calling, "Hey! Hey!" to the guy who'd just parked and was heading toward the kitchen carrying a large green box.

"Care to tell us what this is all about?" asked the driver, turning to Declan.

"Nothing," said Declan. "It's fine."

"It's *fine?*" repeated the driver, sounding as sarcastic as the egg man.

"Oh, Sean, don't be an arse," said the girl. She came over to me. Fine boned and pale, she was even prettier up close. She might have been the most beautiful girl I'd ever seen in real life. "I'm Sinead. This is my cousin Sean. And this is my little brother, Danny." She pointed at the boy next to her, and he gave me a shy wave. I gave him a wave back. "And I guess you already know my brother Declan."

"Hi," I said. "I'm Juliet."

"Hi," said Declan. "Again."

"Thanks," I said. "Again." I gave him a nervous smile.

"No problem," he said, and his face stayed serious.

"Well, this is just fucking great," said Sean, slapping his thigh in frustration. "What are we supposed to do with her?"

"I really appreciate your helping me with that guy," I said. "But I won't bother you anymore. Seriously." I backed away from the van. "See? You won't have to deal with me for the rest of the night. I'm outta here."

But as I turned to go, Sean called out, "Oh no you don't!" His voice was authoritative. I turned back around. "If Mr. Stick Up the Ass finds you on the grounds, he's going to toss all of us out," Sean reminded me. "And I for one don't want to lose a gig I worked very hard to get."

Sinead snorted.

"That's enough out of you, missy," said Sean to Sinead.

"I'm sorry," I said. I said it to Sean, but I meant it for all of them. "I really don't know how I ended up being your problem. I'm just waiting for my friend to finish working." I could hear my voice shaking slightly, but I hoped anyone who didn't know me pretty well wouldn't notice.

I saw Sinead and Declan exchange a look, and then she said, "Are you kidding? You know what a relief it is to get a break from all this testosterone? Not that you have that much, Sean," she added quickly.

"I'm surrounded by comedians," said Sean, walking around the van. From the far side of it, he yelled, "All right, then, you're going to be pulling your weight if you're sticking with us, *Jules*." He hit the nickname hard, like he knew nobody called me that and he was daring me to tell him not to.

I didn't give him the satisfaction of correcting him; I just let Sinead guide me around the van, where I stood with her while Sean kept calling me Jules as he loaded me up with cords and told me to follow Danny up the hill to the stage.

By the time we'd set up all the equipment, I was dripping sweat and my arms and legs ached. I couldn't believe how much work it was to set up for a concert. We'd dragged mics and mic stands and amps and guitars and a drum set up the hill from the parking lot for what felt like hours. But when I checked my phone, it was only eight fifteen. Everyone in the band was calling me Jules, and the unfamiliar nickname only intensified the sense that I was living in an alternate reality, one that was light-years away from my actual life.

I lay on my back staring up at the sky while Danny, Declan, and Sinead tested their mics and Sean hovered over a man Danny had told me was the club's sound guy as he adjusted the levels. Every once in a while there would be the loud screech of feedback, and then everything would go quiet and then they would start again.

My mother either tried to commit suicide or accidentally overdosed.

I lay on the stage, repeating the sentence in my mind as if repetition might make it comprehensible. But the words remained completely unreal to me, detached from any kind of meaning they might try to convey. Overhead, clouds passed slowly in a stratospheric breeze, and I felt as far away from earth as they were.

"Okay, Sinead, let's hear it," called Sean.

"She just went to get some water," Danny answered.

"Oh, well, that's great then," said Sean. "I guess we'll all sit around twiddling our thumbs while we wait for Her Highness to return."

"Just give me a second and I'll do it," Declan said. He was taping wires down with bright blue tape.

"How about you, Jules? You don't exactly seem to be over-worked."

63

I sat up. "What?"

Sean was standing next to the guy at the soundboard, his arms crossed over his chest, a beer in one hand. "Talk into the mic," Sean said. "Testing: one, two. Just like in the movies."

I got to my feet, crossed the stage, and stood at the microphone. The perfect lawn stretched out all around me, as if the stage were a ship floating on a broad emerald ocean. Beyond the edge of the hill, the actual water appeared, then disappeared into the horizon.

"Testing: one, two," I said. "Testing: one, two." There was a loud screech, and suddenly Danny was at my side.

"Here," he said, moving the stand about a foot away from where it had been. "Try this."

"Thanks," I said, following him and standing at the mic in its new location.

"Keep going," Sean called out.

"Um, testing. One. Two. Testing." On the second *testing*, my voice boomed out, shockingly loud.

"You're killing me with that testing," said Sean. "Sing something. Sing 'Happy Birthday.'"

Obediently, I started singing. "Happy birthday to you. Happy birthday to you. Happy birthday dear . . . someone. Happy birthday to you."

There was silence. In the distance, Sinead appeared, a pyramid of water bottles balanced in her arms.

"Let's have that again," said Sean, but he didn't say it with quite the same venom with which he'd said everything else.

I sang "Happy Birthday" one more time. By the time I was finished, Sinead was standing beside Sean. "Holy shit," she called out. "Jules, you have a great voice."

"Thanks," I said.

"No joke, Jules," said Danny from over by the drums. "You can really sing."

"Okay," I said, not really able to process their compliments. They were all staring at me. "Do you need me to sing it again?"

"Ah, yeah," said the sound guy, who had a mustache so big I was pretty sure it was ironic. "If you could sing it one more time, that would be great."

I sang the song for a third time. It didn't sound like anything special, certainly no different than it sounded every other time I'd sung it. When I was finished, everyone clapped. I felt weird standing up there with people looking at me, so I just asked if we were finished, went over to the edge of the stage, and sat down.

When it was time for the concert to start, everyone but me went off to change. Contrary to gender stereotypes, Sinead was the first one done, wearing a tight black dress and a pair of high-heeled black pumps. She stood at the edge of the parking lot, and a minute later the boys joined her. They walked toward the stage, where I was sitting, the guys in black suits and white shirts, Sinead in her dress. I wondered what it was like to be a member of their let's-be-in-a-band-together-and-bicker-but-really-all-get-along-and-love-each-other family. You could tell just by looking at them that all of their parents were happily married, that nobody in their family had tried to commit suicide or overdosed, that they gathered around the piano at holidays and sang seasonal songs.

I kind of hated all of them.

I looked out at the lawn. Little lights were strung up in the few trees scattered picturesquely across the grounds. People were wandering around eating hors d'oeuvres and drinking from tall glasses. All of them looked happy and carefree, enjoying a warm summer's night at their club. I wondered what would happen if I opened my mouth, started screaming, and refused to stop. Would the roasted-egg guy throw me out? Would he have me arrested?

Would the police put me in a hospital bed with restraints on my arms?

My phone buzzed and I picked it up. Sofia.

Sofia: how r u?

I reread our previous exchanges.

Sofia: how r u?
Me: im ok.
Sofia: how r u?
Me: i am okay.

66

Here it was for the third time, and I typed a new response.

Me: i am fucking freaking out, sofia, how do you think I am?

I stared at the screen of my phone.
Don't make a scene, Juliet.
I deleted what I'd just typed. *im ok*, I wrote, and I put the phone back on the stage beside me.

"God, this crowd is ancient," said Sinead, standing at the edge of the stage next to where I was sitting with my legs hanging down.

"We'll have them rocking in the aisles," said Declan, surveying the audience along with her. When they were standing next to each other, it was clear how much Declan and Sinead looked alike—even more than they looked like Danny and Sean and Sean and Danny looked like each other. Declan and Sinead even stood the same way, both arms crossed over their chests, each hand holding the opposite bicep.

"Are you guys twins?" I asked, staring at them.

"Irish twins," said Sinead. Her teeth were very white against her bright red lipstick. "We're eleven months apart. And Danny's our little brother. He's going into first form."

"They don't call it that here," said Sean, who was standing on the ground just below us. The way he said it made me think it wasn't the first time he'd had to tell her. "It's ninth grade. And you are going to be a junior and Declan's going to be a senior." He popped open the beer he was holding.

"Right," said Sinead, snapping her fingers. "Junior. Senior. It sounds so American."

"We *are* American," Declan reminded her. He gave me an apologetic look. "We've been living in Beijing for the past seven years. Our dad just got transferred back to New York in June."

"Start spreading the news!" Sean sang, and he took a swig of beer.

"I thought you were British," I said, confused. "You have British accents."

Sinead laughed. "We were born in London. We lived there before we moved to Beijing."

The sound guy came over to the stage. "Okay, you guys start at nine?" His mustache was truly astonishing.

"That we do," said Sean.

"I guess it's time, then," said the guy. "Break a leg."

"Thanks," said Sinead.

Suddenly everyone was moving around the stage, gathering instruments, talking into a mic, doing a quick roll on the drums. I felt idiotic sitting up there and being in the way. I hopped off the stage just as Declan called out, "Hey! Jules!"

I turned around. He was holding a tambourine out in my direction. "Do you want to play with us?"

I shook my head. "I really can't."

"A cat could play the tambourine." He shook it lightly. "Haven't you ever dreamed of being a rock star?"

Even if I'd wanted to play with them—which I didn't—I was sure that shaking a tambourine would shake loose something inside me that was already barely staying attached. "No. But thanks. Really."

He looked at me like he wanted to ask me something, then dropped the arm holding the tambourine to his side. "See you after the show," he said.

The show was completely insane.

At first, none of the people on the lawn were even remotely listening to the band. Sinead said, "We're the Clovers" into the microphone, and I was literally the only person who noticed. As Sinead counted them in for the first song, I had enough time to try to think about how I'd have to find something nice to say when they came offstage knowing they'd bombed, and then Sinead finished the count and Declan started playing the guitar.

The notes were crisp, almost twangy. Danny joined them on the drums and Sean started playing the bass, and by the time Sinead started singing, people were already filing toward the stage. "I found a picture of you," she began, and her voice was beautiful but there was a slight growl to it, almost like she was mad about what she was singing. "What hijacked my world that night . . ."

I'd heard "Back on the Chain Gang" before, but it wasn't a song I stopped to listen to if I happened to be playing the radio in my car and it came on. Now, for the first time, I could feel how good it was, how the notes pushed into your blood and bones. By the time the song ended, there must have been a hundred people standing on the lawn in front of the stage, and the audience kept getting bigger. Sinead was right—it was an older crowd. But I spotted some younger people, maybe junior high kids, and they were dancing along with their parents.

They went right into a song I didn't know. "Been running so long I've nearly lost all track of time," Sinead belted out, and by now there was no one on the lawn who wasn't listening to the band except for an elderly couple standing about as far away as they could get without actually leaving the grounds of the club.

I edged around to the back of the stage where no one could see me. I'd been right about the music shaking something loose inside me, and as they played I let myself sob, grateful that the band was loud enough that no one could hear me cry.

6

Afterward I felt better, as if the music and the crying had purged me of something heavy and dark. By the time the show was over, I didn't feel like crying anymore; I was just tired, and when I'd helped them bring the equipment back to the van and we were all standing clumped together in the parking lot and Sinead asked me for my number, I had to think to remember what it was.

"That way we can hang out," Sinead explained, gesturing with her phone. "Declan and Danny and I don't know anybody here besides Sean. And he's so old."

"Hey, watch it," said Sean. He'd been drinking steadily, and now he sat in the open door of the van, an empty can next to him, a full one in his hand.

The phone she was holding buzzed, and Sinead looked at

the screen. "Oh, damn. That's Mum," she said. "She's here to get Danny."

"You're coming swimming with us, right?" asked Declan.

Sinead made a face. "I don't know. I'm kind of tired. And I've got to get up early tomorrow. I might just call it a night."

"Pussy!" said Sean.

"Wanker," snapped Sinead.

"Okay," said Declan. "Thanks to both of you for your edifying verbal interplay."

"I'm going," said Sinead, reading something on her screen. "Mum says she's been waiting." She gave me a hug. "You'll give these guys your number, right? So we can hang out. And you should seriously think about joining the band. You have an awesome voice."

"Sure," I said, knowing it would never happen. I let Sinead hug me and then I returned Danny's fist bump as they hustled off to meet their mother.

My phone buzzed. It was Sofia. *sorry i havnt txtd in so long. crazy here maybe not out until 12:30 u want keys 2 my house?*

I was so tired. All I wanted to do was close my eyes. But the idea of going back to Sofia's and getting into the bed I'd slept in last night made my heart pound with terror. I couldn't go back there by myself. I just couldn't.

"You want to come swimming with us?" asked Declan.

"Um . . ." I looked at my phone. It was just after eleven. "Where?"

"Right here," said Declan, gesturing toward the water with his chin. "In the sound."

"I don't know," I said. I remembered the egg's sunburned head, how he was packed into his too-tight chinos. I pictured him having my car towed, though when I looked around, there were still a lot of cars parked in the lot.

Sean made clucking noises, then added, "Chick-chick-chicken," like maybe I hadn't gotten the hint.

"Don't be such a wanker, okay, Sean?" I asked, the word coming to me out of the ether.

"Nicely done," said Sean. He gave a loud burp. "You're an honorary Clover now."

Sean, Declan, and I crossed the wide lawn behind the stage down to a narrow flight of wooden steps. In the distance, I could hear the sound of people talking and the tinny clink of silverware on plates, but we didn't see anyone as we made our journey. At the bottom of the steps was a narrow beach, and I took off my shoes and socks and dug my toes into the cool sand. For some reason, Jason had never taken me here. When we came to the club, we always ended up at the pool.

Sean instantly stripped to a pair of boxer shorts and dove into the water, yelping as he came up for air. "That's fucking cold!" he cried.

"Shhhh," I hissed. "We're going to get caught."

"Shhhh," he mimicked, "we're going to get caught." Then he dove back down and emerged, blowing a fountain of water out of his mouth. Finally he swam back to the shore and lay down. "Who wants to get me a beer?" he inquired.

"Dude, you're wasted enough as it is," said Declan, taking off his shoe and throwing it at Sean.

"Ya bastard," said Sean. He grabbed the shoe and shoved it under his head. "Thanks for the pillow. Oh, I do love the great outdoors." A second later he was snoring.

Declan took off his other shoe and his socks, then rolled up his pants and walked to the edge of the sound. He picked up a rock and skipped it across the surface of the water. The moon was enormous, and it made the beach almost as bright as day.

"Thanks for helping us out," he said. "With the sound check, I mean. And carrying all that stuff. You really do have a beautiful voice."

I sat on the sand and watched the ripples Declan's rock had made slowly disappear. "Thanks," I said.

He threw another rock. "Have you ever sung before? I mean in a band or anything?"

"No." I couldn't see how I was going to make small talk for the next hour and a half while I waited for Sofia to get off work. The thought of continuing to chat gave me a tight feeling in my chest, like maybe now was the moment I'd just start screaming. "Let's swim," I said, getting to my feet. "I feel like swimming." Without waiting for Declan to say anything, still in my shorts and tank top, I walked to the edge of the water and did a shallow dive into the sound.

The water was cold, but I warmed up as I swam, the familiar rhythm of the strokes soothing me. It had been too long since I'd swum, but after commuting home from the city and then doing practice SAT questions or meeting with Glen, my tutor, the last thing I'd felt like doing at the end of every day was putting on my suit and hitting the pool in our backyard. Now, reaching for the dock, I felt the result of my inactivity as I lifted my heavy arm to touch it before turning and heading back toward the beach.

Halfway there I passed Declan, who was swimming out the other way. By the time I got to the shore, he had already climbed onto the dock, and I watched him do a smooth dive into the water. I wondered if he was on his swim team. Thinking about it made me realize that I knew nothing about him: not where he went to school, not where he lived. Not even his last name. It occurred to me how stupid it had been to come down to the beach with two complete strangers, one of whom clearly had a drinking problem. What had made me think this was such a happy family? For all I knew, Declan and Sean were serial killers. This was exactly the kind of story you read about on the front page of the *Post*. "Girl's Body Washes up on Long Island Shore."

If I died, everyone would say how full of promise I'd been.

When he got to the beach, I saw that Declan had taken off his white shirt and his tie, which confirmed my imaginary text to Sofia. He *was* hawt. His shoulders were broad, and they tapered to a narrow waist. Water streamed off his pants, which shone black in the moonlight.

"Hey," he said, dropping down beside me on the sand and not sounding much like a murderer. "When I first met you, you seemed kind of upset." I was focused on squeezing water out of the bottom of my tank top, but I could tell he was looking at me. "Are you okay now?"

I rubbed my wet hands on my equally wet thighs. "Why do people always ask if you're okay? What kind of a question is that?"

"Um, I take it you feel it's a dumb one?" he offered.

I shrugged.

"Look, if you want me out of your business, just say so. I only wanted to know if you were still upset about . . . whatever it was?" He reached his hand out and lightly tapped me on the knee, his tap a physical manifestation of his question.

I turned to look at him, trying to imagine his response if I told him why I'd been so distracted I'd almost hit his van earlier.

As I rotated my body to make eye contact with Declan, I realized just how close we were sitting. His face couldn't have been more than six inches from mine, and our knees were almost touching. We looked at each other.

"Jules?" he said.

Don't do it, I said to myself. *Do* not *do it.*

But instead of answering his question, I leaned across the few inches that separated us and kissed him.

"Jules . . . wait . . . ," he said, trying to talk and kiss me at the same time. But I ignored the talking part, and almost immediately he stopped saying anything and just kissed me back.

At first, as our lips touched lightly, I felt detached from what we were doing. Analytical. I had never kissed anyone but Jason, and Declan kissed differently. His lips were softer, and his tongue traced the outline of my mouth very gently. *This is interesting*, I thought. *This is not what I'm used to.* It was funny how I could be kissing Declan and analyzing kissing Declan and it felt almost like a science experiment I was conducting.

And then, suddenly, it didn't. Declan slipped his arm around my back and I pulled myself onto his lap, my legs wrapped around his waist. I put my hands on his chest.

"Jules," Declan whispered, kissing up the side of my neck. When he got to my ear, he repeated the question. "Who are you?"

But there was nothing about me I wanted Declan to know.

"Shhh," I whispered. "Don't make a scene."

"What?" he asked, his mouth gentle against my ear.

I shivered and pulled him up so that our lips were level with each other, and I kissed him even more deeply. As we kissed, I could feel his questions—along with the rest of the universe—floating away, like the clouds I'd been watching overhead earlier.

7

I woke up to the sound of my phone buzzing like an angry beach insect.

Declan's arm was still under me, and I was curled into him, my legs intertwined with his. As I slipped out of his embrace, he stirred, but he didn't wake up. It was dark and cold, and the moon had dropped behind the trees. A few feet away, Sean was still snoring. I dug my phone out of my bag. Sofia was calling, and it was 1:08 a.m.

"Hello? Sofia?" I whispered, sidestepping away from Declan. My foot made contact with my tank top, which was a sodden mass of salt water and sand. I picked it up and shook it, scattering sand everywhere.

"Where *are* you? I've been calling you for twenty minutes. I'm at your car."

"I'm . . . I'm at the beach." I tucked the phone between my chin and shoulder and rubbed frantically at the fabric of my shirt, as if the sticky wet sand were a bright, scarlet *A*.

"The beach? What beach?"

"Um, here. I'm here. At the club."

"Juliet, are you okay?"

"I'm fine," I said, giving up on cleaning my top. I dropped it over my head and winced as the cold, wet, sandy fabric slid over my bare skin. "Where are you?"

"I said, I'm at your car."

"Right," I said quickly. "Sorry. I'll be there in two minutes."

"Okay," said Sofia. "I'll be here."

I hung up and turned to where Declan was lying.

He was fast asleep. I put my hand on my hair, which was gritty with sand. Images of what had happened with us came at me fast and furious . . . my taking off my tank top . . . his saying, *We have time. Let's not rush this*. . . . I squeezed my eyes shut, willing the movie to stop.

What had I done?

"Declan?" I whispered. When he didn't move, I said it again. "Declan?" This time he stirred slightly, and I held my breath, not sure if I was more scared that he'd wake up or more scared that he wouldn't. He shifted slightly in the sand and threw his arm out as if using it to fill the space I'd just vacated.

What had I *done*? I pressed my hand to my forehead. My mother was in the hospital tied to her bed. My boyfriend of

79

four years was innocently sleeping in France. My best friend was working her ass off, barely able to focus on her job she was so freaked out about how I was.

Meanwhile, I was merrily getting with a complete stranger on the beach.

Declan stirred again, and I froze. If he woke up, what was I going to say to him?

You know, this was amazing, but I'm not really into relationships. Except with my boyfriend.

Did I mention that my mother might have tried to kill herself earlier today?

Do you mind pretending this never happened?

Declan stopped moving, and I held my breath, frozen as an animal sensing danger. Was he waking up? He breathed deeply, then settled his head on his hand.

There was no way I could face him after what had just happened. I could barely face *myself* after what had just happened, but I was stuck with me.

Please don't wake up, Declan. Please do not wake up.

He kept sleeping. I forced myself to stay where I was for a count of ten, then ran silently across the sand, barely slowing down to grab my shoes as I raced to the stairs that would carry me up to the lawn. I was sorry, and I knew Declan would think I was a head case, but that was better than having some awkward conversation with him.

Maybe he'll be relieved, I thought to myself. *Maybe he'll be just as glad that you're gone.*

But his saying *We have time* came back to me, and I squeezed my head between my hands, willing my brain to delete it.

Sofia was leaning against the side of my car, but she stood up as soon as she saw me.

"J, are you all right? What happened?" Puzzled, she touched the ends of my hair. "You're all sandy. And . . . were you swimming or something?"

"No! I mean, yes. I went swimming. I had to . . . I had to clear my head." I forced a smile. "I just wanted to be in the water for a little while."

"Juliet, that's dangerous. You can't go swimming when no one's around." She shook her head. "Seriously." Sofia and I were on the swim team together, so we'd both been listening to Coach Kalman's lectures about water safety for years.

"I know," I said, nodding. "You're right." Declan's van was still parked next to my car, and I was terrified that any minute he was going to come running across the lawn holding my underwear and screaming my name.

That's ridiculous, Juliet. You're wearing your underwear.

It was true.

Barely.

Sofia was still looking at me with a puzzled expression on her face. "Are you okay, J?"

"Not really," I admitted. It felt like the first true thing I'd said in the past ten minutes, even though I knew Sofia would think I meant something other than what I actually meant.

"Let's go home, okay? Follow me."

I got in my car and watched Sofia walk across the lot to hers. As I drove out behind her, I thought about confessing what I'd done. If anyone would understand, it would be Sofia. She was my oldest friend, one of the only people besides my family who'd known me really well before Jason and I started going out.

Sofia, I have to tell you something.

We turned out of the driveway, Sofia's taillights guiding me along Milltown Lane.

If you make out with a guy on the beach and nobody knows, did it really happen?

As much of a relief as it would be to confess, if I didn't tell her—if I didn't tell anyone—then it could be like I'd never made out with Declan. I did a quick mental check. He didn't know my last name. He didn't have my phone number. He didn't know what school I went to or where I lived. My sandy shoes were safely on my feet.

Even the prince in Cinderella had more to go on than Declan.

Sofia held the door of her building open for me, and I followed her into the lobby. When we were younger, her mom would let us come downstairs and sit on the sofas in front of the fireplace, and we'd pretend we were grown-ups living in our own apartment.

Inside the elevator, she pressed the button for her floor. "So what did you do that whole time?"

I leaned against the cool mirror on the back wall of the elevator and closed my eyes. The whole night was taking on a dreamlike quality. "Nothing, really. There was a band, and I listened to them."

"I heard they were smoking hot," said Sofia. "Everyone was talking about it."

"Yeah," I said noncommittally. "I guess they were okay."

For the second night in a row, I borrowed a T-shirt and boxers from her and used my finger to brush my teeth. Sofia wanted to talk about my mom, but as soon as we got in bed I told her I was so tired I had to go right to sleep. I thought I was lying when I said it, but apparently I wasn't, because as soon as my head hit the pillow, I conked out, almost as if my mind couldn't take being awake anymore and needed to hit the off button.

8

The next thing I knew, my phone was ringing, waking me for the second time in less than twelve hours. I reached for it, groggily registering that sunlight was streaming through the blinds and that Sofia wasn't in her bed. The number wasn't one I recognized; I registered a lot of extra digits before putting it to my ear.

"Hello?" I said, my voice hoarse with sleep.

"Juliet, honey, did I wake you?"

"Grace?" I felt so out of it, like I was underwater and trying to swim to the surface. Why would Jason's mother be calling me?

"Juliet, I just got off the phone with your dad."

"You talked to my dad?" Grace and my dad never talked. If ever there needed to be parental communication, it was always between our moms.

She ignored my question. "We agreed that you're going to

stay at our house until your mother . . . until everything is worked out. I know your aunt is arriving today, and she's going to stay with you until we're back, and then next week you'll come to us, okay?"

"Next week?" My tongue felt heavy and it was hard to form words. I needed to pull myself out of my grogginess and focus. I sat up. "Wait, Grace, my mom will be home by then."

"Well, if she is, that's wonderful." Grace said it like, *If she is, I'm a pole dancer.*

"When did you . . ." I squeezed my eyes shut and opened them wide, hoping that would wake me up. "When did you talk to my dad?"

"I just got off the phone with him," said Grace. "He said you were at Sofia's for the night, but that you needed a place to stay more long-term, and he felt it might not be a good idea for him to move back into the house."

I knew I'd been the one to say my dad shouldn't move back into the house, but the fact that he'd listened to me and was just going to foist me off on the Robinsons made my body go cold all over. Last year Michael Priest, a second-semester senior whose dad had been transferred to California, had stayed with Chris Cho's family for the last few months of school. But that was different. My dad lived in New York. And what gave Grace the idea that my mother wouldn't be home in a week?

"Grace, I don't think—"

She wasn't listening. "Let me give you to Jason. He's eager to talk to you."

If the news that my father was boarding me out like our old golden retriever had made me go cold, the thought of talking to Jason turned me to ice. I could *not* be on the phone with him. Not until I'd had a chance to get my thoughts together. If I had to talk to him now, I was going to confess everything. I was going to ruin everything. "Grace——" The word was high-pitched, almost a scream.

But Grace was gone. The voice on the other end of the line was Jason's. "Hey, J."

If I lived to be a hundred, could there ever be two syllables that were more familiar to me than those? I must have heard them a million times. Ten million. They'd been shouted at me down the corridors of Milltown High, hummed quietly in my ear while we were kissing, written across the screen of my phone.

They were more familiar to me than the sound of my actual name.

I hugged the arm holding the phone tightly to my chest. "Hey, J," I echoed. It was all I trusted myself to say, but hearing the words come out of my mouth sounding almost normal gave me hope.

I could do this.

"Are you okay?" he asked.

I pushed away the memory of Declan asking me that same question last night, and I pushed away what had happened after. "I'm okay," I lied.

"How's your mom?" he asked.

"She's . . . I don't know how she is today. She was sleeping when I saw her last night."

"It's going to be okay, J. *She's* going to be okay." Jason sounded calm and confident. I remembered how freaked Sofia had been when I'd told her the news, and how I'd imagined Jason reacting exactly the same way. But of course he wouldn't. Jason never got freaked out about anything.

"I don't know, J," I said. I reached forward and grabbed my foot through the tangled sheet, the pressure of my own hand strangely comforting. "I don't know how you're all right after something like this."

"It was just an accident, J. I'm sure of it. Remember how messed up I was after my knee surgery? My mom wouldn't even let me have the pain pills because I kept forgetting how many I'd taken. It could have happened to anyone."

I started to cry. "J, I just love you so much," I said. My nose was running, and I pressed against it with the tips of my fingers.

"I love you too, J," he said, and when I gave a loud sob, he laughed softly. "Is my saying I love you going to make you cry now?"

In response, I just gave a little squeak.

"I'll be home soon," he promised. "Everything's going to be okay."

I remembered seeing the country club yesterday and how

it had made me feel like I was being wrapped up in something warm and safe. I'd thought of cashmere, but the warm and safe thing the club reminded me of wasn't an expensive sweater.

It was Jason.

Grace said something in the background. "My mom says you're supposed to go and meet your aunt or something," Jason translated.

I forced myself to take a breath and let it out slowly. "Yeah." I'd gone from being scared to talk to Jason to being scared to hang up the phone. But the clock on Sofia's night table said ten thirty, which meant Aunt Kathy was probably already at my house.

Jason lowered his voice. "I miss you."

My eyes stung. "I miss you too."

"Remember: J power," he said.

It was all I could do not to start bawling again. "J power," I whispered. And then he was gone.

When I was a little girl, my parents tried to get me to like *I Love Lucy*, which they and my brother thought was hilarious. To their surprise, I hated the show, how Lucy and Ethel's plans seemed foolproof but were really anything but, how you had to watch, helpless, as they got tangled up in their own complicated incompetence. It made me mad and anxious, and after assuring me for several episodes that *this* was the one I was guaranteed to like, my parents finally stopped trying to make me a convert.

Years later, I hardly ever thought of the show, but as I drove home, an image from it appeared to me. It was Lucy, standing in a vat of grapes, holding her dress high and stomping on the fruit to make wine. In my memory, her expression was pained, as if the grapes were a bed of hot coals on which she was being forced to dance.

Now I felt like Lucy, my memories of last night grapes I had to press down, down, down until they liquefied and fermented and finally turned into something else entirely, something completely unlike what they were—turned into a dream I'd had or a story I'd heard from a girl at school or a scene from a movie I'd watched late one night when Sofia and I were channel surfing at my house.

Anything other than what they were, which was something gross and mean and stupid that I had done.

My dad called as I was pulling into the driveway of my house.

I didn't bother with hello. "Why did you tell Grace Robinson I'd stay at their house without asking me?" I tucked the phone under my chin as I put the car in park.

"What?" He sounded genuinely shocked. "I never said you'd be staying with the Robinsons."

"That's not what Grace said. She said the two of you had agreed I'd stay there until Mom gets home. Which, by the way, Grace seems to think is going to be in about a thousand years."

My dad sighed. "I asked Grace if you *could* stay there if

you had to. I wanted to know what your options were. I have no idea what possessed her to call you and present it as a fait accompli."

"Okay, Dad? Just so you know, when Grace Robinson is involved in something, it *is* a fait accompli."

"I'm sorry, honey. I wasn't thinking straight. This morning, I realized I can just rent an apartment near school and you'll stay with me, okay? I'll get a three-bedroom and call Hofstra or Adelphi and see if there's a college student who could stay in the apartment when I'm traveling for more than a night or two."

I couldn't believe what I was hearing. "A *babysitter?* You want to get me a *babysitter?*"

My dad fumbled for a response. "Not a babysitter exactly, a—"

"Dad, this is absurd," I said, snatching my keys out of the ignition. "I'm seventeen years old. I don't need a babysitter. Why can't I just stay at home? Or at Sofia's?"

"I'm not comfortable with your staying in the house alone, and your mother and I don't like you staying at Sofia's when her mother is working nights."

I snorted. "I love how all of a sudden when it comes to saying no to me, you and Mom are a team."

Another sigh. "Juliet, I'm doing the best I can. We're all going to need to be a little flexible right now."

The way he said that, like being flexible was something

90

he'd been handed that was very heavy and that he was preparing to carry for a long time, brought me up short. There was silence for a minute, and then I said, "I should go, Dad. Aunt Kathy's waiting for me."

As soon as I pushed open the front door, I smelled coffee. Unlike my parents, Kathy and her husband, Sam, didn't care about wine or furniture or where their kids went to college, but they were obsessed with incredibly strong coffee. Whenever I was at their house, I had to make my own because theirs was too strong for me to drink.

"Hello?" called Aunt Kathy.

I put my bag on the table in the foyer and headed through the dining room and into the kitchen, suddenly wishing I were someplace else. Everything I looked at had the power to hurt. I had never understood arsonists, how you could burn down something whole for no reason at all. But now I did. If I'd had a can of gasoline in my hand, I would have happily poured it everywhere, then tossed in the match behind me and pulled the door shut. I would have sat on the hood of my car and watched until my house burned to the ground.

"Hey," said my aunt when I crossed the threshold into the kitchen. She was wearing jeans and a T-shirt with a bright floral print on it and she was barefoot. She got up from the table and gave me a hug. "Oh, Juliet," she murmured as she held me tightly, rocking me back and forth slightly as we stood together. Then she pulled me over to the kitchen table and sat down next to me. There was a piece of paper next to her coffee cup, and on it I saw the words *milk, cereal, bread,* and, in a separate column, *clothes, music (?).* I averted my eyes, not wanting to think about who she might be getting the clothes and music for.

"How are you?" she asked. She tucked her hair behind her ear and folded her legs under her on the seat.

"I'm . . . I don't know. I'm okay, I guess."

"It's a stupid question, isn't it?" she acknowledged.

"Yeah," I agreed. "It is, kind of."

I'd always known that my aunt looked a lot like my mom. They were both tall and very pretty with long hair and eyes such a light brown they were almost gold. The funny thing was that my mom was older but (normally) she looked younger because she dyed her hair and she was obsessed with not getting any sun on her face. My aunt's hair was going gray and she had wrinkles that she didn't try to hide. Still, they looked enough alike that all of a sudden it was eerie sitting at the table next to Kathy, almost as if I were sitting with my mom's ghost. I looked away.

"I want to know what happened. Did she take the pills on purpose, or was it an accident? Don't lie to me," I added quickly. "I can take it."

My aunt made a clucking noise in the back of her throat. "Of course you can. And I would never lie to you. But it may not be that simple. I just spoke with the attending psychiatrist. Your mom doesn't remember exactly what happened."

"*What?*" I turned to stare at her. "How is that possible?"

"Well, it sounds like she's been taking a lot of different medications—" Kathy started hesitantly.

"My dad told the social worker my mom was abusing her medication," I interrupted, my voice sharp.

I expected Kathy to be outraged, but she just sighed and put her chin in her hand. "Yeah, I think that's probably true."

"What is going on?" I stood up. "What is going *on* here? He said she was mixing drugs and alcohol, too. Is *that* true? I mean, her doctor *prescribed* her everything. It's not like she's some kid at Milltown getting Ritalin from her friends."

"Oh, honey." Kathy reached for my hand. Her voice was quiet. "It's complicated. I know her doctor prescribed everything she was taking, but I also know he wasn't supervising her very carefully. And I know she was doing some self-medicating—a little extra Ambien when she couldn't sleep, a little more Klonopin when she was feeling anxious. And drinking."

"Mom doesn't *drink*," I corrected my aunt. "She has, like, a glass of wine with dinner."

"Well . . ." Kathy raised her eyebrows and nodded slowly, almost reluctantly. "You're really not supposed to drink at all when you're on those drugs, Juliet. She and I have talked about it in the past. And I don't think it was just a glass. Whenever I was here, it seemed more like it was closer to a bottle a night. Every night."

"So, what are you saying? 'Hey, Juliet, guess what? Your mother's an alcoholic and a drug addict'?"

Kathy grimaced. "Your mom's unhappy, Juliet."

"Yeah! Because her husband *left* her."

"She was unhappy before that. And taking pills and drinking took the edge off that unhappiness."

Suddenly I felt as if I couldn't hold my body up for another minute. I dropped heavily into my chair. "I can't believe you're telling me this. I can't believe I didn't know this was going on."

"Sweetheart, she's still your mom," Kathy started. "She's still the person you thought she was."

I raised my eyebrow and stared at Kathy. "Are you serious?"

"What I mean is she still loves you."

I had no idea what I was supposed to say to that, so I just sat there and let Kathy talk. She toyed with the pad of paper as she spoke, turning it around and around on the table. "They're still trying to figure out how much of everything she was taking so they can start weaning her off of it. These medications are serious, and you can't just stop taking them on a dime." Abruptly she pushed the pad away, as if she hadn't realized she'd been touching it. "The doctor is recommending that your mom be transferred from the hospital to a long-term facility. Someplace she can get some help."

The word *long-term* felt like a punch in the stomach. I swallowed and forced myself to sound calm. "How long-term are we talking about?"

Kathy reached over and put her hand on mine. Her fingernails were cut short and unmanicured, nothing like my mom's perfect, oval nails with their sheer polish. And unlike my mom, who wears a lot of jewelry, Kathy only wore a plain gold wedding band. It was easier to look at my aunt's hands than at her face.

"My guess is once they find a space for her somewhere, we're talking about six weeks to three months." I didn't say anything as the time my mother might be away washed over me like a huge wave, leaving me shaky and scared. Kathy took my other hand in hers and leaned forward. I could tell she wanted me to look at her, but I stayed focused on her fingernails. "Juliet, I want you to consider something. I want you to consider coming to stay with me and Sam and the boys until your mom's better."

Now I did look at her. "What?"

"I'd like you to think about moving to Portland."

My lips were dry, and I licked them. "You're not serious."

"I am."

There was silence, and then I said as calmly as I could, "You think she meant to do it. To kill herself."

Kathy shrugged sadly. "I can't say that for sure. I don't know enough to know. I don't even know how we got to this point. I blame myself. I knew she was in bad shape, but I was busy, and I put off coming out . . ." She shook her head. "The point is I want to make a real plan. I want to take care of you."

"Aunt Kathy, it's my senior year. I can't just pick up and go to another school."

"I know this is hard," she said, her eyes bright. "If you were younger, it would be so much easier. I'd be upstairs right now packing your suitcase. Not neatly enough for you, of course." We both laughed at that. Once, my parents went away to Vancouver for a weekend while Oliver and I stayed with Aunt Kathy and Uncle Sam and my cousins, Andrew and William. I was eight, and apparently I organized and color-coordinated Andrew and William's drawers. I also delivered a lecture on tidiness to the whole family.

I guess you're never too young to be type A.

"I'm worried about you, Juliet." Aunt Kathy's voice was gentle. "I know you're super competent and responsible. But I'm worried. Your dad travels so much. . . ." She bit her lip and looked around the kitchen. A few years ago, my parents had done a big renovation on the house, pushing out the back wall to create the eating nook we were sitting in now. I remembered them sitting with the architect, looking over the plans in the dining room, cheese and crackers and a bottle of wine open on the table. "Think about it," Aunt Kathy finished. "Just tell me you'll think about it."

I stood up, walked over to the window, and stared out at

the line of trees that marked the far border of our perfectly manicured backyard. "Okay," I promised. "I will."

The hospital didn't allow psychiatric patients to have visitors who were under eighteen, so only Aunt Kathy could go see my mom. She suggested I might want to write my mother a note, so I went upstairs to my room and tried to think of something to say. *Dear Mom.* I sat and stared at the paper for a while. Then I wrote, *I love you and I miss you.* I looked at the words. They seemed so meager on the page. I ripped the paper up and started again. *Dear Mom, I really hope you're okay.* That was worse; obviously she wasn't okay. I ripped up the second draft also, and when Kathy headed to the hospital, I just told her to tell my mom that I loved her.

9

I went on autopilot.

Every morning I woke up at seven, had breakfast with my aunt, got dressed and took a train into the city. Then I walked across town to the UN, where I snapped on my ID badge and got my agenda for the day. Some days I sat in on low-level meetings. Other days I listened to the General Assembly debate. There were information sessions about specific countries and there were lunches in the glass-walled cafeteria overlooking the East River. Meetings with NGOs working on girls' education. Papers to read and discuss. Access to the UN's library and database. Sitting on the 5:48 train headed home, I would realize I had no idea what I'd seen or said or done all day. I would get off the train and it would be raining and I'd think, *Was it raining this morning when I left the house?* and I wouldn't be able to remember.

Aunt Kathy went to visit my mother at the hospital every day. Apparently she was still fairly dopey from the different medications they were giving her. I couldn't see why the doctors couldn't just figure out what she needed to clear her head and ask her if she'd tried to kill herself, but Kathy told me I needed to be patient. I reminded her that patience was not one of my virtues. Oliver finally arrived at some spot in the Adirondack Park with cell service, got the ten million messages we'd left for him, and came home. He went to visit our mom, then met our dad for dinner in the city and stayed with him. Somehow his choosing to stay in the city instead of at the house felt like a decision to align himself against me and Aunt Kathy, and when he called and asked me to have dinner with him and our dad, I said I had plans. He asked me how I was and I said I was okay. I asked him how he was and he said he didn't know. Part of me wondered if he might offer to stay at the house with me after Aunt Kathy left, but he didn't. I guess I shouldn't have expected him to. It wasn't like he didn't have a life in New Haven. And school was starting for him soon, too. We promised to talk in a couple of days, but after I hung up, I had the strangest feeling—so strong it was like a premonition—that I would never see him again.

Friday when I got home the house was empty. I tried to do my SAT homework. Glen, my tutor, was on vacation, but when he came back, he was going to want to see all the progress I'd made while he was away. There was also preseason coming, which

I was totally unprepared for. Out my back window, I could see the pool. It was pristine, shimmering red and gold with the light of the setting sun, and I thought about the pool guy and how he kept coming every week even though nobody used the pool and how he'd keep coming even though soon nobody would be living in the house. The pool guy, the gardener, the housekeeper . . . my house was its own little economy. All these people working so hard to make everything clean and pretty and well-manicured.

And with all that, my parents still hadn't been able to be happy together.

I turned away from the window. The thought of motivating myself to get off my bed, go outside, and swim laps was exhausting, and instead I lay down and tried to get through a reading passage on the creation of the EPA.

I must have conked out, because the next thing I knew, Aunt Kathy was shaking me awake gently. "Juliet," she whispered.

I sat up, sweaty and disoriented. She was sitting on the edge of my bed, smiling at me, and she looked so much like my mother that it hurt to see her. I closed my eyes and leaned back against my pillow.

"You were really asleep there," she said, patting me.

"I was having the strangest dream. . . . I was on a boat, and you were there. And Mom. And we'd forgotten something, and I think we had to go back to get it, but I couldn't figure out how to work the sails. . . ." I shook my head. "I can't remember.

Maybe you weren't there." The dream receded, leaving in its wake the sense that I'd done something wrong.

"Come on," she said, when I didn't say any more. "Let's go have some dinner."

Downstairs Kathy stood at the counter chopping while standing on one foot, her other foot against her knee, like a flamingo. I sat on a stool, watching her and trying to wake up. "Have you given any thought to my suggestion? About coming to Oregon." She was leaving Sunday morning. I wondered if she'd made me a reservation just in case.

"I have." I wasn't lying, either. I'd imagined packing a suitcase and taking a plane to Oregon with Aunt Kathy. Waking up in the guest room. Going to the high school Andrew and William would go to in a few years.

"And?" She dropped the tomato cubes in a bowl and sprinkled some feta in with them. I got up, went over to the cabinet, and took out two plates.

"I can't," I said. I tried to explain why. "I'm already registered to take the SATs here and—"

"Juliet, you must know that you can take the SATs in Oregon." For the first time since she'd arrived, Aunt Kathy sounded impatient with me. She shook the colander holding the pasta roughly.

"But I'm taking them at Webster High." I put the plates down on the table more heavily than I'd meant to. "Because everyone knows you have to take them at Webster High, not at Milltown, because there's always some kind of problem with the proctoring at Milltown. And if I come live with you, I won't know the right place to take them." She started to interrupt me, but I talked over her. "And there *is* a right place to take them in Portland, Kathy. Trust me. You just don't know about it. Plus I've got all my AP classes *and* swimming *and* debate *and* my SAT tutor—I can't leave all that behind. You have to understand that."

She added the pasta to the feta and tomatoes. "Is this about Jason? Because I know he's a wonderful boyfriend, and I'm sure the idea of living with him is very exciting, but you can't let that cloud your decision."

"It's not about Jason," I said firmly. "I'm not even sure I'm going to live with the Robinsons."

Kathy didn't look completely convinced, but she didn't push it. Instead, she brought the pasta over to the table and gestured for me to sit down. "There's something else I'd like to talk about. And that's your seeing someone." She reached behind her and took a piece of paper off the counter, then slid it across the table to me. "Her name's Elizabeth Bennet, and she's apparently terrific."

I made a face. "Her name's Elizabeth Bennet? Like the Jane Austen character?" I'd done an independent study with my English teacher last year, and we'd read *Pride and Prejudice*, *Emma*, and *Sense and Sensibility*.

Aunt Kathy laughed. "You know, I didn't even notice that."

"I'm not seeing a therapist named Elizabeth Bennet." I rolled my eyes. "Please."

"Juliet, don't be like that. She's a good therapist. I think she could help you." Kathy turned the paper toward herself, like maybe the woman's name would have changed since she wrote it down.

"Aunt Kathy, *I'm* not the one who needs help. My *mother* is the one who needs help, okay?" It came out really nasty.

"It's okay to be angry," said Aunt Kathy, her voice quiet and calm. "Even if all she was was irresponsible about her medication, your mother did a horrible thing."

"No, she didn't," I corrected her. I was embarrassed by how emotional I was being, and I tried to get my voice under control so Aunt Kathy wouldn't think I was freaking out. "It's not her fault. I feel bad for her, not angry at her."

"Juliet, it's not your job to take care of the grown-ups in your life." Aunt Kathy reached her hand across the table. "And it's okay to be angry."

"Don't tell me how to feel," I snapped. "I mean . . . I know it's okay to be angry, okay? But I'm not angry. Not at Mom, anyway."

She studied my face for an uncomfortable minute. "I'd feel better if you'd see someone."

"If it's not my job to worry about the adults in my life, then it's not my job to see a therapist so you feel better, right?" I raised an eyebrow at her to show how impressed she should be by my flawless logic.

Kathy threw her napkin up over her head. "Okay. I surrender. You win." She stood up and walked over to the refrigerator, clipped the piece of paper with Dr. Bennet's name on it under a magnet, and came back to the table.

"Just so we're clear, you know you can always change your mind, right?"

It wasn't clear to me if she meant I could change my mind about Dr. Bennet or about moving to Oregon, but since neither of those things was going to happen, there was no reason to ask which she was referring to.

"I know," I told her. And this time I was the one who reached my hand across the table to hers. "Thanks."

That night I put on my bathing suit for the first time in weeks. I was planning on swimming laps, but I just ended up sitting by the dark pool with my feet dangling in the water, trying to make a decision.

My dad kept leaving me voice messages about apartments the HR person at his consulting firm had found for him. Some had pools. One had a tennis court, which his mentioning as a selling point was kind of hilarious given the fact that my mother was the only person in our family who played tennis. I tried to imagine living in some random apartment complex with my father and the college girl he'd found to stay with me while he commuted back and forth to Ohio where a hospital had hired his firm to restructure it. Would she try to be friends with me? Would we all have dinner together when he wasn't traveling? Would the two of them fall in love?

Could my life possibly get even more melodramatic than it already was?

Sitting there, staring at the few brave leaves that had fallen since the pool guy had cleaned, I knew that I was going to move in with the Robinsons. I made the decision without making it, just like the summer Sofia and I vowed we weren't going to eat any refined sugar and then we'd been at the diner one night and found ourselves ordering dessert.

I sat back on my hands, looking through the glass doors at my aunt, who was sitting at the kitchen table talking to my grandparents on the phone. From the little bit I'd overheard before coming outside, I could tell they wanted to come down and that Aunt Kathy was trying to get them to wait. I hoped she would convince them not to come. I loved my grandparents, but my grandmother was fairly nervous and my grandfather's idea of intimate family conversation was asking you what route you'd driven to his house in Connecticut and how much traffic there'd been. I couldn't exactly see them being helpful in the midst of a mental health crisis.

As I watched my aunt, I wished it were my mother sitting there instead of her sister. I understood that the social worker was right, that now my mother was going to get the help she needed. And I knew I should be happy about that. But if I was being honest, I had to admit that I wished my mom were sitting at the kitchen table, buzzed on muscle relaxants and white wine, while I swam laps, blissfully ignorant of all the sadness inside her pretty head.

10

It was strange to pull up in front of Jason's house with an overnight bag on the seat next to me and to know I'd be sleeping there tonight and tomorrow night and every night for the foreseeable future. How many times had we sat on his couch, wrapped up in one of the fuzzy blankets his mom kept in a cedar chest in the den, fantasizing about what it would be like when we lived together someday?

And now we were doing it.

But walking across the lawn, I couldn't get excited about moving into his house. And it wasn't because of what had happened at the club that night with Declan. Every time I started to think about that, I forced myself to think about something else. It had been a horrible night, I had done a stupid thing, no one knew about it, and soon I'd have forgotten about it completely. Already the whole twenty-four hours felt unreal, as if I could just as easily have dreamed it as lived it. Last night, right before going to bed, I'd gotten up the nerve to ask Aunt Kathy about my mom's restraints.

"Restraints?" she'd asked, surprised. "What restraints?"

"On her wrists. Little blue restraints. With Velcro." I illustrated with my hand where they had gone. "She was wearing them that first night in the hospital."

"Oh, honey," said Kathy, hugging me. "She doesn't have anything like that now. If you could see her, you'd see she's just in a regular hospital bed. As soon as they transfer her to a long-term facility, you'll get to visit her, and you'll feel so much better." She shook her head. "Restraints," she said quietly. Then she perked up. "Are you sure you weren't just looking at a hospital bracelet?" She made a gesture similar to the one I'd made. "White and blue plastic?"

"Nooo . . . ," I said slowly. I was pretty sure I'd asked the social worker about them, but now I couldn't remember. "I don't *think* that's what it was."

But because Kathy was convinced I hadn't seen restraints on my mom's wrists, I'd started to wonder if maybe I was wrong and they hadn't been there at all. Maybe I'd imagined not just the restraints but everything about that night—finding my mother passed out on the floor of her bathroom, the fight with my father in the ER, the near accident with the van, singing "Happy Birthday" onstage, kissing Declan.

Had any of it actually happened?

So it wasn't the fact that I'd cheated on him that made moving into Jason's house feel weird. What made it weird was that it was proof of how fucked up my family was. Part of what had made me and Jason so special all these years had been that our families were so alike—he had a younger sister; I had an older brother. His parents had met in college; my parents had met in college. He had a stay-at-home mom; I had a stay-at-home mom. Our lives were identical, and we knew that our lives together were going to be identical to the ones we'd grown up with (except for the stay-at-home mom part).

We were equal.

I stood on the lawn staring up at his house, just as I'd had two weeks ago when he was leaving for France. Jason had never expressed any opinion about my parents getting divorced outside of sympathizing with me. He'd never been anything but supportive and loving and concerned.

But he must have had feelings about it. He must have had feelings about *me* and it.

What were they? What was he thinking about my family now? What was he feeling about *me* now?

I pulled my bag higher up on my shoulder. Somehow its weight was comforting, a reminder that I existed outside of Jason's parents' charity. Maybe I didn't have parents who could take care of me or a house I could go to. But at least I had a bag.

I crossed the lawn and rang the bell.

. . .

The Robinsons had a guest room, but it didn't exactly surprise me that I wouldn't be staying in it, since it was right across the hall from Jason's room and on a different floor from his parents' room. Bella's room, on the other hand, was next door to Grace and Mark's.

Sitting on the trundle bed, which Bella had made with bright pink sheets and her old My Little Pony comforter, and looking at Jason standing in the door of the bedroom wearing his sweatpants and a Brown T-shirt, I couldn't believe I'd been nervous about seeing him. From the second I'd walked in the door and Jason had put his arms around me and whispered, "Hey, J," in my ear so softly it made me shiver, I'd known everything was going to be okay.

Maybe I wasn't living in my house. But I was definitely home.

As soon as we'd come upstairs, Bella had insisted on helping me unpack all my stuff, marveling at what a neat folder I was. It inspired her to take everything out of her own drawers, and we'd spent half the afternoon organizing her clothes. That had made me feel better about being a guest, as if I was contributing to the family rather than just taking from them.

"So," said Jason, smiling at me from the doorway.

"So," I repeated, smiling back at him.

"Nice jammies," he said, nodding at my yoga pants and T-shirt with a silkscreen of the Buddha on it. Aunt Kathy had bought both for me last Thanksgiving when we'd gone out to Oregon and she'd convinced me to take a yoga class with her. I'd hated the class (being told to relax about ten thousand times in an hour made me tense enough to punch someone), and Aunt Kathy had irritated me by saying I wasn't *surrendering* to it, but even though few things were more annoying to me than Aunt Kathy on a yoga spiel, when I'd slipped on the clothes in the bathroom earlier, I'd felt heavy with loneliness for her.

I glanced down at what I was wearing. "I had the feeling your parents wouldn't dig seeing me in boxers and a tank top."

"Maybe not," said Jason. "But I would." He gave me a wicked grin, even though he'd seen me in a lot less than boxers and a tank top. "Movie?"

"*Really* movie?" I asked, because normally when we talked about watching a movie we meant channel surfing until his parents went to bed and we could go up to his room to have sex.

But Bella interrupted before Jason could answer. "What movie?"

Jason rolled his eyes. "I was thinking of me and J," he said. "You should get some sleep. You're probably pretty jet-lagged."

"You need sleep more than I do," countered Bella, kneeling on her bed and pointing at Jason to emphasize her point. "You both start preseason tomorrow. And anyway, Mom said you guys aren't allowed to exclude me the whole time Juliet's here."

Jason took a step toward his sister. "She *also* said you had to give us some time alone, so don't be a total brat!"

"*Mom!*" Bella shouted. "Jason called me a brat."

"Guys! Guys!" I said, and I couldn't help laughing. "Enough." Being here with Jason and Bella suddenly felt like being at home with my brother before he left for college. "We'll *all* watch a movie together tonight. Then tomorrow, Jason and I will watch a movie alone."

Bella sat down on her heels. "And the next night you and *I* will watch a movie alone. That's fair."

"Well, we definitely want to be fair," Jason said sarcastically.

Bella and I filed past Jason (who patted me lightly on the ass as I walked by), and the three of us headed down to the den. Except for the fact that I wouldn't be getting in my car and driving home in the next two hours or so, it was just another normal night at the Robinsons': Grace in the kitchen cleaning up after dinner. The glow of the computer screen letting us all know Mark was at his desk working. My entire life had exploded, and the Robinsons were doing exactly what they'd been doing every night since I'd met them.

Or were they? As we walked by the open door of Mark's study, it occurred to me that while he was sitting at his computer, none of us had any idea what he was actually doing. Maybe he was in a chat room picking up fourteen-year-old girls. Maybe he was online, gambling away the family's every last dime. Maybe twelve hours from now he'd be arrested for insider trading while Jason was at soccer practice and Grace and Bella were at Roosevelt Field Mall buying Bella's school clothes.

I couldn't get the idea out of my head. As Bella and Jason bickered about what we were going to watch and who would hold the remote and whether Bella, Jason, or I got to sit in the middle, I pictured Grace discovering Mark's secret, their screaming fight, Mark loading his belongings into the trunk of the Lexus and driving off to his new home. I imagined Grace's perfect hair with the roots showing, her spin-class-thin frame blowing up on Oreos and takeout.

The thought was awful. It really was. But it also felt strangely good, like finding out a test you'd been dreading had been canceled.

"You okay?" Jason's arm was around me, and Bella was squeezed up on my other side.

"Me? Yeah." I made myself stop thinking about what Mark might or might not be doing on his computer. I didn't want anything bad to happen to Jason's family. I loved Jason's family. And they loved me.

Jason and Bella had settled on a channel, and we watched a commercial featuring a line of dancing tissues that conga'd across the screen. I snuggled up to Jason, and he squeezed my shoulder more tightly. Bella laughed when one of the tissues sneezed.

"This is so romantic," said Jason.

"We're living the dream."

Bella wanted me to come upstairs while she washed her face and brushed her teeth, and by the time she went to sleep, Mark and Grace were already in their room.

"Sneak out," Jason whispered, hugging me. "Sneak out once they're in bed."

"I can't," I whispered back. Bella was supposedly asleep, but I had the bad feeling she was listening to every word we said. "I don't want to make your parents mad." I felt very conscious of being a guest in the Robinsons' house.

"Okay, I know when I'm beaten," said Jason sadly, and he kissed me on the lips. I kissed him back, but I was distracted. I needed to tell him what my dad and my aunt had told me about my mom and her drinking. And the medication. I always told Jason everything, but somehow this felt different. When you got right down to it, divorce was mundane. An accidental overdose was careless. A suicide attempt was tragic.

A problem with drugs and alcohol felt gross to me. And even if it was stupid, I couldn't help feeling like Jason would accept all the other scenarios more easily than he would accept that one.

A door closed. It was probably just a closet, but both Jason and I tensed. "I should go," he said.

"You should go."

We kissed one last time, and he headed down the hall.

. . .

I crawled under the covers, making a mental list of what I had to do tomorrow. Preseason. Then Bookers with Sofia to do some SAT prep. I had to call Glen to see if he could tutor me later on Thursdays like he had in the spring, because once school started, I'd have debate on Thursdays, and that went later than swim practice.

As the list formed in my mind, I thought about my mother and how she'd always helped me juggle my life. For years, she'd kept a big whiteboard calendar in the kitchen with my schedule and Oliver's. It had our whole lives: lessons and tutors and vacations and finals, what time a performance started and what time we had to arrive if we were performing. When Oliver left for college, the calendar just had my activities, and sometimes stuff that my parents were doing. *Dinner with the Chapmans. Tennis, court reserved.*

She was so together. That was the most impossible thing about all of this. Except for Grace Robinson, my mom was possibly the most together mom in my whole school. Okay, she wasn't, like, the president of the PTA. But that was because she thought the PTA was idiotic. The point was: she was a great mom. When it was time for me and Oliver to go to sleep-away camp, she interviewed camp directors. When it was time to redo my room, she hired a decorator. When it was time for me to look at colleges, even though she assured me every second that I'd get into Harvard, she also drove me all over the

114

Northeast so I could tour every college in New England and have a dozen backup schools on the off off off chance (as she kept putting it) that I got rejected.

Lying on Bella's trundle bed, I missed my mother so much I could taste it—something hard and metallic on the back of my tongue. My perfect beautiful mother with her soft sweaters and her gentle hands and her fresh flowers on the kitchen counter and her whiteboard with my life on it that I'd been looking at for so long I couldn't plan something without it appearing in my brain written out in dry-erase marker in my mother's clear, blocky letters.

I missed her so much, but what I missed wasn't even real. It hadn't even existed. That woman I'd loved and counted on had been miserable and drunk, her beautiful face hiding a brain full of rot and worms.

Just think about something that's not your mom, I said to myself. *Just think about something that's not your mom.*

And out of nowhere I thought of Declan.

The thing that hadn't happened even though it had, the thing I'd tried to turn into something else, the thing I hadn't let myself think about since I'd told myself never to think about it again came back at me, faster and bigger than the sun. I could feel his lips on mine, could feel his muscular body heavy and hot and pressing against mine and mine pressing back against his, as if all the energy I'd put into forgetting what had happened had only served to distill the experience, making the

115

memory of it even more potent than the thing itself. As if the memory were stronger than I could ever be.

I pressed my hands against the sides of my head, willing myself not to think about anything but to think about nothing.

And somehow, somewhere in between the remembering and the trying not to, I managed to fall asleep.

11

At preseason, I didn't tell anyone on the swim team about my mom. I knew Sofia and Jason wouldn't say anything either, but I had the feeling word was going to get out—gossip at Milltown was a varsity sport. Every day when I walked into the locker room, I looked at my teammates' faces, and every day that they casually waved hello to me was one more day I knew that they hadn't heard. I wasn't exactly relieved, though. Once they found out I was staying at the Robinsons', people were going to want to know why. I thought about Elise and Margaret, my closest friends besides Sofia, whispering theories about my parents. I thought about all the people in my grade who I knew but didn't really know. Sofia wasn't the only one of my friends who had been jealous of my family. People were always saying how good-looking my parents were, how smart and successful my brother was, how lucky I was.

Now were they going to pity me instead of envying me?

There was a surprising amount of back-and-forth about whether what my mom needed was a psychiatric facility or rehab, but apparently everyone decided that given the possibility that she'd made a suicide attempt, what she needed was a psychiatric facility. Jason, still holding out hope that the whole thing had been a dosing error on my mom's part, couldn't believe that they were really going to put her in the hospital for weeks just because she'd accidentally swallowed a few too many painkillers. When I told him that any day now she'd be going from Long Island Hospital to a mental hospital, he put his arms around me and kissed my neck. "It's crazy, J," he said quietly.

"You mean *she's* crazy," I whispered.

"Shh," he said, gently rubbing my shoulders. "Don't say that."

"You're right, I shouldn't say that," I agreed. I let my head drop down as he rubbed the back of my neck, then kissed it. "She might just be a drunk."

"Hmmm?" asked Jason, sliding my shirt collar down and kissing my shoulder blade.

"Nothing," I answered quickly. He kissed me again, and I turned around and kissed him back, relieved he was too distracted to follow up on what I'd said. I still hadn't told him what Aunt Kathy and my dad had told me about my mom's drinking and pill popping, but I knew now wasn't the right time.

Taking skeletons out of the family closet isn't exactly anyone's idea of foreplay.

Aunt Kathy called me the night before the first day of school to tell me that my mom's transfer to a long-term facility had been approved by her health insurance company and that she'd be moving to a place called Roaring Brook the next morning. She said she'd email my dad and keep him updated on what was going on and that she'd call my brother and tell him, also.

I was alone in Bella's room. Bella had insisted on picking out what I'd wear for the first day of school, and now she was downstairs watching TV while I folded up the outfits she'd considered and then rejected.

"They won't let your mother have visitors for the first two weeks," said Aunt Kathy. "It can be hard for patients. To see their families."

"Oh." Starting when we were in middle school, my parents had constantly given me and my brother some variation on an identical theme. *We never see you anymore. You're always with your friends. We miss you.* Sometimes, when my mom was frustrated with how little one of us was around, she'd say, *This isn't a hotel, it's your home, and we want some time with you.*

And now it would be "hard" for her to see me?

119

Through the phone, I heard a teakettle whistle and then abruptly shut off. I pictured Aunt Kathy in her bright yellow kitchen, the flowers in the window boxes bobbing in the breeze. "I'm sorry," she said. "I know it's difficult for you not seeing your mom. . . . Juliet? Are you there?"

I'd been hearing my mom's voice in my head. "Sorry," I said, tuning back into my conversation with Kathy. "I'm here. Thanks for letting me know."

"You doing okay with the Robinsons?"

"Yeah," I said, looking around the room. Bella had given me two drawers in her dresser and had vowed to use my staying with her as motivation to be a neater person. The Robinsons kept saying *Our home is your home* and telling me to have my friends over, but except for Sofia, nobody knew I was living with them. "They're being really nice," I said truthfully.

"But . . . ," Kathy started.

I shrugged. "But it's not my *home*." I felt my eyes well up. It was weird how talking to Aunt Kathy almost always made me want to cry.

"This is all going to be okay," Aunt Kathy said softly. "I promise."

"Yeah," I said. I swallowed my tears down. "I know."

There was a pause. "It's not too late to get in touch with Dr. Bennet."

"Her number's at the house," I said, adding, in case she didn't understand what I meant, "At my house."

120

"Oh," said Kathy. "And you couldn't possibly go back to your house and get it, could you?"

"Ha-ha."

From downstairs, Bella called, "Juliet, come watch with us!"

"I should go," I said. "Bella's calling me to watch TV with her and her mom."

"Well, I'm glad they're treating you like family," said Aunt Kathy. "That must help a lot."

"It does," I said. "It really does."

"Can I ask you to call Nana and Papa when you have a minute?" she asked. "They're worried about you and Ollie."

"Sure," I said, putting that on my list of things to do. "I'll call them tonight."

"Thanks."

Almost the second I hung up with Aunt Kathy, my phone rang. It was my dad, and I was about to answer it, but then I decided to let it go to voice mail. There was something exhausting about talking to my father lately, and it wasn't just that I couldn't help blaming him for what had happened to my mom. It was partly that, but it was partly something else. He'd call and ask how I was doing, and I'd give him a list of everything I'd accomplished. If I had made good time at swimming, I told him about that. And if I'd done well on a practice SAT, I'd tell him about that. Then I'd ask him how he was doing, and he'd say he was okay but tired. Then we'd try to find a

121

time when I didn't have my SAT tutor and he wasn't traveling and we could have dinner together. Then, when we couldn't, we'd agree to talk again soon. The empty routine of our conversations was what made them so tiring, but it didn't seem to bother my dad at all.

The crazy thing was, if you'd asked me six months earlier, I probably would have said that my dad and I were close. That even though he worked a lot and we didn't see each other all that much, we had a great relationship. That we knew each other really well. When I was younger, my grandfather—my mother's father—had teased me about being a daddy's girl, and even though I didn't like being teased, I'd liked the idea. I was a daddy's girl. My daddy and I were super close.

But apparently it turned out that we were so close that when my mother had to go into a mental hospital, I decided to live with my boyfriend instead of with him, and when he called me, I didn't pick up the phone.

Some daddy's girl.

It was Grace's idea that we tell people that I was living with the Robinsons while my mom explored job options out of town. On the drive to the first day of school, I prepared answers to their imaginary questions.

Massachusetts.

Not until after graduation.

Wetland conservation—she was an environmental studies major in college.

I imagined the small nonprofits where my mom was interviewing, the B and Bs where she would spend her nights on the road. In my head, I heard our conversations each night as she called me. *They're doing really interesting work,* she'd say. *I think I could be happy here. And if you get into Harvard, you'll be really close.*

The alternate reality felt so good that I started to hope people *would* ask me about my mom so I could make the fantasy feel even more real by talking about it.

None of our friends was interested in where my mom was, though. Everyone was too focused on it being the first day of senior year to ask me questions about my family. I got through homeroom, four classes, and morning break—more than half my first day—without anyone asking me anything that might necessitate my saying I was staying at Jason's. And then, at the start of lunch, right after we decided to go to the deli and were all walking across the senior parking lot to our cars, Stefan asked where Jason's car was. Jason said he'd driven to school with me, and Elise said, "Isn't that kind of out of the way?"

"I'm staying with Jason's family," I said, feeling my cheeks get hot. "My mom's job searching. In New England." Despite my practicing, the words were transparently a lie. I steeled myself for Elise to call me on it.

"Excellent," said George to Jason. "Sex on tap."

Elise turned around and slapped George—who was walking with Jason and Stefan a few feet behind us—on the arm.

"You're a pig, George." Elise and George had been going out almost as long as Jason and me, but unlike me and Jason, they were always fighting and almost breaking up.

"Ouch!" George objected, but Elise ignored him. She was looking at my schedule, which she'd grabbed from my hand as we exited the building. "Jesus. Your schedule is even busier than mine."

And just like that, my story stood. I wasn't sure if I was relieved or disappointed.

Sofia and Margaret were waiting for us by my car, and I waved to them.

"Do you have *no* free periods?" Elise asked, her finger tracing a line through my week. "Oh, wait, Thursday after lunch."

I shook my head. "I'm going to try and schedule a peer tutoring thing."

"Dude, you're going to have a nervous breakdown," said George.

"No," Jason corrected him. "She's going to get into Harvard early action." He closed the distance between us and hugged me from behind. "Then she can have a nervous breakdown."

"I'll pencil it in," I said.

"Come on, man," said George. "Let's grab some burgers." He and Stefan turned off toward George's car at the far end of the parking lot.

Jason kissed me, then held out his pinky. "J power."

"I'm going to barf," said Elise, who'd barely acknowledged George's leaving. I ignored her and linked pinkies with Jason. "J power."

The line at Jaybo's Deli was long, and by the time we got back in my car, it was going to be tight to make it to sixth period. As Elise and Margaret and Sofia talked about how much it sucked to be back and who'd done what over the summer and whether or not Elise should apply early to Princeton, I tried to follow the conversation, but every few minutes I realized I'd tuned out and had missed something. I glanced at the clock on my car's dashboard. Twelve thirty-five. Had my aunt said my mom was being transferred to Roaring Brook in the afternoon or the morning? I couldn't remember, and not being able to remember made me feel awful. I had one mother. She was being transferred from the psychiatric ward of a hospital to a long-term psychiatric facility. Was it so much to ask that I'd remember when that was happening?

"Did you hear about the exchange student from China?" asked Margaret from the backseat. "He's doing a year in America and apparently he is *ha-awt*!"

"There's an exchange student from China?" Sofia handed me a potato chip out of the bag on her lap. "I can't believe we have exchange students now."

"Asian guys don't do it for me," Elise announced.

"Oh my God, that is so racist," cried Sofia. "And anyway, you have a boyfriend."

"It's not racist if I'm Asian," Elise corrected her. "Which I am." She reached between the seats and took a chip out of Sofia's bag. Sofia slapped her wrist and Elise jerked her hand away.

"Hey, driving here!" I said. I was pretty sure Kathy had said my mom was being transferred in the morning, which meant she'd be there by now. What did her room look like? What were the other patients like?

Did she miss me? Or was she glad she couldn't see me for another two weeks?

"You're only half Asian," said Sofia.

"Dude, I'm Asian enough that I can say Asian guys don't do it for me," Elise informed her.

"I don't think you can say an *entire* ethnicity doesn't do it for you," Margaret argued. "Like, I'm sure there's *one* Asian guy out there in the world who you would be hot for."

"Yeah," said Sofia, handing me another chip. "And George better watch out, because maybe he's the guy who's spending the year at Milltown."

We were two minutes from the bell by the time I pulled into the parking lot, and Sofia and I raced down the corridor, dodging through the two thousand other students trying to get to their classes, our bags slapping against our thighs. People were clustered around the door to room 108, and I breathed a sigh of relief. We weren't going to be the last ones inside.

"Made it," I said to Sofia.

"You doing okay?" she asked, her voice quiet.

I nodded, and as she put her arm around me and gave a squeeze, I felt how lucky I was to have a friend like Sofia. She'd never breathe a word about what was really going on with my mom, and she'd never push me to talk about it, but she wouldn't pretend it wasn't happening either. I leaned my head on her shoulder as we moved toward the door of the classroom.

The line to get into the room was moving slowly, and I couldn't figure out what was going on. Mr. Burton was known for being quirky, but I couldn't see him holding people up at the door instead of letting them file into the classroom.

As I got to the front of the line, I saw what was causing the holdup. Mr. Burton was talking to a student, and they were standing just close enough to the door that people had to slide past them single file. The student wasn't the problem. It was Mr. Burton, who was practically standing *in* the doorway, but he was so engaged in what he was saying that he had zero awareness of the bottleneck he was causing.

"To say that interpretation of *Hamlet* is legitimate is simply grotesque. It's nothing short of an *outrage*. I admire your teacher for thinking freshmen could tackle the play, but I feel you have been done violence, yes *violence* by being fed such an absurd analysis of the text." Mr. Burton's arms flailed wildly. As I got to where he was standing, I had to duck in order to avoid getting whacked in the head by one of his hands.

I saw Jason sitting at the far corner of the room, and he saw me see him and gestured at the empty desk next to him. I turned slightly to point to Sofia, who was right behind me, and as I did, Mr. Burton said, "I am quite troubled, my boy. *Quite* troubled."

Apparently feeling he had made his point, Mr. Burton finally moved toward the front of the room, opening up the space he had been blocking between the doorway and the student he was talking to. And as he did, someone said, "Jules!"

I snapped my head to look.

"Oh my God," I whispered. It was as involuntary as breathing.

Standing there in my Honors English classroom was Declan.

12

He looked both exactly the same and ever so slightly different, as if I'd been remembering a blurry photo and here he was in focus. We stared at each other, neither of us saying a word, as my body registered what my mind had acknowledged the very first time I'd seen him—he was *hawt*. In his low-slung jeans and ancient CBGB T-shirt and black Doc Martens, he was smoking hot. Standing in front of him in my Honors English class, I could feel his hotness, just like I'd felt his hands on my body that night on the beach.

And suddenly, as if it were the answer to an SAT problem I'd been struggling with, I heard Sinead's voice in my head. *We've been living in Beijing for the past seven years.*

"You're the Chinese exchange student." My voice was strangely breathless.

"What happened to you the other night?" he asked, ignoring my non sequitur and leaning toward me to be heard over the chaos of the classroom. "What are you *doing* here?"

"What am *I* doing here? I've gone to school here since I was six. What are *you* doing here?" I hissed. We were close enough that I could smell something deliciously lemony on his skin. Soap? Laundry detergent? My nose struggled to place it.

"Do you guys know each other?" asked Sofia, eyes flickering between me and Declan.

"Do we—" Declan began.

The floor was tipping, slipping away from me, and I had the urge to grab Sofia before I toppled over. "We met at the club," I said quickly, hysterically. I pulled my eyes from Declan's and looked at Sofia, willing her somehow to know and not to know. "The night. That I had to wait for you. He was with the band. *In* the band. He was in the band. I hung out with them."

I couldn't tell if Sofia registered how strange and panicky I sounded. Eyes on some blank spot in the air between my face and Declan's, she said, "Hi. I'm Sofia." Her voice was pitched higher than usual, and her cheeks were ever so slightly pink.

"Ladies, Mr. Brennan. If you would be kind enough to take your seats." Mr. Burton's voice made it clear we could take our seats or take a hike.

So that was his name. Declan Brennan.

"Come sit with us," whispered Sofia. She led Declan over to where Jason had saved the two of us seats.

130

I went first, Sofia followed, and Declan took up the rear. James Gross was sitting in the empty seat next to the one Sofia sat in, but she said something to him and he moved over one desk. I sat down next to Jason and focused on the board, my eyes boring into it so hard they should have drilled a hole straight through to the next classroom.

My heart pounded in my chest, and my hands shook. This was impossible. For two weeks I had told myself to forget what had happened, and now what had happened was sitting two seats away from me in my English class. It wasn't fair. I followed the rules *all the time*. Then one night I did *one* stupid thing because my entire fucking life was falling apart, and now I was being punished for it. Wasn't it enough that my parents were getting divorced? That my mother was in a mental hospital? Declan's showing up was such an insane and unfair twist it was all I could do not to put my head down on the desk and weep.

"Welcome to Honors English," Mr. Burton announced. "And let us hope that the honor is not all yours."

I wasn't looking at Declan, but my body hummed with his closeness.

"This is Jason," whispered Sofia, and Jason whispered back, "Hey, man."

"Hey, man." I felt Declan's voice someplace deep in my lower back.

"For our purposes, the English language begins *here*." Mr.

Burton slapped the map hanging in front of the blackboard. "And *here*." He held up a book. Even if I hadn't been having a complete and total nervous breakdown, I would not have been able to read the title of the book he was holding. "With *Beowulf*, an Old English heroic epic poem. And when I say Old English, I mean capital *O*, capital *E*. Why is that, Mr. Chang?"

Behind Jack Chang's answer, I heard Sofia whisper, "Jason is Juliet's boyfriend. But she probably told you all about that when you met her." Something dropped to the floor. There was the sound of a metal chair sliding slightly on linoleum, and out of the corner of my eye I saw Declan lean forward and retrieve a pen.

"No," Declan answered Sofia. "I don't think she mentioned him."

Mr. Burton gave a single sharp clap. "Excellent, Mr. Chang. That is correct. How nice to start the year off with an intelligent response."

As soon as class ended, I shoved my stuff into my bag and got to my feet. "I've gotta run." My back was cold with sweat. All through class, I'd barely been able to hold my pen in my damp, twitching fingers.

"We're going to the same place," said Jason, slowly gathering up his stuff.

But if I had to stay in that room for one more second, *I* was the one who was going to end up in a mental hospital. "I have to get some water. I'll meet you in Latin."

I was looking at Jason, but all I could see was Declan sitting next to Sofia.

I kept my eyes on Jason. He smiled. "Suit yourself."

I tried to smile back, but nothing happened.

"Call me later!" Sofia yelled after me.

I barely nodded, just gathered my bag to my chest and tried not to drop anything. I could feel Declan watching me as I left the room. All the way down the hallway, long after it was possible, I felt his blue eyes on me, two bright flames burning against my back.

I'd had some idea that the sprint from English to Latin would clear my head, but all it did was make me breathless.

"Hey," said Jason, sliding into the seat next to mine a minute behind me. "Did you get your water?"

"Yeah," I lied as Ms. Croft entered the room.

Now was not the time to get confused about my priorities. Latin was my number one challenge for the year. If anything stood between me and Harvard, it was this class.

Last year, Latin had been, without a doubt, my worst subject. According to my report card, I had a ninety-six average, but the truth was that our teacher, Mr. Racine, was a little scared of our class. The Latin kids had a reputation for being the Smartest Kids in the School, so if I didn't know something or didn't do very well on a test, I felt like Mr. Racine somehow got the idea that I really *did* know it or maybe he figured he hadn't given a very good test or something. In the end, my real average was probably more like an eighty-five than a ninety-six, but somehow he'd factored in class participation or, I didn't know, the cookies my mom and I gave him at Christmas, and so I got my A.

I'd wanted to drop Latin, figuring I'd quit while I was ahead, but Jason had convinced me not to. He said that even though I was a third-generation legacy, I shouldn't do anything that would give Harvard a reason to put me in the "maybe" pile.

"Welcome to AP Latin," announced Ms. Croft. "This is the *sanctum sanctorum*, and you are the high priests of the study of an ancient and beautiful language, the keepers of the flame."

On my notebook, Jason wrote, *Is she for real?* but I pushed his hand away, took out my pen, and started taking notes as Ms. Croft continued to talk.

The Aeneid *is a Latin epic poem.*

Declan Brennan does not exist.

Written by Virgil.

No one will ever find out about that night.

Dactylic hexameter

I love my boyfriend.

29–19 BCE

Jason drew a heart around the date, which I'd written at

the top of the page. Inside it, he put two Js, one facing forward, one backward.

J power.

"Want me to walk you to the pool?" Jason offered when class ended.

There was a strange buzzing in my head that made it hard to hear. "Sure," I said.

I was going to get caught. Naturally I was going to get caught. It was delusional to think no one would find out, to say Declan didn't exist.

Of course he existed. He was in my fucking English class.

Jason put his arm around me as we walked. "What time are you done? Should I just get a ride with Stefan or do you want to coordinate?" He drew out the syllables of *coordinate*, like he was being ironic.

I shook my head. "I'm going to Sofia's." I sounded jittery. Jason was sure to notice.

Why do you sound so nervous, J?

Just scared you're going to find out I cheated on you.

"I didn't know that," said Jason. "Did you tell me that?"

I stopped walking. My heart stopped beating in my chest. "Wait, *what?*"

Jason cocked his head at me, a confused look on his face. "That you were going to Sofia's after practice. Did I know that?"

My heart started beating again, but inexplicably, relief made me irritable. "Dude, since when do I clear all my plans with you?" As soon as I said it, I smiled, like, *JK!*

But I wasn't JK. Not exactly.

Jason tucked my hair behind my ear. "Just call my mom and tell her you won't be home for dinner, 'kay?"

"Seriously?" I asked. My voice had an edge to it.

"Well, I mean . . . she's expecting you." Jason shrugged.

What was wrong with me? It wasn't as if it came as news to me that Jason's family had dinner together every night at seven. Now that I was living with them, of course Grace expected me to be at home by then or let them know I wouldn't be. It wasn't her fault that I was distracted by the fact that the boy I'd cheated on her son with had just shown up at school and shattered my world.

"Sorry," I said quickly. I reached into my bag. "I'm just being crabby. I'll text her right now." We started walking again.

"Thanks," said Jason, and as I took out my phone, he kissed the top of my head. "Sorry you're feeling crabby. Is it about your mom?"

"No," I said, "It's just—"

Oh my God, what was I *doing?* It was like I *wanted* him to ask why, *wanted* to tell him about me and Declan. "Yeah," I said, doing a full one-eighty. "I guess it is about my mom."

I didn't look at him as I lied, focusing instead on writing my text to his mom about dinner. I hit send just as we arrived at the door to the pool. "Done," I said proudly, holding up my phone so he could see I'd sent it.

"Thanks," Jason said. He reached out his pinky, and I intertwined it with mine. "J power."

"J power," I repeated. I watched him heading down the hall to the locker room, and I remembered when we were first going out and I would go to Jason's soccer games. Sofia and Margaret and Elise and a bunch of these other girls we were friends with would sit in the stands and I would watch Jason and I would think, *We are a couple.* It made me feel safe and special, and watching him now, I felt the very same way. *We are a couple.*

Nobody was going to mess that up.

Not even me.

13

On the way to school the next morning, Jason abruptly turned my car into the parking lot at Jaybo's.

"I am in urgent need of a bacon, egg, and cheese sandwich," he declared. "And I would be honored to buy you an enormous cup of coffee."

"I could use it," I said, rubbing at my eyes, which felt raw in the harsh morning light. I hadn't finished my Latin homework until almost one in the morning, but that wasn't the reason my eyes burned and my head felt too heavy for my neck. After getting in bed, I'd lain awake for hours trying to figure out what to do about the situation with Declan. Finally I gave up on sleep, threw my covers off, and tiptoed over to my backpack. I slipped a piece of paper out of my notebook, wincing as the paper tore with a screech guaranteed to wake Bella. But she hadn't stirred, and I'd gotten the paper out and written a note by the light of my phone. *Declan, I need to talk to you.* At the bottom I'd put my name and my cell, hesitating for a while about whether to write *Jules* or *Juliet*. Finally I'd written *Juliet*. It was my name, after all, and it wasn't like he and I knew each other well enough for him to have a nickname for me.

Well, not really, anyway.

"I'll go in and get the stuff," I said. "Salt and pepper on the sandwich?"

"You know it," said Jason, "and buy yourself something nice." Winking, he handed me his wallet.

Jaybo's was crowded with kids from Milltown and guys in work boots and paint-spattered pants, and I waited on line for Jason's sandwich before getting my coffee. My whole body ached with sleepiness; I had to squint to read the labels on the different coffee carafes. Aunt Kathy had emailed me that she'd talked to my mother's doctor, who'd said my mom was settling into Roaring Brook and doing well and that she could have visitors in two weeks. I hadn't seen my mom since that night in the emergency room, and I tried to imagine what it would be like to visit her at a mental hospital. All I could think of was parents' weekend at Yale a year ago, how my parents and I had gone up to see Oliver and he'd shown us his room and introduced us to his roommate and then given us a tour of the campus. Was that what visiting my mother was going to be like? The image was parodic, but somehow it didn't make me laugh.

"Are you going to explain what happened the other night?"

I gave a little yelp, jumped, spilled my coffee on my hand, and gave an even bigger yelp. Heads all over the deli turned to look at me. "Shit!" I said, shaking my hand, which stung from the hot coffee. "Shit!"

Declan handed me a wad of napkins, and I didn't look at him as I wiped off my hand and the counter, not bothering to deal with my T-shirt, which was black anyway. I thought of the note I'd spent so much time composing and how it was at that moment in my bag in the car.

Why was it nothing ever turned out the way I planned it anymore?

I wadded up the soaked napkins and tossed them and the half-empty cup in the hole in the counter where the garbage went. Finally, I forced myself to look at Declan.

He was standing a foot or so away from me, wearing a pair of black jeans and a red T-shirt so faded it was almost pink. His hair was damp. I couldn't smell the lemony scent over all the other Jaybo smells, and I was grateful for that. Still, there was something about his physical presence that my body reacted to. I *sensed* his nearness, like bats echolocate walls and doorways. It was disconcerting—to feel him without touching him—and as we stood there, looking at each other, I was sure that when I opened my mouth to say something, no words would come out.

Amazingly enough, though, they did. "Look," I said, my voice reassuringly level. "I was really . . . that was a very bad night for me, and I'm sorry for what I did. I really am." In books, characters are always communicating with their eyes, but even though we stared at each other for at least a count of five, I had no idea what Declan was thinking and I was pretty sure he wasn't reading my mind either.

"Yo, Declan!" Rob Noel, a guy in our class I didn't know very well, was standing at the door.

"Whatever," Declan said finally. "It was no big deal." I watched him follow Rob outside and head to Rob's BMW, the little bell dinging when the door of the deli swung shut.

The car was cool, and I slid gratefully into the smooth leather seat. I took the bacon, egg, and cheese sandwich out of the paper bag and handed it to Jason.

"Thanks, J," he said. "Where's your coffee?"

I looked out the window. Everything on the other side of the glass looked as hot and wilted in the September heat as I felt.

"J?" said Jason.

"Yeah?" I asked, startled.

"Your coffee?"

"Oh I . . . I realized it wasn't what I was in the mood for," I said. "I should probably drink less coffee anyway."

Jason took a bite and put the sandwich in his lap. "Not first semester senior year you shouldn't," he said. He put the car in drive and pulled out of the parking lot. "Now is not the time to make major changes to your routine." We eased into the traffic on Judson Road.

"You're right," I said, still looking out the window. "Now's not the time."

14

I sensed Declan everywhere.

Tuesday, he walked into English, and my heart slammed against my chest as he looked over and nodded at Sofia and me and then went and sat in the back of the class next to Christian Donaldson. Even though he was on the opposite side of the room and behind me, I could feel him back there, as if there were an invisible thread connecting us. The whole first week of school, as soon as I forgot about him even for a minute, I'd pass him in the hallway or I'd see him across the lawn or he'd walk into Mr. Burton's class and I'd feel the gentle tug. *Declan. Declan.* After that morning in Jaybo's, though, we never spoke to or looked at each other.

I was glad that Elise had been right—my schedule *was* nearly killing me. I spent my days racing from class to class, then to practice, then home for homework or tutoring sessions with Glen or writing drafts of my supplemental college essays. I'd collapse into bed long after midnight, setting the alarm for six so I could finish whatever I hadn't done the night before. I barely had time to think about Declan. I barely had time to think about my mom and the countdown to my visit with her. When my dad called, I barely had time to tell him I didn't have time to talk on the phone.

How u holding up? my brother texted me. *Don't stress college 2 much.*

The summer before my brother's senior year of high school, my mother drove him up to Yale so he could meet with the squash coach. All fall, on the kitchen calendar, she kept a list of his major assignments and when they were due. She cross-referenced his applications so that if he didn't get into Yale early, he would know which parts of which supplemental essays he could use more than once. In late October, when he got strep throat, she emailed his teachers to make sure he got every assignment, and then she emailed them back, attaching the work he'd done while she brought him soup and Ritz crackers so he could keep up his strength. Until he got the letter saying he'd gotten into Yale, she made sure he never missed a class, was never late with a paper, was never unprepared for even the most minor reading quiz, and even after he got accepted and we celebrated with a huge family dinner, to which we all wore Yale T-shirts, hats, and scarves that she'd had FedExed overnight from New Haven, she stayed on top of him so that he wouldn't be one of those kids you heard about whose grades dropped so much that a college rescinded his acceptance.

And now she was in a mental hospital and he was texting me not to stress college too much.

Thanks, Ollie, I texted back. *I'll try not to.*

Two weeks into school, when we were talking about trying to squeeze in an extra debate meeting before the competition the following weekend, Kenyatta suggested some of us get together at his house on Saturday.

"I can't do morning," I said. "I have a practice SAT. Oh, and then I've got a meet. What about afternoon?"

"I can do that," said Sebastian, who was a junior and probably going to be captain next year. "But only from three to five. I've got my math tutor after." A few other people said they could do Saturday and took out their phones to write it down.

Jason cleared his throat. "Saturday afternoon's not really good," he said. "What about Sunday?"

"What's wrong with Saturday?" I asked.

He was staring at me, his eyes bulging unnaturally. "Don't you have that, um, thing?"

Macy was studying her iPhone. "I could do Sunday between twelve and two," she said. "Or I could stay late next Thursday."

"I can't stay late next Thursday, I have my SAT tutor," I said, still looking at Jason. *What?* I mouthed.

Your mom, he mouthed back.

145

"Um, let's do Sunday, guys, 'kay?" I asked quickly.

"Sure," said Sebastian. "What time? I have squash at five."

Later, when Jason and I were walking to his car, I mock-slapped my forehead. "I can't believe I almost forgot to visit my mother in the mental hospital."

He shook his head and took my hand. "I'm glad you think it's funny." He'd offered to come with me to Roaring Brook, but only immediate relatives were allowed in the hospital. I was glad the choice wasn't mine to make. I wouldn't have thought there was something more intimate than sex, but if there was, it was definitely visiting a person's mother in a mental hospital. I wasn't sure I was ready to share that part of my life with anyone, not even Jason.

"Well, I mean, it's not *funny* funny," I corrected him. "It's, you know, crazy funny. It might be the *definition* of crazy funny, actually."

He clicked his key and the alarm gave a brief squawk. Then he opened the car door for me. "I love how your mind works, J," he said.

"Translation: You think I'm a nutcase."

"I'm saying I wouldn't change a thing about you." He kissed me and gestured for me to get into the car.

Unfortunately, my sense of humor deserted me on Saturday afternoon, and for the life of me I couldn't remember what I'd found funny about visiting my mother in a mental hospital.

Roaring Brook was on a wooded piece of land next to a brook that trickled more than it roared. Something about the elegant private road reminded me of the drive up to the Milltown Country Club, and thinking about that drive made me think about everything that had happened before I saw Sofia and everything that had happened after.

Once upon a time, my mind had been a happy block where all the kids played together and nobody locked their doors at night.

Now it was a bad neighborhood I tried to avoid going into alone.

The road forked, and I followed the arrow on the sign that read VISITOR PARKING, which landed me in a small but surprisingly crowded lot. *All these people know someone in a mental hospital*, I thought. I wondered if any of the other visitors had taken a practice SAT that morning. What was the Venn diagram of people with a mentally ill family member who took the SATs?

It would have made a good SAT question.

The hospital was an odd building—the stairs leading up from the parking lot took me to what looked like an old house, but there were more modern wings coming off on both sides. Had people gotten crazier over the years, so they had to make the place bigger? Was there a tour guide I could

147

ask, like in Colonial Williamsburg?

Our family had taken a trip to Colonial Williamsburg the summer I was fourteen and Oliver was sixteen. Standing on the wooden porch of Roaring Brook, I had a sudden, powerful memory of my dad lifting his glass at an old-timey restaurant where we'd eaten. There had been some kind of crisis that day. Had we booked a hotel room and it hadn't been available? Had the car broken down? I couldn't remember what had happened, just that my parents had been on their cell phones a lot and it had been very tense and then we'd finally gotten to the restaurant. Both of my parents ordered drinks before dinner, which they didn't normally do, and neither of them said anything when Oliver and I attacked the basket of rolls the waitress put on the table.

When my parents' drinks came, they lifted their glasses at each other and my dad made a toast. He said, "To my beautiful wife who never loses her head in a crisis," and then my parents kissed.

I remembered the toast because at the time it had embarrassed me that my dad had called my mom beautiful, and when he'd kissed her, I'd only been more embarrassed. Was it because Jason and I had already started going out, so I knew more about what kissing meant than I had before? Whether or not that was why, the memory had stayed with me—my dad smiling at my mom, his glass raised in her direction. My mother's glass clinking gently against his. Their kiss.

Had they been unhappy then? Because that moment looked a lot like happiness to me.

I pushed open the thick glass door, glad that the place felt more like a house than a hospital. Behind an elegant wooden desk was a youngish woman, maybe in her thirties, who looked up when I walked in.

"May I help you?" She reminded me of a salesclerk in a store.

"I'm here to see my mo—sorry. I'm here to see Barbara Newman."

"Of course," she said. She stood up and came around the other side of the desk. "She's expecting you." The woman led me down a corridor lined with small old-fashioned tables and chairs. The floors had antique runners, and there were small, glass-shaded lamps along the walls. It really did feel like we could be in somebody's home until we got to the end of the hallway and she had to type a code into a keypad in order to open the door.

On the other side of the door, an older woman in a nurse's uniform was waiting for us. "Thanks," she said to the first woman. And then she held out her hand. "I'm Grace."

It was startling to hear Jason's mom's name come out of the nurse's mouth. I shook her hand and said, "I'm Juliet."

"Come," she said briskly. "Some of the patients are at therapy now, and others have time to themselves. We have group sessions in the morning and the afternoon. It's a chance for the patients to get to know one another and talk about . . . well, some of the issues that brought them here." Grace was acting as if I didn't know what I was walking into, like maybe I thought my mom really was out of town looking at jobs.

We must have crossed over into the newer part of the building, because all the charming molding and carpets of the corridor were replaced with linoleum floors and walls painted a flat, institutional pale blue. There was a faint smell of some kind of cleanser. Along the corridor were doors, each one with a small window in it. I was scared of what was behind the doors, but when we passed an open one, I saw that there was just a bed and a table and a small chest of drawers in the room. I felt better until I saw that the large window had bars on it.

"Here we are," said Grace, stopping in front of another door, this one glass without any keypad. She turned to me, and her voice was cheerful. "When's the last time you saw your mother, honey?"

"When she was in the hospital. The night she . . . was admitted." As I said it I felt guilty, but then I reminded myself that I couldn't have seen her between then and now because no one would let me.

"Well, you may find her a little changed," Grace continued in the same chipper voice.

Given the fact that the last time I'd seen her she'd been tied to her bed and the time before that she'd been half-naked and unconscious on the floor of her bathroom, *changed* didn't exactly seem like a bad thing.

"Okay," I said. "Thanks. I'll be ready for that."

Grace placed her hand on my arm. "I'm going to suggest that we keep the visit brief. I'll be back in half an hour." She patted me lightly, then turned and headed back down the corridor.

As soon as she was gone, I realized there were about ten million questions I should have asked. Were there things I wasn't supposed to talk to my mom about? How was I supposed to act? If she started getting upset, what was I supposed to do? Change the subject? End the visit?

The realization that I was scared to talk to my mom made me feel heavy and tired in a way that even my swim meet and practice SAT hadn't, and I had to work to push open the door, which led into a sunny room with walls and windows that were almost entirely glass. It made me think of the greenhouse in the botanical garden.

I spotted my mom immediately even though she was sitting in a chair that was slightly hidden by a large potted tree. She was wearing a blue cotton sweater and a pair of linen pants, and the *New York Times* was open on her lap. I hadn't realized until this minute how much I'd missed her, and I crossed the space between us quickly, almost at a run.

"Mommy!" I cried. I hadn't called her that in years, but the word flew out of my mouth. There she was. My mommy.

She turned her head slowly. Except for the long roots of her hair, she looked totally normal. I figured she'd stand up and hug me, but she just took my hand and squeezed it. "Hi, sweetheart," she said.

I felt weird standing—almost looming—over her, but she didn't make any move to get up and there wasn't another chair nearby. Finally, I went over to a card table where two people were playing chess while a third one watched. One of the guys playing was young, maybe even my age. Was he a visitor or a patient?

I decided I wasn't going to think about that.

"Can I take this chair?" I asked.

"By all means," said the older guy who was playing. The younger guy didn't look at me.

"Thanks," I said, sliding it out from under the table.

"Our pleasure." He smiled at me. I smiled back. He seemed totally normal. Everyone in the room seemed totally normal— the older woman knitting in the corner, the guy watching the chess game. No one was rocking back and forth or moaning or shouting.

Maybe none of them were crazy at all. Maybe all these people were locked up because of some kind of clerical error.

I pulled the chair up next to my mom's. The newspaper was still on her lap, but she wasn't reading it. I realized she was sitting in the same position she had been when I first saw her, which meant she probably hadn't been reading it then, either.

"So," I said, excitement at seeing her still running through my veins, "how are you? I'm sorry," I added quickly. "Do you not want to talk about how you are?"

"No," she said, "it's fine to ask." Her voice was thick, almost as if she'd been drinking, which seemed unlikely.

"I just took a practice SAT," I said. I thought she would ask about the test, but she didn't, so I said, "Do you like it here?"

She looked around as if she needed to be reminded of where she was before she could answer my question. "I do, actually. It's very restful. It reminds me of summer camp."

"Oh," I said. "Well, that's . . . you must like that." My mom had gone to the same summer camp practically her entire childhood, first as a camper for a million summers, then as a counselor for about a million more. She'd seemed a little disappointed when neither my brother nor I was especially into the summer camp we went to.

I had one question and only one question that I wanted to ask my mother. *Did you mean to do it?*

But the words stuck in my throat.

There was silence. It was an awful silence, something cold and dark with tentacles that were pulling me down into it.

"Mom?" I whispered. "Mommy?"

I looked at my mom. She was facing me, but her eyes were focused on something just above my head, as if she were looking into the eyes of a taller version of me.

I reached out and touched her hand. It was dry and cool, and I was startled to see that she wasn't wearing her wedding band or her engagement ring. Her engagement ring was a huge diamond, and she took it off to play tennis and wash dishes, so it wasn't weird to see her without it on, but I'd never seen her hand without her wedding band, a thin ring of diamonds set in platinum that she'd kept wearing even after my dad moved out. Had she had it on the night of her . . . the night we went to the hospital? I tried to picture her hand that night, but all I could see was the blood on the floor, her thigh, naked up to her underwear.

"Mom," I said quietly. "What happened that night? What . . . happened?" I repeated vaguely.

If she heard me, she didn't indicate it. The minutes ticked by until it became clear that if I wanted an answer I was going to have to repeat the question. I opened my mouth to ask it again and almost immediately closed it. This was insane. The woman sitting here was not my mother. She didn't know any more about what my mother felt than I did.

Time seemed to have stopped, and when I finally saw Grace out of the corner of my eye, I felt as if decades must have passed since she'd left me at the door to the glassed-in room.

She came over to where my mother and I were sitting. "I hope you had a nice visit."

My mother turned her eyes to Grace and gave a vague smile. I recognized it.

It was the same smile she'd smiled at me.

I stood up. "Mom," I said. "I have to go." I reached down and took her hand. She gave me an anemic squeeze back.

"Thank you for coming," she said, as if I were a guest she'd just met at a cocktail party.

I could feel tears burning at the corners of my eyes, and I just turned and walked out, several feet ahead of Grace until I got to the locked door, where I had to wait until she punched the code into the pad.

At the front desk, the woman smiled at me. "I hope you had a good visit," she said.

"Not really," I said. I pressed my fingers to my lips to stop their shaking, then added, "My mom's pretty out of it."

"I'm sorry," she said, and she seemed genuinely sorry.

"Thanks," I said, and I raced out the front door so she wouldn't see me bawling.

As soon as I got outside, I dialed Kathy's number. She picked up on the first ring.

"How'd it go?" she asked.

"She's like a zombie." I was crying hard enough that I wasn't sure if my aunt would understand what I was saying.

"I'm really sorry, honey. I'm so sorry you had to see her like that. The doctors are trying to get her medication right, and it's tricky. Psychotropic drugs are an art, not a science."

"What does that even mean?" I wailed. "What kind of fucking art does that to a person?"

"It's going to take a little time," said Aunt Kathy. "Why don't you wait to visit her again until I'm back? I don't know how much she'd really get out of it, and it's just going to upset you. Okay?"

I nodded, and Kathy said, "Juliet."

"Sorry," I said, wiping my eyes with my knuckles. "I was nodding. Yes. Okay."

"I'd really like you to think about seeing Dr. Bennet."

"Why don't you understand that I *can't*," I almost shouted. "I can barely do everything I have to do as it is."

Aunt Kathy wasn't flustered by my yelling. "Sometimes we have to make time for things that are really important."

When I got back to Jason's house, I was sorry to see Grace's car in the driveway. The last thing I felt like doing was pulling myself together and interacting normally with anyone. But when I walked into the kitchen, Grace took one look at the expression on my face, put down her iPad, and came over and gave me a hug. I'd thought I was all cried out, but as soon as she put her arms around me, I started to sob.

"Shhhh," she whispered. "It's okay."

Standing there, smelling her clean hair and the perfume she wore—light and floral, like a bush of lilacs in the beginning of summer—I let myself fantasize that she was my mom. I imagined I was standing in my own kitchen, having just come home from visiting some crazy aunt. I remembered my first night at the Robinsons'. Bella had said, *Now we're like sisters*, and Jason had joked, *I think we're getting into a gray area.* The memory made me laugh a little, and Grace pulled away and nodded approvingly.

"That's better," she said, pushing some hair out of my eyes. "As long as you can laugh, everything is going to be okay." Then she reached over to the counter and handed me a tissue from the pale gray box on the counter. It was a slightly lighter gray than the granite counter and a slightly darker gray than the glass backsplash. Even the tissues were a pale, pearly gray, and the blouse Grace wore had a band of gray piping around the neck. It didn't surprise me. Everything about the Robinsons matched perfectly.

Grace went to the cabinet and took down two glasses, then filled them with water and ice from the door of the fridge. I wasn't thirsty, but I accepted the glass.

"Thanks," I said. I took a deep breath.

"You're welcome. Want to talk about it?"

I shrugged. "I don't know. My aunt said they're trying to get her medications right, but she seemed pretty out of it." *Pretty out of it* felt like a bit of an understatement considering my mother's near catatonia, but I couldn't bring myself to be any more explicit.

"Well, Roaring Brook's got an excellent reputation, and I'm sure she's getting wonderful medical care." Grace shook her head. "You really got dealt a bum hand, didn't you?"

"I sure did," I agreed. We both smiled. I was starting to feel better.

"Just remember, Juliet. Your mother made her choices, and you'll make yours. You're your own person." She took a step closer to me and put her hand on my shoulder.

Grace's confidence in my mental health should have made me feel good, but instead it made me mad. What did she know about my mother? What did she know about me?

She squeezed my shoulder and smiled at me, then turned back to her iPad. Over her shoulder I could see she was looking at a website with a recipe. I stared at her back.

"Dinner's at seven," she said, half focused on me, half focused on what she was reading.

On the counter beside her was a slab of butcher block with slots for knives. There was an enormous cleaver that I'd used once when Jason and I were cutting watermelon. I imagined taking it now and cleaving her head in two, leaving her perfect kitchen spattered with her perfect brains.

"Maybe you'll help set the table," she continued, making a note of something on a gray Post-it.

"Sure," I said carefully, almost as terrified by what I'd been thinking as Grace would have been.

As I walked through the foyer, I heard the tinkling of the ice in my glass, and I realized my hand was shaking. Grace was so confident I wasn't like my mother.

But wasn't I?

15

I had Latin first period Monday, and I completely bombed a quiz. After, Jason kept telling me I'd probably done better than I thought I had, and even though I let him think I believed him, I knew he was wrong. I couldn't get my head into anything, and even Mr. Harris, my history teacher (who never yelled at anyone), snapped at me for checking my phone in class. I'd been looking to see if Kathy had talked to my mom's doctors and called to tell me about it, which was pretty dumb considering it was seven a.m. in Oregon and she probably hadn't even tried to reach the doctor yet. At swim practice, I could not find my rhythm at all. Coach Kalman kept blowing her whistle and shouting things at me, but it was like she was speaking Swahili.

I finished a lap, surfaced, and found myself face-to-face

with Coach Kalman. "Newman, where's your head?"

"Sorry," I said automatically.

"Yeah, well. Sorry's not good enough," she said. Then she blew her whistle. "Okay, that's it for today. Let's hit the showers."

I stayed in the water and let myself sink down, down, down until my feet were touching the bottom of the pool. All I wanted was to stay down here, to not have to make any decisions—not about my mother, not about my father. Not about swimming or debate or college. If I could just let everything slip away. It would be so easy. . . .

Was this what it had been like for my mom? This sense that it was easier to sink down than to swim up? I thought of the Sylvia Plath poem we'd had on our first practice AP exam. *Dying / Is an art, like everything else. / I do it exceptionally well.* Maybe my mother hadn't done it exceptionally well. Maybe she'd really wanted to die, only she'd screwed up the dosage.

Maybe they'd get her all cleaned up and healthy and she'd get home and do it again.

Do it right this time.

By then my lungs were bursting, and it seemed like a force other than my own body pulled me up to the surface. I bobbed, gasping for air, coughing a little when I accidentally swallowed a mouthful of water.

Killing yourself really was harder than it looked.

• • •

Walking out of swim practice, I ran smack into Sinead. It shouldn't have surprised me—obviously, if Declan went to Milltown High, so did his sister and Danny. The surprising thing was how long it had taken me to run into one of them. Two thousand students was a lot of people, but it wasn't enough to keep you from running into someone indefinitely. Still, seeing her threw off my already tenuous equilibrium. I hadn't thought about Declan since English, and now it was like Sinead was here to remind me not to forget him.

If I was surprised, Sinead was shocked. She did a double take. "Jules? Wait, this is so crazy." She was with two girls I didn't know, and they hesitated, clearly unsure of whether to stay or go. "Do you . . . do you go to school here?"

"Yeah," I admitted. "I'm a senior."

My saying I was a senior must have decided Sinead's friends, because they scuttled off. "See you later, Sinead," they called.

"Later," she called. We stood there awkwardly for a minute, and then she threw her arms around me. "This is amazing! I can't believe I haven't seen you yet. You know, Declan's a senior too."

I hugged her back. "Yeah," I said. "I have a class with him, actually."

She stepped away. She was wearing a short red skirt and a black top. There was nothing particularly special about the outfit, but something about the cut of the skirt looked cool

161

and British to me. "Serious?" she asked, her accent suddenly very pronounced.

"Yeah. Honors English." I realized how weird it was that I'd never asked Declan about his siblings. If he and I hadn't fooled around that night, if I hadn't been so eager to avoid him, I would have asked about them. Maybe not Danny, who was just a kid, but definitely Sinead. Not asking about her suddenly felt as suspicious as anything else I'd done with Declan.

She was still looking at me with those blue, Declan eyes. "He never told me that."

"He probably forgot. I mean, that we'd met and everything." I was rocking back and forth uneasily, my bag clutched to my side.

"My brother's a total wanker," she said finally.

"So how are you?" I asked, eager to change the subject and glad to let her blame everything on Declan's absentmindedness. "How are you liking life as an American?"

She shrugged a very Declan shrug. "It's okay. Are you coming to the show on Friday? At the Coffeehouse? Or did he forget to tell you about that, too?"

"I didn't know you were having a show," I said, struck by how chill Sinead was. She was someone I could imagine hanging out with, maybe even being friends with.

One more thing I'd blown by getting carried away that night on the beach.

"Yeah, bloody Danny's supposed to be putting up posters,

but he's about as reliable as his brother." Sinead laughed and squeezed my arm. "It was so much fun hanging out with you at the club that night. I was really pissed when Declan forgot to get your number. I had this crazy idea you'd join the band."

"I wish I could," I said, which was true in its way. "I'm too swamped to join a band right now. You know, with college and everything. But I had fun hanging out with you, too."

She hugged me again. I'd had some idea that British people were standoffish, but apparently I was wrong. "See you at the show," she said.

I hugged her back. "Definitely," I said, meaning *Not on your life.*

On my way home, Kathy called. I knew I shouldn't answer while I was driving, but I did anyway.

"They were trying a new drug," she said after we'd said hello. "But she didn't respond well to it, so they're taking her off it."

"Okay," I said. What else could I say?

"Their goal is to get her off everything and then see where we are," Kathy explained.

"Okay," I said again. I turned onto Jason's block. I glanced in my rearview mirror and saw a police car behind me. I thought about hanging up quickly, so he wouldn't see me on my phone, but then I would have had to explain to Kathy that I was talking to her while I was driving, and I knew she'd be angry. I pulled up in front of Jason's house, and the cop drove on. Apparently we both had bigger things to worry about than my breaking the law.

"You sound mad," said Kathy. "Which is understandable," she added quickly. "It's maddening."

"I'm not mad," I said.

We talked for another minute, and then Kathy reminded me to call my grandparents and I said I would and we said good-bye and I went inside. Nobody was home, but I could smell something cooking, which meant either Tammy (the housekeeper) or Grace had started dinner before going out to get Bella and take her to tennis. I was starving, but I knew better than to eat. Dinner was in an hour.

And suddenly, standing in the Robinsons' perfect, gray kitchen, I *was* mad. But not at my mother's doctors. I was mad at Grace Robinson. Why did we have to eat at seven? I was hungry now. I wanted to eat something now, but if I ate something now, I wouldn't be hungry for dinner. Then Grace would be all, *Don't you like the chicken, Juliet?* and I'd feel bad because maybe I would like the chicken or maybe I wouldn't. But the point was, I didn't want to eat at seven, I wanted to eat at six, but if I ate at six, I was going to be causing a problem for the perfect family.

I took an apple from the basket on the counter, went upstairs, and flipped open my Latin book. *Do your hardest homework first.* That was what my dad had always told me.

Hardest work first. It's when you're freshest. Leave the easiest for last. I'd only been doing that for a decade. In middle school, I'd always started with math. Then, when science got really hard, that came first. And for the past two years it had been Latin.

Fucking Latin.

I sat staring at the passage in front of me. *Infelix o semper, oves, pecus! ipse Neaeram . . .*

I heard the front door open and, a minute later, Jason's familiar tread on the stairway. I didn't feel like seeing him now—I didn't feel like seeing anyone now—but there was nothing I could do about it, because this was Jason's house, and if he wanted to see me, I was going to have to see him.

"Hey." He poked his head in the door. "How was practice?"

"It was okay."

Jason came over and put his hands on my shoulders, rubbing them gently. I leaned back against him. "That feels good," I murmured, relaxing into his touch.

"How's it going with the Latin?" he asked. I realized he was looking at the textbook open on the desk.

"Fuck Latin," I said, leaning forward, which had the dual effect of covering up the book and letting him massage lower down on my back.

"You know it makes me crazy when you talk dirty," he said, kneading my spine with his knuckles. He started to ease my shirt up, and I tensed.

165

I didn't think Jason had noticed, but then he said, "You okay?"

"Yeah," I said immediately. "I'm fine." I felt a little guilty for how not into having sex I was lately, though the truth was, Jason was so busy he barely seemed into it either.

He started rubbing my back again, this time under my shirt, but almost immediately there was the sound of the garage door opening.

"Drats," said Jason. "Foiled again."

"Anyone home?" Grace called out.

"We're up here, Mom," Jason answered.

A minute later, Bella appeared at the top of the stairs. "Mom said you guys should come set the table in five." She scampered back down the hallway as soon as she'd said it.

"Sure," said Jason. He kissed the top of my head and headed toward the door.

"Jason!" It came out louder than I'd intended, almost a scream, and he instantly swung around to face me. "Sorry," I said, smiling embarrassedly.

"It's okay." He put his hand on his chest. "That's my cardio for the day."

"I really am thinking about dropping Latin."

"J, I think that's a huge mistake," he said, running his hand through his hair. "We'll do the work together. We'll—"

"You mean you'll do the work *for* me."

He walked back to where I was sitting, shaking his head.

"You think you can't do it, but you can. And it's worth it, J, at least for first semester. You don't want to turn around in April and say, *I wish I hadn't dropped Latin.*"

"What if I turn around in April and say I wish I *had* dropped Latin?"

He grinned. "Not going to happen," he promised.

I wanted him to be right. Oh, I *so* wanted him to be right.

From downstairs, Grace called, "Guys! Could you come down and help me?"

Jason held out his hand, and we locked pinkies.

16

Danny must have finally put up the posters for the Clovers' show (unless Sinead had gotten tired of waiting for him to step up and had done it herself), because by Thursday the school was covered with them. The poster looked very eighties and very awesome: a black-and-white photo of Declan, Danny, Sean, and Sinead, the guys dressed in their black suits, Sinead in her black dress. Underneath, it simply said *The Clovers* in a sans serif font and, below that, in smaller letters, *Friday night, the Coffeehouse*. It didn't say which Friday, and it didn't tell where the Coffeehouse was, like if you had to ask, you weren't cool enough to go.

People were talking about the show with an excitement normally reserved for prom.

"He's hot, but I've heard the sister's a total bitch," said

Elise. We were at our lockers Friday afternoon, and she and Margaret had been talking about the Clovers since we'd walked past a poster in the lobby.

I was wondering if I should defend Sinead when Sofia came running over to us. "Declan Brennan just *personally* invited me to the show tonight." She leaned against my locker. "I'm in love."

"Don't get too excited," Elise warned her. "He's going out with Willow Raffei."

Something shifted in me, as if a door I hadn't realized was open had abruptly blown shut.

"*What?*" Sofia shrieked. "He's been here, like, a minute. How can he have a girlfriend already?"

Elise shrugged. "They hooked up at Rob Noel's party last weekend."

I realized my mouth was hanging open, and I snapped it closed.

"Rob Noel's an idiot." Sofia slammed her foot against the locker.

"I bet the little brother's still available," Elise offered. "What is he, a freshman?"

"You're hilarious," said Sofia.

Elise went off to find George. I looked over at Sofia. "Fuck Willow Raffei," I said, though it seemed a bit undeserved considering that Willow had allowed me to dodge the awkward bullet of Sofia's being crushed out on the guy

I'd secretly cheated on Jason with.

"Yeah, well. I guess Declan is." She closed her eyes and leaned her head back against the locker again. "I really liked him," she said quietly. "He's funny and nice. I thought he liked me too." She shook her head. "I'm such an asshole."

"You're not an asshole," I said, adding (perhaps a bit too emphatically), "He's an asshole."

"He's *not* an asshole," she snapped. "He's a nice guy. When's the last time a nice, cute guy showed up at Milltown? Third grade? It's hard sometimes. Elise has George. Margaret has her thing where she hooks up with Topher practically every other weekend. And you and Jason are, you know, the world's most perfect couple. I'm like the"—she frowned and calculated—"seventh wheel."

I put my arm around her waist. "If it's any consolation, my mom's in a mental hospital."

"Thanks." Sofia leaned her head on my shoulder. "That helps, actually."

Later, when she asked me to go to the Clovers' show with her, I said I would. Because that's what best friends do.

The Coffeehouse was packed. Jason and I squeezed around a tiny table with Sofia, Elise, Margaret, George, and Topher. I hadn't ever thought about how it might be tiring for Sofia to hang out with the six of us, I guess, because I never thought of Topher and Margaret as a couple. But Sofia was right—they did hook up at almost every party. So they weren't a couple but they were. I was glad when Lucas and Marco Miller, twins who were on the soccer team but who we didn't normally hang out with, came and smushed themselves into the group at our table. When Lucas said hello to us, I noticed that he'd had his braces taken off; he'd had them on since about seventh grade, and now his teeth looked preternaturally straight and white.

I had never been to the Coffeehouse before. Like Bookers, it had a lot of small tables and couches. Bookers had posters up on the walls of book covers, and the Coffeehouse had posters of bands, but the big difference was that the Coffeehouse served alcohol and Bookers didn't. Tonight, though, there were a lot of handwritten signs everywhere saying *YOU MUST BE AT LEAST TWENTY-ONE TO DRINK ALCOHOL* and *ANYONE CAUGHT USING A FAKE ID WILL BE PROSECUTED TO THE FULLEST EXTENT OF THE LAW.* As far as I could tell, no one was trying to test how serious the bartender was. He was a big guy with a beard, who stood at the end of the bar reading a book that he wrote in every once in a while with a pencil he kept tucked behind his ear.

As if to make up for the work the bar wasn't doing, half a dozen waitresses were racing from table to table delivering trays of potato skins and chicken wings, burgers and fried calamari. Looking around, I saw that the place was getting more crowded by the second. No wonder Lucas and Marco had sat down with us; there was no place else to sit. Half of Milltown

High must have been there. The room buzzed; people were laughing and talking loudly, the energy level somewhere between a theater before the movie starts and the courtyard at school during morning break.

The stage was lit, and there were instruments on it, but none of the band members were up there yet. I was nervous about the show. It was hard enough seeing Declan every day and running into Sinead; what was seeing the whole band together going to feel like? Jason's arm was around me, and I leaned against him, trying to shut out the room by thinking about everything I wanted to get done over the weekend. Lately, instead of just making a list, I imagined a whiteboard like the one my mom used to keep for me and Oliver. First I visualized the days as blank boxes, and then I filled the boxes with everything I had to do. I put my practice SAT in the top of the Saturday box, and under it I wrote *buy shampoo/razor* because I could stop at Dodge's Drugs on my way home from the test. Then I wrote *Latin* and *math* under that with *Harvard supplement* under that with a question mark after it. Picturing completing each task and crossing it off my list felt good; the weekend took shape, and I saw myself Sunday night looking back at everything I'd anticipated doing and knowing it was done. It felt satisfying to do that. It made me feel like me.

An older guy wearing a shiny leather vest and a pair of jeans hopped up on the stage.

"I want to welcome you all to the Coffeehouse," he said.

Everyone cheered and clapped. "Just to let you know, tomorrow night we'll be featuring Beanmeister Fuller and the Jazz Hands, and a reminder that Sunday night is open mic night at the Coffeehouse." There were a few claps and some whistles, and then the man said, "So without further ado, I give you . . . the Clovers."

My stomach clenched as the band came through a door I hadn't even noticed. They were dressed the same way they had been that night at the country club: the guys in suits and ties, Sinead in a black dress. Sean came first, then Danny, then Sinead. Declan came last, and as soon as I saw him, I felt dizzy. I'd thought I remembered how good he'd looked in a suit, but clearly I hadn't. He pushed his hair off his forehead and slipped his guitar over his neck. Then he stood there, so handsome I had to turn away.

Everyone went crazy, clapping and screaming and whistling. The floor shook as people stamped their feet, and Jason took his arm from around my shoulder to clap. I just sat there, frozen, but nobody seemed to notice.

Danny started playing a hot beat that got into your blood and made you want to move. Almost immediately, the people up at the front of the room got to their feet, and seconds later half the room was standing and clapping along to the drums. Danny said something into his mic, and then Declan started plucking a tune out on his guitar. That got pretty much everyone who wasn't already standing to get up. Sofia was the first person at our table to start dancing as Declan gave a wolf whistle and said, "Yeah." And then he did it again, and everyone in the room sang out, "Yeah." And then he started singing. His voice was deep, and it filled the space until you could feel it in your chest. "Yeah. I love you. I do. I love you. All I'm saying, pretty baby. La la love you, don't mean maybe." Sinead joined him, high and sweet and flirtatious. "All I'm saying, pretty baby. La la love you, don't mean maybe." By the time Sean joined in on the bass, it felt as if the room could spontaneously combust from all the energy it was trying to contain.

I let my gaze settle on Declan. He was singing into the mic, his lips so close they were almost kissing it. His eyes were half closed in a way I remembered, but not from the last time I'd seen him play. Tonight the thread connecting us was more like a rope, and I felt myself being pulled toward him.

I looked down and saw that Jason and I were holding hands and I hadn't even noticed.

When the set ended, people swarmed the stage. I wanted to stay at the table, but Sofia dragged me forward with her to go congratulate the Clovers, and Jason wanted to come along with us, so I didn't know how I could get out of it. Declan was so swarmed with people that I couldn't even see him, and standing at the foot of the low stage, I found myself looking at Sean, who was leaning against an amp not talking to anyone. His shirttail had come untucked, and he'd loosened his tie; he didn't look relaxed so much as he looked unkempt.

I wondered if he'd even remember that we knew each other, but as soon as he saw me standing there, he raised his beer can in a sort of salute. "Hello there, Jules," he said. He looked me up and down in a way that would have been offensive if it weren't somehow so . . . Sean. "You're looking lovely as ever tonight."

"Hey, Sean," I said. "You guys were great."

He nodded. "We were, weren't we?"

"How do you know each other?" asked Jason, who was standing next to me.

"Oh, Jules and I go way back," said Sean, giving me an exaggerated wink.

I rolled my eyes. "You're hilarious." The stage was mobbed with people, but for a second the crowd opened up, and I saw Sinead, who glanced my way just at that moment. I gave her a thumbs-up. She beckoned me over, but I saw that Declan was standing right behind her, and I didn't feel like I could make small talk with him right now. I was glad when, almost immediately, people came between us and we couldn't see each other anymore.

"J, we should really go," said Jason. He sounded irritated. "It's late and you've got the practice SAT tomorrow."

"Yeah," I agreed. "We should go. See you, Sean."

"Nighty-night." He gave a smug little wave, which I ignored. Sofia, Lucas, and George were standing by the far corner of the stage talking, and we said good-bye to them. Lucas's smile was really bright, and I almost congratulated him on getting his braces off, but then I thought maybe I shouldn't call attention to it.

Jason was quiet as we walked out of the Coffeehouse, but as soon as we got into the car, he turned to me. "What's the deal with that guy in the band calling you Jules?"

That Jason thought something might have happened with me and Sean would have been funny if it hadn't hit so close to home. "The night that my mom . . . that she went to the hospital, I met Sofia at the club. But she couldn't get off work, so I just waited for her, and I ended up hanging out with the Clovers. They all called me Jules. I really don't know why." Even though I was telling the truth, it sounded like I was lying.

"I think the whole thing's weird," said Jason, holding the steering wheel at ten and two as if he were driving instead of parked. "I don't like it."

It wasn't Jason's style to be possessive, and I was scared. What if he wasn't talking about Sean? Had he seen the way I was looking at Declan while he was singing? Had he noticed something about the way I never met Declan's eyes in English class? Was there some kind of rumor going around school that I didn't know about? "What don't you like?" I asked, tentatively.

"I don't like the way that guy Sean was looking at you." He

turned to me angrily. "Did he make a pass at you that night?"

I was so relieved that Jason's question made me burst out laughing. "J, is that what you were mad about?" I leaned across the space that separated us and kissed him. "God, no! And anyway, he's disgusting."

Jason kissed me back, then put his hand on my knee and gave me a squeeze. "He is kind of disgusting, isn't he?"

"Totally," I said, taking his hand and kissing it.

He started the car, pulled out of the parking lot, and drove home. The two of us held hands the whole way, and this time, I noticed.

17

According to Aunt Kathy, the doctors were playing with my mom's medication. That was the exact phrase she used: *playing with.*

"'Playing with' doesn't exactly inspire confidence," I pointed out. It was Wednesday evening, and I was walking to my car after swim practice. A gust of wind made me wish I'd dried my hair before I'd left the building. When had it gotten so cold?

Um, sometime between your mother going into the looney bin and your last practice SAT, answered the voice in my head.

"I know it's frustrating," Aunt Kathy acknowledged. "But we have to trust the doctors a little."

"You realize it was doctors who prescribed her the sleeping pills she OD'd on, right?"

"Just as long as nobody's angry, Juliet."

"Sorry." I got to my car and dug around in my bag for my keys.

"You don't need to be sorry. You just need to be honest about how you're feeling." I didn't say anything, just rolled my eyes.

"Are you rolling your eyes at me?" Kathy asked, and I had to laugh.

"Maybe," I admitted. I got into my car. Part of me was focused on the call with Kathy, but a lot of me was thinking about the work I had to do later. Latin. History essay. Calc. I allotted minutes or hours for each task, picturing the hands on the clock circling forward through blocks of time that changed color as I slid through the assignments. As it always did, organizing my night ahead of time felt productive, as if I had somehow started the work simply by planning.

"What's on your agenda for tonight?"

I tuned back into the conversation and told my aunt about the one thing I hadn't put on my mental whiteboard. "Dinner with Dad," I said. "I'm meeting him in half an hour."

"I'm glad," said Kathy. "I'm glad you're making time to see each other."

"Yeah," I said, but really, I wasn't so sure.

My dad was sitting at a table for two, chatting with Mario, the owner, when I walked into the restaurant. When I got to the table, my dad stood up. Mario squeezed my hands and told me how beautiful I was getting. He asked how my mother was, and I froze for a second, and my dad said, "She's doing well," and he and I made eye contact, and I thought about how weird it was to feel close to someone not because you are really close to that person but because you're partners in duplicity.

"So, how are you?" asked my dad when Mario had left. He hadn't even offered us menus; if you were a regular at Mario's, you never looked at the menu.

"I'm okay," I said. "How are you?"

"I'm okay," he said. He smiled. "It's good to know we're both so okay."

The waitress brought our drinks, a Peroni for my dad, a Pellegrino with lime for me. There was silence as she put them down, and it stretched out even after we'd each taken a sip. My dad loosened his tie. "I got an A on my English paper," I blurted out.

His face broke into an enormous grin. "Juliet, that's wonderful. I'm so proud of you."

"Thanks." I couldn't help smiling back at him. I loved everything about As—how perfect and symmetrical they were, how they looked as if they were saying, *Good job, Juliet!*, how they made my parents so happy and proud of me. Sometimes, when I stared at an A, I felt as if I were looking at a little house I wished I could climb into and live inside.

"To your A," said my dad, lifting his glass.

"To my A," I echoed, lifting mine.

Mario came to the table with two small plates. He itemized the ingredients in the mushroom and tomato sauce on the polenta, and I was happy to let him talk. When he left, my dad and I dug into the tiny portions.

"This is delicious," I said, mopping up some of the sauce with a piece of soft bread.

"You can't beat Mario's," said my dad. He ripped a small piece of bread off the loaf and I did the same. A man sitting behind me said, "Undoubtedly," and the person or people sitting with him laughed.

I took another sip of my Pellegrino even though I wasn't thirsty.

"Juliet," said my dad, pushing his plate away from him, "I'd really like to revisit the possibility of my taking an apartment in Milltown and your living with me. If you don't want someone else living with us, maybe you could stay with the Robinsons when I have to travel."

Just sitting across the table from my dad was miserably awkward; the thought of living with him was exhausting. "I don't know, Dad." I toyed with a nugget of bread, rolling it between my fingers. "I don't want to have to keep going back and forth all the time." The bread was a tiny hard ball, and I forced myself to put it down on my plate and look at my father. "And anyway, with your schedule and my schedule, we could probably see each other more if we just met for dinner once a week."

"Well . . ." He shrugged. "I'd certainly like to do that." He reached across the table and took my hand. I was glad I'd put the bread down. "Just because I don't live at home anymore doesn't mean we can't still be close. I love you, Juliet."

There were so many things I wanted to say, but all I said was, "I love you too, Daddy." Because I didn't have the energy to try to figure out whether the vast chasm separating us had been created or exposed by my parents' separation.

The truth was, I didn't have the energy for any of it: for listening to my aunt tell me that psychiatry was an art, not a science; for talking to my dad about our relationship; for being polite when my brother told me not to sweat college. I didn't want to do any of those things. All I wanted to do was turn back the clock, to drive home to my house and find my beautiful mother making dinner in her beautiful kitchen, to know that my father was due home from work any minute, and to be told to go upstairs and make sure the As kept rolling in like the tide.

I wanted everything in my life to be exactly the way it had been six months ago.

Perfect.

18

Friday morning, Sinead was standing outside my English class. I assumed she was waiting for her brother, but as soon as she saw me, she called, "Jules!" and met me in the middle of the hallway. I was glad I wasn't with Jason. What had possessed me to let the Brennan clan call me by a nickname?

"Hey," I said. "You guys were amazing. Everyone's been talking about it."

It was true. If the Clovers had had a show every night, I was pretty sure they could have packed the Coffeehouse for each performance.

"Thanks," she said. But she seemed distracted. "Can I talk to you for a sec?"

"Sure," I said. I let Sinead lead me to a small alcove by the windows. Just as we got tucked inside, Declan walked into English.

Would there ever come a time when seeing him didn't make me catch my breath?

Sinead hadn't noticed her brother. "So," she began, "I got accepted to this voice program at Boston Academy of Music."

"Congratulations," I said, happy for her but not sure why she was telling me. "I mean, I don't know anything about music, but I'm sure it's really impressive."

She laughed. "Thanks. It is, actually. But the problem is, I have to go up to Boston every weekend starting in January. And the Clovers just got offered a standing Friday night gig at the Coffeehouse starting whenever we want. So I was wondering if maybe you'd think about taking my spot. Being the lead singer."

"Really?" I asked. I was flattered. "But . . . how come? I mean, why me?"

"We all agreed you'd be the best person."

We all agreed.

That meant she'd asked Declan. He'd had to talk about me.

This is stupid, Juliet. You have a boyfriend. Stop thinking about Declan.

But I realized I was smiling, and I made myself stop. "I'm sure there are lots of people at Milltown who are way better singers than I am."

Sinead bit her lip thoughtfully. "The thing is, being in a band isn't *just* about singing. I mean, you're a great singer," she added quickly. "We know a lot about music, and it doesn't take much to tell when someone has the chops to sing. But it's also the Sean factor."

"The Sean factor?" I echoed. "Is that some kind of musical thing?"

Sinead rolled her eyes. "I wish. Look, I love Sean. He's my cousin, and he's had some rough times in his life—his dad, that's my mum's older brother, is pretty messed up and his mum's not around anymore and Sean's taking some time off from college and he's supposed to be figuring out what he wants to do and all that, but it's hard for him. And, you know, all things considered he's a really great guy. But not everybody can . . . handle him." She sagged against the window slightly.

"Seriously?" I couldn't hide my surprise. "Because, I mean, he's not my favorite guy in the world, but he's clearly harmless."

"*That's* why we want you to sing in the band," Sinead said with excitement.

I shook my head. "I'm sorry. I'm not following you."

"Four out of five girls do *not* find Sean harmless," Sinead explained. "Believe me."

The warning bell rang. "Sinead, I'm really sorry. I'd like to help you guys out, and I'm totally flattered. But I've got the SATs coming up and my life's kind of . . . insane right now. To put it mildly. I just don't have time to sing in a band."

"Will you think about it?" she pleaded. "Just overnight?"

I shook my head. "I know what my answer is going to be.

The SATs will still be there tomorrow. And then I might have to take them again if I don't do well, and I have applications and homework and . . . I just can't." I put my hand on her shoulder. "I know you'll find someone awesome. Everyone loves you guys."

"Thanks." But Sinead didn't look comforted.

"See you around." I turned and headed into English.

"Yeah," Sinead said quietly. "See you around."

Aunt Kathy flew into New York the night before my SATs. I'd had some idea that it would be good to sleep in my own bed before taking the test, but when I pulled into my driveway after picking her up at the airport, I wondered if I'd made a mistake. I hadn't slept at home in weeks, not since Kathy's last visit. As Kathy and I walked across the front lawn and I felt the weight of her bag on my shoulder, I remembered walking across Jason's lawn with my own bag. It was like existing in the kind of split screen they have in the movies; pushing open the front door, I was half sure I'd find myself standing in Jason's foyer instead of my own and that it would suddenly be August instead of October.

Oliver arrived about an hour after we did. He came into the kitchen where Kathy and I were making dinner, and he hugged her so hard he lifted her off her feet, then gave me a slightly gentler hug, probably because I was stirring tomato sauce on the stove.

"It smells good in here."

"Thanks," I said, turning around to look at him. "Hey! You grew a beard."

He touched his chin, as if he wasn't quite sure it would still be there. "Yeah. It's easier not to shave when you're camping and then . . . I don't know. After the summer I just kept it."

"It looks good," I told him. "You look older." He did, too, and somehow that made me sad, like even more time had passed since I'd last seen him than actually had. I remembered my premonition the last time we'd talked, when I'd had the feeling I'd never see him again. And here I was, seeing him, but he looked so different it was almost as if he were someone else.

"I don't get carded as much," he acknowledged.

"Not that you'd ever order alcohol, given that you're not twenty-one," said Kathy, laughing.

"Of course not," Oliver assured her. He hopped up on the counter. "Dad's growing a beard too. His is lamer than mine, though."

Hearing that my father had decided to grow a beard was even stranger than my brother having grown one. College guys were supposed to experiment with facial hair. But dads weren't.

"When did you see Dad?" I asked. "Because he was clean shaven the last time I saw him." I tried not to think too much about sitting across the table from my father at Mario's, attempting to make conversation with him as if he were a complete stranger.

"He came up to New Haven last weekend." Oliver said it like it was no big deal.

"He *did?*" I dropped the spoon into the sauce and spun around.

"He did," echoed Oliver, making his voice whiny and high-pitched and nothing like mine. "Why is that so outrageous to you?"

I couldn't bring myself to give the real reason I was so shocked that my dad had spent the weekend with my brother. Instead, I crossed my arms over my chest and said, "Frankly, I can't picture him making the time."

"According to Dad, *you're* the one who's too busy to see *him.*" Oliver leaned back on his hands.

"Wait, he said that?" I couldn't believe my father was talking about me behind my back.

Something about my voice must have warned Oliver that he'd gone too far, because he corrected himself. "He just said you're really busy. You know, working hard and stuff."

"Well, I am," I snapped. "Maybe you've noticed that Mom's not around to work as my personal assistant during the college application process."

"Okay, okay," Kathy said, literally stepping between us. "That's enough, you two. We're making dinner. Juliet, stir that sauce. Oliver, wash your hands and start slicing cucumbers."

We made dinner together, and Oliver and I managed not to bicker. The three of us were supposed to go visit my mom the next day, after I took the SAT, and as we ate, Oliver and Kathy debated whether he should try to meet his old squash coach for breakfast or if the timing wouldn't work out. I was too distracted by my own calculations about the next day to register what they decided. But just before bed, I told my aunt what I'd decided.

"I'm not going to go with you and Ollie to see Mom tomorrow." I didn't explain that over dinner I'd realized that there was no way I'd be able to focus on the SAT if I was planning to visit my catatonic mother as soon as it was over.

"I understand," said Aunt Kathy. She was sitting on the bed in the guest room. It wasn't a very comfortable room—before my dad left, my mother had been planning on redecorating it, and it was one of the only rooms in the house that still looked the way it had when we'd first moved in ten years ago. There was no overhead lighting, and Kathy and I sat in the dim glow of a small desk lamp. The bed she was sitting on was narrow and uncomfortable; I knew because I'd slept on it last year when my room was being painted.

There was no reason my aunt shouldn't have just slept in my mother's bedroom, but neither of us had suggested it. The door to her room remained closed, though Kathy assured me the cleaning woman had dealt with the bathroom.

"But just so you know, she really is better," Aunt Kathy

promised, touching my forearm lightly. "The doctors think they've gotten her medication right. She's much more alert and focused now."

"Does that mean they're going to send her home?"

I knew what the answer would be even before Kathy said it. After more than a month of dealing with doctors, I found their decisions much less mysterious than they'd once been.

"They're hoping to send her home soon, but they can't say exactly when," said Aunt Kathy. "It's—

"I know, it's an art, not a science," I interrupted her.

She smiled and reached over to tousle my hair. "You should get some sleep. Tomorrow's the big day. Got your pencils and your ID?"

I nodded.

"Sleep tight," she said.

"Sleep tight," I echoed.

Oliver wished me luck before going into his room and closing the door. When I thanked him, it felt like a truce, and as I listened to him puttering around next door, I found there was something comforting and familiar about being in my own bed in my own room in my own house. Still, I couldn't sleep. And it wasn't because of having the SATs the next morning. In some ways it seemed unreal to me that the actual test was really here, that tomorrow wasn't one more of the millions of practice tests I'd taken since last January, when I'd started getting tutored.

As I lay in my bed, watching the hour on my digital clock change from ten to eleven to twelve, what kept me awake was that I couldn't stop thinking about my dad going up to New Haven for the weekend.

I pictured my father and brother at the restaurant my parents and Oliver and I had eaten at parents' weekend of his freshman year, but instead of the awkward silence that had characterized my dinner with our father, Oliver and my dad were happily chatting and laughing. They raised their glasses and toasted to how close they were, how untouched their relationship was by everything else that had happened in their lives.

When my dad and I had had dinner, the two empty chairs where my brother and my mother should have been sitting had felt like ugly, gaping wounds. When Oliver and my dad were together, I couldn't imagine them caring that they were alone.

19

My SAT tutor called me right after the test.

"Soooo, how'd it go? Did you kick ass and take names?"

I liked Glen, and he'd brought my scores up hundreds of points on all the practice tests I'd taken, but he was still the kind of guy who said things like, *Did you kick ass and take names?*

"I did, Glen," I said. "I kicked ass and took names."

Sofia snorted. She was driving us to Bookers, where we'd agreed to go for a post-SAT celebratory latte.

"Seriously," said Glen. "Tell me how it went."

"I think it went okay. You know I can never tell." Glen had been trying to help me evaluate my performances more accurately, but on my last practice test I'd still had a section that I thought I'd aced and I'd actually done poorly on, and I'd aced two sections I was sure I'd bombed. I tried to think carefully about today's test and how it had gone. "It was weird. The whole time I kept feeling like I'd been there before."

"Déjà vu, dude," said Glen, and I could picture him nodding his head approvingly. "That's a good sign. Means you were in control of the moment."

"Yeah, maybe." I didn't have the heart to tell Glen I was having that feeling a lot lately, not so much because I was in control of my life but because my life—school, swimming, homework, sleep, school, debate, homework, sleep—felt like a hamster's wheel.

Sofia pulled into the Bookers lot.

"So you'll call me as soon as you get your scores, right? Couple of weeks?"

"Right," I said, getting out of the car. "I'll call you as soon as I know."

I hung up and walked over to where Sofia stood in the doorway of Bookers checking her phone. When she looked up at me, she had a confused expression on her face, as if she'd gotten a text in a foreign language. "Lucas Miller just texted to ask me how the test went."

"Really?" I said. "Let me see." I took her phone from her and read the screen. *how'd it go? lucas.*

I tapped her phone. "This is significant," I told her. "Trust me. How does he even have your number?"

"Science," said Sofia, reading the text over my shoulder. "Dr. Pao made us all write down our cell numbers and then he xeroxed the list for the class so nobody could say they couldn't get the homework if they were absent."

"*Veddy* interesting," I said, handing her back her phone. "Ve must to analyze zis at great lengz."

"I don't know." Sofia shrugged, went to put her phone away, pulled it out of her bag at the last second, reread his text, slapped her hands (one of them still holding the phone) to her face, and gave a little scream. "I can't deal!"

I took her by the arm and guided her inside. "You gather your thoughts, and I will get us each a latte," I said, gently placing her at one end of a sofa covered in a loud floral pattern. I'd turned to go up to the counter when I saw Sinead and Declan sitting at the table just around the pillar from where I'd sat Sofia. Their heads were close together, and they were talking quietly. My stomach tensed as it always did when I saw Declan, and I did a quick inventory of what I was wearing: faded jeans, hoodie, hair up in a messy ponytail. I wanted not to care that I looked completely blah. But I cared.

I was about to slip past their table when Sinead saw me.

"Hey, Jules," she said. Declan nodded at me. I nodded at Declan.

"Hey," I said, trying to look like I hadn't noticed them sitting there until now. "Hi. How are you?"

On the other side of the pillar, Sofia was studying her phone.

"Pretty bad, actually," said Sinead. Declan didn't say anything.

"What's up?" I asked. Sinead's head was leaning heavily on her hands, and she shrugged.

"Sean strikes again," she explained.

I was intrigued. "Meaning?"

"We asked this sophomore, do you know her, Anika Dunbar?"

The name wasn't familiar, but I didn't know many underclassmen. I shook my head.

Sinead continued. "Yeah, well, she's got an amazing voice, and we had a great rehearsal yesterday *without Sean*, and then today he showed up and he was just such a complete and total wanker that after about twenty minutes . . ."

"She ran screaming from the house," Declan finished.

"She didn't run screaming from the house," Sinead corrected him. She looked up at me. "She was crying."

"I'm impressed." I tried to think of what Sean could have said to make a girl cry. "Did he tell her her voice sucked? Or, wait, he said she was fat."

Sinead stared at me. "It's too awful."

"Just say it," said Declan impatiently, leaning back and crossing one ankle over the opposite knee.

Sinead dropped her head into her hands. "I can't," she said from behind her fingers.

"It's no big deal," Declan assured her. He looked directly at me for the first time in weeks. I had to work hard to focus on what he was saying. "It's really no big deal."

"So then *you* say it," snapped Sinead, her face still buried.

Declan sighed, raised an eyebrow at me, and said, his voice matter-of-fact, "Sean told her that to sing punk rock, you have to look like you enjoy getting fucked."

I burst out laughing.

Sinead jerked her head up. "Oh yes, it's all very funny. Mind you, the girl learned to sing in the choir. *At her church.*"

Sofia poked her head around the pillar, then slid over to a chair at Sinead and Declan's table. "What's up?" she asked.

I filled her in on what had happened during the Clovers' latest attempt to find an alternate lead singer. "What an asshole," said Sofia.

I shrugged. "He's fine."

"No, to *you* he's fine," Sinead corrected me. "To everyone else, he's a monster. That's why you've *got* to take my place. Things are getting desperate."

"Wait, you want Juliet to sing with the Clovers?" asked Sofia. "Oh my God!" She put her hand on my arm. "Juliet, that would be the coolest thing ever. You'd be a rock star."

I rolled my eyes. "I'm getting us lattes."

When I came back carrying the drinks, Sinead and Declan were getting ready to go. Sofia was telling them something, but she got quiet as soon as she saw me. "Well, great chatting with you." Her voice was fake casual. I put the latte down on the table in front of her.

"Thanks, Sofia," said Sinead. "You're awesome." She and Declan said good-bye, and the tinkling of the chimes on the door indicated they'd left.

I stared across the table at Sofia. "Whatever you promised them, I'm not singing in the band."

"What?" She stirred her drink. "What makes you think I promised them anything?" But she wouldn't meet my eyes. When I refused to say anything and just kept staring, she finally said, "Okay, fine. I told them I'd convince you. But you really should do it," she continued quickly as soon as she saw me shaking my head. "You've had such a bad fall and it would be so much fun. They rehearse every Monday. And you're *free* Monday nights. You're free *every* night now that you're not meeting with Glen twice a week."

"First of all, if my scores didn't go up, I'll still have to meet with Glen. Second of all, I'm getting a Latin tutor. So I'm not going to be free every night."

Sofia rolled her eyes. "The Clovers are so *cool*."

"If you think I'm joining a band so you can get with Declan Brennan, you have *no* idea how wrong you are."

"It's not that. I know he's with Willow now. It's just . . . they're *cool*, Juliet. Seriously, really, no joke cool. And we've never done anything cool in our lives. Not really."

I took a sip of my drink, but it was too hot and I burned the roof of my mouth. I put down the cup. "Getting into Harvard early action is cool."

She stared at me over our drinks. "No it's not. Getting into Harvard early action is a lot of things. But cool is not one of them."

. . .

Sunday afternoon, I dropped Kathy at the airport, promising her I believed what she kept saying about my mother having improved dramatically since her last visit. That night, as I was sitting at the desk in the Robinsons' guest room, where I'd sequestered myself so I couldn't avoid doing Latin, my phone rang. I was one hundred percent sure it was Sofia, and even though I'd *sworn* to myself that I was not going to avoid doing Latin by talking on the phone *or* going online, I couldn't resist the siren song of its ring. I reached into my backpack and pulled it out, promising myself I wouldn't talk for more than five minutes. I even checked the time on my computer and made a mental note to get off the call by ten fifteen, but then I looked at my phone and saw that it wasn't Sofia who was calling.

Dad (mobile).

I traced the letters on the screen, the big fat *D* towering over the little *a*. When the phone finally stopped ringing and the word disappeared, I felt relieved but also a little empty. I waited to see if he'd leave a message. He didn't, and I put the phone down.

But it was hard to focus on Latin. For some reason, I kept thinking of him going to visit Oliver. What had they done? Had they gone to a movie? Had they talked?

They'd probably played squash. My brother had started

playing in elementary school, and he still played, though he'd stopped playing for Yale at the end of his freshman year. My dad had tried to teach me to play a couple of times when I was eight or nine, but I hadn't been very good, and he'd gotten impatient and I'd thrown my racket down and he'd told me not to make a scene and I'd marched off the court in silence. Then he'd tried to get me to take lessons so we could play together, but I was already taking tennis. And piano. And swimming. And ballet.

Thinking about how busy I'd been back in third grade was strange, like stumbling upon a room I'd once lived in but hadn't entered in years. My mom, standing by the car at pickup, a bagged snack in her hand. *Let's go, Juliet!* She must have said that to me a million times in my life. Ten million times. *Come on, Juliet.*

Juliet, we have to go.

Juliet, we're going to be late for dance.

For piano.

For tennis.

For swimming.

Had I ever just gone home from school and hung out? I tried to remember, but I couldn't really remember *anyone* in my family just hanging out. We were all always doing something. Squash. Piano. Homework. Planning a vacation. Packing for a vacation. Unpacking from a vacation. Running errands. Making reservations. Organizing play dates. Soccer. Little League.

Swimming. Redecorating. Visiting colleges.

The only moments of stillness I could think of were my mom, sitting in the living room in the evening, a glass of white wine at her side.

An IM popped up, the ding startling me. It was Jason. He was downstairs doing his physics homework, spread out at the kitchen table. I'd left him there because I was sure if I stayed downstairs, I'd get distracted. Now I was glad for the distraction.

Jason: whatcha doin?

Me: Latin.

Jason: need help?

Me: maybe later. how's physics going?

Jason: done. calc.

Me: J?

Jason: yeah?

Me: does this ever feel pointless.

Jason: what?

Me: idk. everything. school. homework. SATs. college.

Jason: college isnt pointless. it's your future.

Me: my future is where i go 2 college?

Jason: u know what i mean.

Me: lets not go.

Jason: go where?

Me: college. let's just ditch it.

Jason: ha-ha.

Me: im serious.

Jason: and do what?

Me: Sinead asked me 2 join the Clovers 2day. i cud be in the band. u cud be a groupie.

Jason: tell me u r high right now.

Me: u just dnt like the idea of me being a rock star.

Jason: since when do u WANT to b a rock star?

Me: idk. it might b cool.

Jason: i don't like that guy sean.

Me: so don't u b in a band with him!

Jason: u know what i mean.

Me: forget sean. can u see me in a band w/o sean?

Jason: not really.

Me: u r not even trying.

Jason: this is dumb.

Me: not 2 me. try.

Jason: try what?

Me: try 2 picture me in a band.

Jason: u don't have time.

Me: i'd make time. it wud be fun.

Jason: u dnt have time for fun.

Me: i'd make time 4 fun.

Me: hello?

Me: hello?

I waited, but Jason didn't write anything. A text came in from my aunt, and I glanced at it. *Hey, just to let you know Dr. Gulati's really happy about how your mom's responding to her new meds. These may do the trick. Call me when you can.* I pushed my phone away. I was busy. I didn't have time to get my hopes up about my mom.

Me: J? r u there?
Me: J? r u there?
Me: just forget it what i said, k? jk!

And then I felt a hand on my shoulder.

Jason was standing behind me. "I thought if you were making time for fun, I'd better take advantage of it."

I stood up and he put his arms around me and we started kissing. Neither of us said anything else about my joining the band, but somehow between when we started making out and when Jason went back downstairs to finish his homework so his mom wouldn't get suspicious that we were having sex, I made a decision.

I was joining the Clovers.

∽ 20 ∾

There was no way I could ask Declan about rehearsal. Sofia had said the Clovers rehearsed Monday nights. But I didn't know where, and I didn't know when, and I couldn't ask him.

I knew I'd have to talk to him if I joined the band. *Obviously* I'd have to talk to him if I joined the band. And I was pretty sure I *could* talk to him as long as Sinead was around. Better yet, as long as Sinead, Sean, and Danny were around. But one on one with Declan felt off-limits, so I let him walk out of English class without asking him when and where the Clovers were rehearsing, and when I saw him walking with Willow in the parking lot at lunch, I didn't ask him then either. They were holding hands, and her long, blond hair fanned out behind her like a bridal veil.

I told myself I didn't care. That had been my deal with

myself if I joined the Clovers: No more thinking about Declan like that.

I'd had some idea that I'd run into Sinead or Danny and be able to ask them if there really was a rehearsal tonight, but even though I'd been sure that if I was looking for them, I'd run into them, I didn't. By the time Sofia and I were walking out of swim practice, I realized that my dramatic decision to join a band was being foiled by logistics.

"What are you up to tonight?" Sofia asked, squeezing the wet ends of her hair between her fingers.

I shrugged. Now I was glad I hadn't told Sofia I was going to try singing with the Clovers. How dumb would that have been? "I don't know. Home, I guess. Then homework."

She cocked her head. "Hmm," she hummed, and then she smiled as if she had the answers to my math homework in her backpack.

"What?" I asked, irritated.

"Aren't you forgetting something?"

"Such as?"

Her face cracked into a grin. "God, you're such a bad liar. Eleven twenty-two Larkspur Lane. Seven o'clock."

We stared at each other. Sometimes Sofia and I had a crazy mind meld, so I didn't even ask her how she knew what I was thinking.

"It's off Webster," she added. "In case you were wondering."

"I was, actually."

"No need to thank me," she said. "But I'll take comps to your first show at Madison Square Garden."

The address Sofia had given me was a rambling old farm-house with a small bronze plaque next to the front door that said BUILT IN 1784. There were enormous rosebushes along the front porch. Danny opened the door, looking surprisingly unsurprised to see me. "Come on in," he said. "We're still waiting for Sean." I followed him down a wide hallway past a brightly lit kitchen. The whole house felt chaotic in an orderly way, by which I mean there were books everywhere and a pile of shoes by the front door but no spiderwebs hanging from the ceiling and no dust on the banister that I trailed my hand down as we headed to the basement.

"Guys," Danny called, bounding down the steps ahead of me. "Jules is here!" He took the last three steps in a giant leap.

I followed him and found myself in a low-ceilinged room lit by long fluorescent bulbs. There was a huge square rug on the linoleum floor, dark green and fraying at the edges, as if someone had ripped it off an even larger rug. The room smelled warm and basement-y. Danny's drum set sat in one corner. Along the wall with the staircase, Declan was stretched out on a red pleather sofa. Sinead was sitting in a battered recliner by a built-in, empty bar.

As soon as she saw me, she stood up and dropped the sheet music she'd been reading. "Oh my God, Sofia did it."

She clapped her hands with excitement.

"Don't give credit where credit isn't due," I said. "I did this all on my own."

"Does this mean you owe Sofia fifty bucks?" asked Danny, going over to sit behind his drum set.

I couldn't believe it. "You promised Sofia fifty bucks?"

"Only if you survived at least one full rehearsal," Declan said from the sofa.

"And what do *I* get?" His shirt had come up a little bit, and there was a strip of stomach showing above his jeans. I pretended he was Sean and that I didn't even notice.

"Um, fame and fortune?" Declan offered.

"Our eternal gratitude?" suggested Sinead.

The door at the top of the stairs banged open loudly enough that I jumped, and then Sean's voice boomed down the stairs. "Okay, you wankers! Let's get this party started."

I looked from Declan to Sinead and then to Danny. "I'd say Sofia got the better deal."

"Jules, sweetheart," Sean said, stopping the song for what must have been the fiftieth time. "You sound like you're singing in the church choir."

"I'm an atheist," I snapped.

"Yes, but—" Sean interrupted.

"I think what Sean means," said Sinead before he could define punk rock as succinctly for me as he had for Anika, "is that you want to sound a little nastier."

"Nastier like you've gotten laid at least once in your life, not nastier like you're a bitch," elaborated Sean.

"And thank you very much, Sean," said Sinead, turning on him. He made a face at her, and she growled a warning at him before returning to face me. "Hear how I'm doing it?" She curled her upper lip and ripped out the opening of the song. "One way or another I'm gonna find ya. I'm gonna getcha getcha getcha getcha."

Sinead sounded sexy but scary, as if she knew the person she was singing about wanted her to get him but wasn't quite sure what would happen when she did.

"Let's take it from the top," Declan suggested.

"Okay," I said. Declan counted us off and hit the guitar hard, blasting out the opening notes of the song. Then Danny came in, nailing the beat so perfectly it was impossible not to start moving your hips. Sean's bass line was under it all, sewing the song together and pushing it forward.

And then it was my turn.

"One way or another I'm gonna find ya. I'm gonna getcha getcha getcha getcha." I tried to sound mad, and I *did* sound mad. I sounded like I was going to find the person and hurt him very, very badly or possibly even kill him. It wasn't sexy so much as it was terrifying.

"Well, that was better," said Sinead. She'd been smiling at me through the whole song, like she'd given up being the lead singer to be the lead smiler.

"You can say that it sucked," I said, slipping the mic back into the stand. "I might not know anything about punk rock—"

"New wave," Sean corrected me.

"Whatever," I said. "But I have ears. I know when something sucks."

"It didn't suck," Sinead insisted. "You should have heard *me* the first time I tried that song. It was pathetic."

"Worse than pathetic," offered Declan. "I thought you'd be arrested for crimes against humanity."

"Thanks, Dec," said Sinead. "I believe we've made our point."

"Listen," said Sean, and there was something commanding in his voice that made us all look over at him. "Making art is never about being perfect. It's about what Sam Beckett called 'failing better.'"

It seemed to me that Sean's saying that was a sign that I'd passed some kind of test. Like first he'd tried to scare me, but now he was going to help me.

"That's beautiful, Sean," I said. "I've gotta listen to some of his music."

"Whose?" Sean asked, confused.

"Sam Beckett's."

"He's a playwright." Sean reached over, grabbed one of Danny's drumsticks, and mimed driving it through his heart. "Your ignorance is killing me, Jules. It is seriously killing me."

. . .

When I got home to Jason's, it was almost ten. On the counter, leaning against a tinfoil-covered plate, was a note in Grace's handwriting. *Mark and I are at a fund-raiser. Here's some dinner— you might want to heat it up. We'll see you tomorrow.* I'd texted her that I wouldn't be home for dinner, but I hadn't said why, and her note didn't say anything about my having been at band practice. Had Jason told her where I was? I'd texted him also, too chicken to tell him in person that I was joining the Clovers. The possibility that now one or both of them was mad about what I'd done made me uneasy.

"Jason?" I called. I didn't want to yell too loudly, because Bella went to sleep at nine thirty. I walked to the foot of the stairs. "Jason?" I stood still and listened, and from the third floor I heard the sound of the shower running.

I went back to the kitchen and microwaved the plate of spaghetti and meatballs, then sat at the kitchen counter eating it, my Latin textbook open on my lap and my notebook next to my plate. As I tried to translate, I couldn't help being distracted by all the other work I had to do before I could get to sleep. The history paper alone could take a couple of hours. I forced myself to focus on the Latin. If worse came to worst, I'd skip the English reading and only do half the math problems—Mrs. Matthews almost never checked to see if we'd done the homework anyway.

"Hey."

Jason's coming into the kitchen startled me. My notebook started sliding off my lap, and I dropped my pen when I tried to catch it. In the end, both of them fell to the floor.

"Hey," I said back. He was wearing his Harvard T-shirt and a pair of sweatpants, and his hair was wet. Once upon a time, I would have said Jason was as familiar to me as my own family. Now he was actually more familiar to me than they were.

"So how'd it go?" He leaned down and picked up my book and the pen and put them on the counter next to my plate. "You going to be the next Beyoncé?" I couldn't tell from his voice if he was mad about my going or not.

"Hardly." I rolled my eyes. "I kind of sucked."

"I doubt that," he said. He came and stood beside my chair, toying with the tie of my shirtsleeve. "My parents were worried that you don't have time to be in a band. My mom wanted to talk to your dad about it."

"She didn't want to talk to *me* about it?"

Jason shrugged. "I told her she should cut you some slack. You know what you're doing." He gave me a crooked smile. "I didn't tell her about the whole not going to college idea, though. You might want to wait on that."

"J," I whispered. I put my arm around his waist and pulled him toward me, burying my face in his chest, thinking about how he totally agreed with his mom but how he'd defended my joining the Clovers anyway. "Thanks."

He leaned his chin on my head and gently stroked my

neck. "I'm worried about you, J. I don't see how you have time to do everything."

I squeezed him even more tightly. "I know."

He put his hands on the sides of my face and tilted my head up so I was looking at him. "Really. I don't get why you're doing this to yourself."

I shook my head, but gently enough that I didn't dislodge his hands. "I'm not . . . I'm not doing it *to* myself. I'm doing it *for* myself." I laughed. "I sound like someone who does yoga."

He laughed also. "You do, kind of." He leaned down, and we kissed on the lips very gently. "Want some help with this?" He tilted his head to indicate my Latin book.

But I didn't see how I could let Jason defend my being in a band and then lean on him to get through Latin. "I'm okay," I said. "You have your own work to do."

"I don't mind," he said, kissing me again, this time not so gently.

I kissed him back, then pulled away. "*I* do. I've got to do this myself . . . or die trying," I added at the last minute.

Jason took my hand. "Come work with me in the dining room," he said. "We'll get us some J power."

"Let me just put this in the dishwasher," I said, picking up my plate. "I'll meet you there."

The next morning, when I turned on my phone, there was a text from Sinead. *u r gonna rock. check facebook.* I clicked over to

Facebook, and there was a message: *Declan has shared a playlist with you.* I stared at the screen, then shoved my phone into my bag, still groggy from getting too little sleep. The one good thing was that I knew I'd kicked ass on my history paper. I'd had to write about the origins of the Thirty Years' War, and I'd gotten really into all the stuff about politics and religion. If I hadn't had to start it so late, I would have done an even better job, but I hadn't finished my Latin until almost eleven.

Jason said he'd drive so I could proof my paper on the way to class, but I was too tired and the words just ran together on my screen. I flipped to my email and remembered Sinead's message. We were still a mile from school.

"Mind if I put some music on?" I asked.

"Sure," he said. "Go for it."

I hooked my phone up to the USB port, and the sound of Blondie's guitarist rocked the car.

"What's this?" Jason shouted.

"Blondie," I shouted back. "One way or another I'm gonna find ya. I'm gonna getcha getcha getcha getcha one way—"

"But why are we listening to it?"

"I'm supposed to sound like them," I shouted. Sinead was amazing, but Debbie Harry was in a whole different league. Her voice slashed through the words, sexy and mean and playful and cool. I stared at the picture of her—she stood in front of a line of guys in black suits. In her white dress and pearls, she looked tough as nails, as if she wasn't afraid of anything, and anyone who was thinking about messing with her had better think again.

When we stopped at a red light, Jason lowered the volume. "How can you edit your paper and listen to this music?"

"I can't," I said. I took his hand and kissed it, then reached forward and turned the volume back up. "You can't do anything else while you listen to this music." The truth made me laugh, but as the light turned green, Jason was shaking his head.

"It's your funeral," he said.

But driving along listening to Blondie didn't feel like a funeral.

It felt like a party.

# 21

I loved being in the Clovers.

It wasn't just learning the songs. Since Sinead was still going to be singing with the band until January, we'd agreed I'd just do one song at each gig until January, learning the Clovers' repertoire over the next two months. We were even working on a song to sing together until she left, a reggae version of "I Got You Babe" that UB40 and Chrissie Hynde of the Pretenders had recorded. We both thought it was übercool that we were two girls singing a love song.

"Everyone's going to think you're dykes," Sean warned us.

"Maybe we are," Sinead shot back.

"Better tell that Jason guy."

"Sean?" I said.

"Yeah?" he asked.

"Blow me."

It was hard, sure. My voice was okay, but it wasn't like I'd had any formal training, and my throat was always sore no matter how much tea with honey (Sinead's formula) I drank. And the Sean factor wasn't irrelevant. Maybe he couldn't make me run out the door crying, but when I sang something and Sinead said I was getting better and Declan said I was sounding good and Danny gave me a thumbs-up and Sean rolled his eyes and Sinead said to him, "What is your problem?" and Sean said, "Why are you guys *lying* to her?" I felt more kinship with Anika Dunbar than I'd care to admit.

Unlike me, they were all amazing musicians. Danny didn't just play the drums. He played drums and piano and guitar, and he could noodle around on bass. Sinead played the bass too, and one night when Sean didn't show up at a rehearsal because (we later learned) he was sleeping off a bar fight, she just played his part. I could read music, a little, from when I'd taken piano, but they could all sight-read—once, when I got there early, they were practicing a song for their grandparents' wedding anniversary, some old Irish tune none of them knew. Sean was playing a fiddle, which I'd never seen him do, and Declan was playing a tin whistle. Their dad had let me in, so they didn't know I was there, and watching them huddled around the music stand, playing and singing, I tried to imagine me and my brother or maybe me, my brother, and my parents making music together.

It was like trying to imagine us vacationing on the moon.

No, what I loved about singing with the Clovers wasn't about what I could or couldn't do or what the other band members could do better than I could, which was pretty much everything. It was how the music made me feel. Tough. And strong. And sexy. And powerful. When I was at rehearsal, I didn't think about school or my mom or my Harvard application or leaving for college or where my next A was coming from. I just thought about the music. It was like a drug, and I was like an addict. My aunt had told me that my mom's doctors were talking about sending her home in a couple of weeks, but if this was how all those little pills she'd been taking made my mother feel, I was going to be surprised if any doctor anywhere could get her to stop taking them.

The Friday morning of our first gig at the Coffeehouse, I logged on to the College Board website to get my SAT scores. My hands were shaking and sweaty. If my score was low, I was going to have to start all over again. More tutoring with Glen. More vocabulary to memorize. More reading passages, more sample math questions. More practice tests. There was no way I'd be able to study for the SATs, do all my schoolwork, swim, stay in debate and sing in a band.

The thought of dropping out of the Clovers and going back to meeting with Glen twice a week made me feel as if I was being shoved into a cell and someone was slamming the door behind me. But if my scores were bad, I wouldn't have a choice. I remembered the last time I'd logged on to get my scores, back in June, when I'd gotten that crappy, crappy number. Why shouldn't the same thing happen again? It wasn't like my situation was any better now than it had been. If anything, my life was even *more* fucked up. So if my messed-up life was the reason I'd scored so badly in the spring, why wouldn't my scores be even lower this time around?

So much was riding on this one little number. It was like I'd bet my fortune on a roll of the dice, and it either came up high or I lost everything.

Click. I held my breath and hit the button to see what my future would hold.

And what it held was perfection.

Literally.

I stared at the number 2400 on the screen for a long, long moment, watching it blur and then re-form. All those weeks and months of tutoring. All those hours of studying. All those practice tests.

It had all paid off. There it was in black and white: I'd done it. My parents' marriage had imploded. My mother had gone off the deep end. I'd joined a band and bombed as many Latin quizzes as I'd aced.

But none of it mattered. The numbers said it all. In this one instant in time, I had done it.

I was perfect.

I ran, screaming, from Bella's room and into Jason's. We were the only ones still in the house, but I wouldn't have cared if I'd woken the entire family.

"Oh my God, you beat me by twenty points!" he cried when I told him my score, but he threw his arms around me and lifted me up into the air, and I knew that he didn't really care about my having a higher score than his.

"I'm taking you out tonight," he said, putting me down but keeping his arms around me.

"I have the show at the Coffeehouse," I reminded him. His shirt was unbuttoned, and I touched him lightly on the chest.

"Right. Of course." He laughed and ran his hand through his hair. "It's so weird. I mean, everyone's been talking about the show, but I keep forgetting you're playing with the Clovers." He laughed again. "Sorry. I guess it's 'cause you don't really talk about it."

"I don't?" As soon as I said it, I felt bad. I was lying. It wasn't an accident that Jason didn't associate me with the Clovers. I never talked about the band with him. "I guess I just feel like you don't really like that I'm singing with the band, so . . ." I shrugged. "I don't talk about it that much with you."

"Wait, why do you think I don't like the band? I like the band. Declan seems like a cool guy and Willow's great, obviously." He took a step away from me and started buttoning his shirt.

"Willow isn't *in* the band," I said. I'd meant to say it in a teasing way, but it came out mad.

"She isn't?" Jason looked genuinely surprised, as if he'd spent weeks thinking about and listening to the Clovers. "I just assumed since, you know, she and Declan . . ." He tucked his shirt into his jeans.

"No," I said, and this time I managed to keep my voice light. "She's his girlfriend, but she's not in the band. And before, when I said you didn't like the band, I didn't mean that you don't like the individual members of the band per se. I meant that you don't like my *being in* the band. I get the feeling you don't want to talk about it."

"J, I totally want to talk about it. Are you kidding?" Whenever Jason lied, his voice got slightly higher.

"Look, let's just change the subject, okay? Can we go out for breakfast? Just cut first period and you can take me out. We'll celebrate."

"I want to finish this conversation," said Jason. He went over to his drawer and took out a perfectly folded gray sweater.

I shrugged. "There's nothing to finish. I thought you didn't want to talk about the band. You, in fact, have been secretly dying to discuss my experiences with the Clovers but keeping your desire to know more about rehearsals under wraps for some mysterious reason. I can see I was wrong, and I retract my accusation."

"J, if you want me to ask you about band practice more often, you should just say so." As he pulled his sweater over his head, Jason's voice was calm, on the verge of being condescending. It was his tone more than anything else that pissed me off.

"Why do you do that?" I snapped.

"Do what?" he asked, looking genuinely bewildered.

"Make it seem like *I'm* the one with the problem. I don't *want* you to ask me about band practice, okay? I'm just saying that the fact that you never do leads me to believe you aren't particularly interested in my experience as a member of the Clovers. This stands in sharp contrast to your *obsessive* concern, for example, with how I do on every fucking Latin quiz Ms. Croft gives us."

"J, you're being—"

"I am not *being* anything," I shouted. "I'm *being* myself. And now I am *being* myself going to school."

"J—"

But I didn't want to talk to Jason. I knew it wasted gas and was bad for the environment, but I just took my car to school alone. The whole drive, I tried to figure out how we'd gone in under five minutes from Jason's sweeping me up in his arms and kissing me to my storming out the door and driving to school by myself.

My fight with Jason had dampened my spirits, but I was sure that telling my dad about my SAT scores was going to feel as good as seeing them had. Sitting in the parking lot, I took my phone out and dialed his number.

He picked up on the third ring. "Juliet?"

For the first time in weeks, I was glad to hear his voice. "I got my SAT scores."

"How'd you do?" he asked, nervous.

"Twenty-four hundred."

He gave a cry of delight. "That's fantastic, Juliet. Why don't I take you out to celebrate? You and Jason. Or you and Sofia. I'll make a reservation for tonight if you'd like."

"Actually, I have a gig tonight. It's my first one."

"A *gig?*" my father echoed.

I'd never told my father about the Clovers. "I'm singing in a band. We're performing."

"Oh," he said, sounding hurt. "Maybe I could come and see you play and then I could take you and your friends out after."

I tried to imagine my father at the Coffeehouse, then taking me and Jason and Sofia out after. It would be so awkward, everyone either wanting to hang out or to go party at someone's house. What would I do with my dad there?

"Maybe another time, Dad," I said.

"Well, break a leg," he said. "I'll be thinking of you." His saying that made me feel sad, like he'd spend his night sitting in a dark room somewhere trying to imagine me playing with the Clovers. "And Juliet?"

"Yeah?"

"Thanks for calling. I'm really proud of you, honey."

Normally my dad's saying that made me feel warm all

over, but suddenly it struck me as a strange thing to say. *I'm so proud of you.* In the past, I'd always thought of what his being proud said about me, but now I thought about what it meant to be proud of something. It wasn't just that he was impressed by what a good job I'd done or that he thought I was a hard worker or a good test taker. It meant *he* took pride in work *I'd* done. That he felt it was something he'd done also. You weren't proud of something that had nothing to do with you. Like, I wasn't proud of the Panama Canal or the Special Olympics.

Or was it *me* my dad took pride in? Did he feel that anything I'd done was something he could take pride in because he was my father and so I was something he'd made?

I walked into the building thinking about how weird it was that I could feel so distant from my dad that I couldn't figure out how my brother filled a weekend with him, but he could feel so close to me that he saw my SAT scores as proof that he'd done something good.

Which one of us was right?

Neither Jason nor I liked to fight in public. Not that we fought all that much, but when we did, we kept it private, unlike, say, George and Elise. When I got to Latin, he'd saved a seat for me, and I slid into it the same way I did every day. When class ended, I asked him if he wanted to go for ice cream after school.

"Soccer practice," he said.

"Come on," I said, tracing a line up his arm. "Cut practice.

You cut practice; I'll cut practice. I'll let you buy me an ice cream so you won't feel bad about my having a higher SAT score than you have."

Jason shook his head. "I can't bail on practice. How about after?"

"I have to shower and get ready. We're doing a sound check at seven." I didn't really want to bring up the Clovers, considering where that had gotten us last time, but it wasn't like there was some other reason I couldn't go out with Jason after practice.

"I guess we'll do it another time," he said. He kissed me lightly on the cheek. "Break a leg tonight. I'll be cheering for you."

"Thanks," I said. Watching Jason walk away, I felt uneasy, as if there was something I needed to tell him. But if I'd gone running after him and grabbed him and turned him around and said, "I need to talk to you," what would I have said?

After school I didn't feel like swimming. I'd been weirded out all day by my fight with Jason, and I couldn't seem to get back the feeling I'd had when I first saw my scores, the feeling that I could do anything, that the whole world was suddenly perfectly aligned with me and my goals. Maybe Sofia would want to celebrate. She'd kicked ass too. Why shouldn't we treat ourselves to insanely fattening, gross, overpriced sundaes at Bookers?

On the way to swim practice, I took my phone out to text her and saw that there was a missed call from Aunt Kathy and also an email from her. I checked the email first.

Good morning (well, morning my time)! I just left you a vm. I spoke to Dr. Gulati, and he feels your mom is ready to come home from Roaring Brook next Saturday. She'll keep going to group and individual therapy and she'll be taking medication, but he feels she doesn't need to be an inpatient anymore. I'll come in for the weekend to help her get settled. Let's talk later today, okay? I love you, sweetheart! xoxo Aunt K.

I read Aunt Kathy's email twice, then listened to her voice mail, which said basically the exact same thing, except that listening to her talk I could hear how relieved she was.

It was clear that she expected I'd be relieved too. At the end of her message, she said, "Call me," and the words were almost a song.

I stood, leaning against a random locker, not calling her. Instead of making me feel great, Aunt Kathy's message had filled me with a sense of doom. I told myself I was being crazy, but I couldn't shake the feeling.

I didn't want to be at home alone with my mother.

It was an awful thing to think, and as soon as the idea formed itself in my head, I hedged. I was just worried about her. What if the doctors thought she was ready to come home but she really wasn't? What if being back in the house where our whole family had lived, where she'd been so happy once, sent her into a downward spiral? I wanted to believe that everything that had happened to my mom had been a terrible mistake, that she'd overmedicated herself and then accidentally overdosed. But what if she'd really tried to kill herself? And what if, as soon as she got home, she took advantage of her freedom and tried to kill herself again?

I felt antsy, almost physically itchy. I couldn't stand there thinking about what it would be like to live at home with my potentially suicidal mother. I dialed Sofia.

"Where are you?" she asked. "I'm opening the door to the pool."

"Let's bail on practice," I said. "I want to do something radical."

"I'm closing the door to the pool. What do you want to do?"

"Well, at first I was thinking ice cream."

"Not so radical."

"Not so radical," I acknowledged. "But then I had another idea. Meet me at my car."

"I'll be there in five."

Six minutes later, we were pulling out of the parking lot, the mild sunshine making patterns on our faces as we headed south.

"Now what?" asked Sofia.

I had my iPhone with Declan's mix playing. The Clash's "London Calling" came on, and instead of answering her, I blasted it.

Sofia tolerated the song, but as soon as it ended, she lowered the volume. "Are we just going to drive around all day listening to the music of our parents' generation?"

"It's the music of *our* generation," I corrected her. "It is the music of eternal youth."

Sofia groaned. "I want to do something," she said. "I want to do something to mark the fact that I am never. Going. To have. To take. The SATs. Again!" She screamed as soon as she said it.

I could tell Sofia was feeling what I'd been feeling when I first saw my scores, but despite the cool music and the sun, between my fight with Jason and the news about my mom I couldn't seem to get back that sense of perfect happiness. As I turned the car into the parking lot of the Milltown Mall, I could only hope that what I had planned would be enough for me to find it again.

"What are we doing here?" asked Sofia. "I thought we'd agreed that ice cream wasn't radical enough."

I pulled into a spot at the other end of the mall from Bookers. "We're here," I said.

Sofia looked at the store we'd parked in front of and hesitantly read the elaborate script on the window of the tacky hair salon. "Dyed and Gone to Heaven." She turned to me. "What is going on in that diabolical mind of yours?"

I popped open the locks and stepped out into the chilly afternoon. "You'll see."

Two hours later, we were walking out of Dyed and Gone to Heaven, and all I could think was, *Mission accomplished.*

"I still can't believe you did it," said Sofia.

"You did it too," I pointed out.

"Yeah, but not the *color*. It's all about the color."

I turned toward the plate glass window. Looking at our reflection, I couldn't deny the truth of what she'd said.

Sofia had gotten her hair cut shorter. When we'd walked into Dyed and Gone to Heaven, her hair had fallen practically to the middle of her back, and now it fell just below her shoulders. She looked much older, like a college student or even a twentysomething, and the woman had blown it straight, so there was a touch of British princess glam going on there also.

But she was right—her transformation wasn't nearly as dramatic as mine. I'd told the woman to cut my hair to just below my ears in an angular bob. And she'd given me bangs. But what came next was the shocking part. Because once she'd cut my hair and shaped it, I'd told her the real reason I'd come into the salon.

"I want you to dye it," I said. "I want you to dye it black."

The woman was startled. "But you have such beautiful

hair," she said, lifting a strand of it as if to show me. "I mean, it's such a beautiful color."

In the winter, my hair got to be kind of dingy, but now it still had the brightness of late summer. The piece she was holding up was particularly blond, and if I'd had even the slightest doubt about what I was planning, seeing it would have convinced me to change my mind.

But I didn't.

"You know how sometimes you just have to make a change?" I asked.

She nodded.

"I have to make a change."

The woman—her name was Cynthia—looked unsure, but then she sort of squared her shoulders and met my eyes in the mirror. "Well then. Let's pick a black for you."

Now, looking at myself in the window of Dyed and Gone to Heaven, it seemed to me that for the first time since my father had moved out, my outsides matched my insides. I turned my head and felt the ends swish lightly against the back of my neck.

I dropped Sofia off at her house, then headed to the Coffeehouse. It was too late to shower and change, but I was wearing a scoop-necked, long-sleeved green shirt with a black skirt and a pair of black tights that, with my amazing new hair, had a touch of Blondie badass about it. Just before the turnoff to the Coffeehouse, I remembered that half a mile down the road was a shoe store that always carried Doc Martens, and I gunned it, raced into the store, and asked the guy behind the desk if they had any black ones in my size.

"Um, yeah," he said, nodding along to the music playing on the earbud that was in his ear. "You want to try them on?"

I took out my credit card. "That's okay," I said. "I'll just take a pair."

I parked right in front of the Coffeehouse, pushed my seat all the way back, pulled off my clogs, and slipped on the Doc Martens. They were heavier than I'd expected, and as I stepped out of the car, I felt strong and powerful.

If anyone messes with me, I thought, *I will kick their fucking ass.*

It was warm inside the Coffeehouse and dark except for a few lights up by the stage. I saw Declan sitting in a chair, restringing his guitar. He was the only one there.

"Hey!" I called.

He shaded his eyes with his hand and peered into the darkness. "Who's there?" he called. "Sinead?" He stood up and walked over to the wall.

I stepped forward just as he hit the lights. The sudden glare made me squint.

Declan almost dropped his guitar. "Holy shit."

"What?" I asked, looking around to see what he was staring at.

He took a step toward me. "Your hair."

"Oh." I put my hand to the top of my head, suddenly self-conscious. "Sean's going to crucify me."

"Fuck Sean," said Declan. "It's great." He came closer and circled me. "You look really hot but also kind of like my sister. It's freaking me out a little." He laughed and I laughed also, even though I was suddenly very conscious of being alone with him.

He smiled at me. "We're opening up with 'I Got You, Babe,' so get ready."

"I'm opening?" My heart started pounding, but now it wasn't because I was alone with Declan. It was one thing to know in the abstract that I would be performing later. It was another to know I'd be opening.

"You'll be great," he promised, and he put his hand on my forearm.

I'd promised myself I wasn't joining the Clovers to spend time with Declan, and during the weeks we'd been rehearsing, I'd gotten used to being around him. I still sensed his presence, but I'd worked to pretend that my feelings for him were no different from my feelings for Sean or Sinead or Danny. *He's just a guy in the band,* I told myself whenever I *noticed him* noticed him. *He's just a guy in the band.*

But now I felt his touch run all the way up my arm and then spread through my body like an electric current. He must not have felt it, though, because he took his hand away almost as soon as he'd touched me, and checked the time on his phone. My throat felt tight, but his voice was completely normal. "Sean's getting Danny on the way, so big surprise that they're late. No idea where"—suddenly, his phone burst into "Don't You Want Me," which I recognized from the mix he'd made me—"Sinead is," he finished. "Excuse me a sec."

"Hello there, gorgeous," he said, and he walked slowly to the other side of the room. Declan sometimes called his sister gorgeous, but something about the quiet tone in which he was talking gave me the feeling he was on the phone with Willow. My hunch was confirmed when he said, "Willow? Willow? Hang on a sec, I have another call. Yeah, sure. Okay. Right after. Bye." I noticed he didn't say *I love you*, but then I reminded myself that just because Jason and I said it didn't mean every couple in the world had to say it. Jason and I had been going out for years. Willow and Declan had gotten together less than two months ago.

And what did I care about him and Willow, anyway? The person I needed to think about was Jason. Why was I fighting with my boyfriend and getting all excited by Declan's touch? Everything about the way I was acting was completely fucked up, and it stopped *now*. I took out my phone to send Jason a text and tell him that I loved him.

"Hey, Mom," Declan said, clicking onto his other call. "What's up?"

And in an instant, I stopped composing my text to Jason.

"*What?*" Declan's voice was hoarse with shock. I'd been trying to give him privacy (or at least the illusion of privacy) during his conversation with Willow, but now I dropped my hand and stared at him. His fist was pressed against his forehead, and his face was white. "When? . . . Where are you now? . . . Where is that? Yeah. Yeah. . . . I'm on my way." He hung up.

"What happened?" I asked, walking over to him.

"Sean and Danny got into an accident. They hit another car. Danny was sitting in the passenger seat. . . ." Declan took a breath, and I stepped closer to him. "He was knocked unconscious and he has internal bleeding. He's being operated on at Long Island Hospital right now."

Danny. Little Danny. "Is he going to be okay?"

Declan had been staring at me the whole time he told me what had happened to Danny, but now he looked away. "They don't know."

The miracle was that we didn't have our own accident on the way to LIH. We were in my car, which Declan had insisted on driving. He was following my directions but not listening carefully, so twice he crossed three lanes of traffic at once in order to make a turn. The blare of angry car horns was the soundtrack of our drive.

Please let Danny be okay. Please let Danny be okay. I repeated the sentence over and over in my head, realizing only after we pulled into the emergency parking lot at the hospital that the prayer was almost identical to the one I'd been whispering three months ago, when I'd pulled into the same parking lot in an ambulance with my mother unconscious next to me.

The waiting room was unchanged. Even the people looked the same, their eyes glassy with fatigue and worry and boredom. The same stale air I'd smelled the night we brought my mother in seemed to be circulating.

Declan immediately spotted his family gathered at the far end of the waiting room, his mom and dad sitting next to each other staring straight ahead, her hand on his on the armrest between them. Their faces were so expressionless it made me think of my mom sitting in the day room at Roaring Brook. But unlike my mom, the Brennans were innocent victims. Their youngest son might die, but it wasn't their fault.

Not that my mom's overdose or suicide attempt or *whatever* it was had been her fault. She was an innocent victim also.

Was she, though?

I couldn't stop the thought from popping into my head, and once it was there, it stuck. I stood off to the side and watched Declan's mom hugging Declan, squeezing him, and rocking him, their hair the same color except for where hers was streaked with gray, and I thought about my mom. She'd had a choice. Her husband had left her, but he hadn't put a bullet through her brain. He hadn't driven into oncoming traffic with her in the passenger seat. It might have *felt* like he had, but he hadn't.

Danny might die.

As bad as what had happened to my mom was, it wasn't this. It wasn't death. But she'd tried to make it this. Or she'd carelessly almost made it this. How could she have done that?

Declan introduced me to his parents, but I wasn't sure they registered who I was. I thought maybe I should leave, but I felt weird asking Declan if he wanted me to go and even weirder just going, so I sat beside him. Then Sinead showed up and sat with us. After about an hour, I asked if anyone wanted some coffee, and Sinead and both of Declan's parents did. Declan didn't respond to my question, and rather than ask a second time, I just brought them each a cup. Declan's sat on the empty seat between us growing cold.

The hours passed unbelievably slowly. More and more people came—Declan's grandparents first, his grandmother tiny, his grandfather well over six feet tall. His grandmother took my hand and squeezed it. "You're so good to come," she said. "We've heard so much about you." I was pretty sure she had me confused with somebody else, but it seemed impolite to ask who she thought I was, so I just thanked her.

I kept getting texts from people who had gone to the show and found out it was canceled. Jason. Sofia. Elise. Margaret. Jason asked when I was coming home, and I just wrote back *idk.* He didn't respond. And even though texts kept coming in,

I didn't hear from him again.

At some point, we were moved upstairs to the waiting room for patients in surgery. And then, at a little after midnight, a man in white came out and called, "Brennan." Declan's dad shot to his feet, and the man came over to where we were all gathered.

"I'm one of the nurses, and I've just come from the OR. I want you to know that they are still operating on Danny. He's a strong young man."

Declan's dad's face crumpled when the nurse said that, and his mother took a step forward and put her hand on the nurse's arm. "Is he going to be okay?"

The nurse put his hand over Declan's mom's hand. "He's doing very, very well so far. Dr. Rubin wanted to wait to tell you anything until we had a little more information, but I know parents always expect the worst when they don't get any news. So I wanted to let you know what little I could. I'm hoping to be back in a little while with something more concrete." With that, he patted Declan's mom's hand and turned and walked out.

Declan's mom looked around at us. "Well, that was nice. That he came to tell us."

"It was," Sinead agreed quickly.

"It was bullshit," said Declan.

"Declan," said his dad harshly.

"What?" he asked, turning to his dad, his hands at his

sides clenched into fists. They stared at each other, their faces wearing the same tight expression.

"He's doing all he can."

"Well that's just *great*," said Declan. "Maybe he'll come out again in ten *more* minutes and tell us nothing. Maybe he'll keep doing that all night."

Nobody said anything. Declan's parents sat back down.

"Declan, what is your problem?" hissed Sinead.

"Don't you start with me," Declan snapped back.

"Children," said Declan's grandfather. "That's enough."

Declan and Sinead were quiet, but I could tell they were just waiting for an opportunity to snap at each other again. Now was definitely the moment for his family to get some alone time. I stood up. "I should go," I said. "It's getting late and ... I should go."

Declan's parents both reached for my hand. "Thank you so much for waiting with us."

I was touched by how they seemed genuinely glad that I'd stayed and not bewildered by why I'd hung out so long. I shook his dad's hand and then his mom's. I wanted to say something about how Danny was going to be okay, but I couldn't see making them thank me for a useless platitude. Sinead and I hugged. "Thanks for coming," she said into my shoulder.

"He's going to be okay," I promised her, and somehow it felt true.

"I know," she whispered back.

I stepped away and gave a little wave, surprised when Declan said, "I'll walk you to your car."

"I'm okay," I said quickly. "You can stay with your family."

Declan stared at his parents, his grandparents, and his sister, then shook his head. "I should get some air."

Neither of us spoke as we walked down the corridor and waited for the elevator. When we got downstairs and went outside, we both realized we were at the main entrance, not the emergency entrance, which was where my car was parked.

"I can find my way," I said when I saw where we were. "Really."

Declan didn't even respond, just pulled open the door and headed back into the hospital. I wasn't sure if he was going back to his family or if he was going to go with me to my car, but then I saw that he was standing a few yards from the door and waiting.

We looped through the hospital. It was maddeningly serpentine; each time we seemed to have found our way, we'd hit a door we couldn't enter or an elevator that was for staff and patients only. With each wrong turn we took, I could feel Declan's frustration mounting, and I was starting to get scared he'd lose it when a bright red arrow appeared on the wall with EMERGENCY written on it in white letters. I followed Declan along the corridor. Just as we stepped outside, an ambulance pulled up with its lights flashing and its sirens blaring, and at first I was so blinded by it that I didn't notice the person who stepped out of the shadowy area just beyond the cement portico. By the time I saw that it was Sean, he was practically next to me.

He had what looked like dried blood on his arm. At first I assumed it must be his, but then I realized it was probably Danny's.

"Get away from here," growled Declan.

"Dec, I'm so sorry." Sean's eyes were red, and he took a step toward us, stumbling slightly.

"Get the *fuck* away from here," Declan repeated, his voice shaking with rage.

"Tell me he's going to be okay," said Sean. He was crying now. "Please, Dec. Please just tell me he's going to be okay."

And just like that, Declan whipped back his arm and punched Sean smack in the jaw. I screamed as Sean fell backward against the Plexiglas barrier.

"You are such a fucking asshole!" Declan screamed into Sean's face. Sean was crying harder, but he didn't make any attempt to hit Declan back. "You're a drunk and a disgrace, and if my brother dies, so help me I will fucking kill you, Sean Brennan. Do you hear me? I will kill you."

"I'm so sorry," Sean muttered. He wasn't looking at Declan, and when he tried to get up, he fell back, but I couldn't tell if it was because he was drunk or because of how hard Declan had punched him.

"You'd better be sorry, Sean. And you'd better hope to God that my brother lives." Now Declan was crying also. "You'd just better hope that, do you hear me? You'd just better hope that he doesn't die in there on that operating table."

Even though he was crying, I could hear Declan getting angry again, and I pulled on his arm, to get him away from Sean. To my surprise, he let me lead him to my car, and he stood against it crying while I stood next to him.

"Oh, Jesus," he said. "I'm sorry." He leaned forward, his hands on his knees, and he nodded with his head in the direction of the spot where he'd hit Sean.

"Hey," I said. "It's okay. Really." I put my hand on his shoulder. "Really," I said again.

He put his hand on mine and stood up, and I was about to say, "It's going to be okay," or something equally banal, and then all of a sudden he put his hand on my waist and then I seemed to fall forward against him and without either of us saying anything, we were making out.

My mind might have forgotten what it felt like to make out with Declan, but my body hadn't. He scooped me up and put me on the hood of my car, and I wrapped my legs around his waist and pulled him against me as hard as I could. There was nothing in the world that felt as good as this, and I started unbuttoning his oxford as he slipped his hand up the back of my shirt.

His hands were hot against my skin, and he clutched the

back of my neck. I kissed him hungrily; I couldn't get enough of his lips.

"Jules," he whispered.

"We should get inside the car," I whispered back, and then I had my keys in my hand and we had the back door open and I was sliding across the seat as he slid in on top of me and helped me slip my shirt off over my head. My bra disappeared somewhere onto the floor of the car, and I realized that even though Jason and I had been having sex for almost a year, I had never in my entire life really wanted to have sex until this moment.

Declan sat up, slid me onto his lap, and pulled his shirt off over his head. I leaned forward and kissed him on the base of his neck, a spot I'd been memorizing for weeks without knowing I was doing it. As my lips pressed against his skin, he groaned, deep in his throat.

"I've wanted this for so long," he whispered, and I lifted my head. His eyes met mine and he put his hands on my face. "I've wanted this for so long," he said again.

"I have too." I said it so quietly I wasn't sure he'd heard me, but still it felt like putting down something heavy I'd been carrying, and in the lightness I leaned forward and pressed my mouth to his, and I knew from the way he dug his fingers into my hair so hard it was almost painful that he'd heard.

I ran my hands down his bare arms, noticing somewhere in the back of my brain that there was music playing. For a second I thought maybe my car radio had turned on, but I barely had time to wonder how that was possible before it stopped. My fingers intertwined with Declan's as the song played again. This time, Declan froze.

"What is it?" I whispered. The music played a third time, and I recognized the song I'd heard that afternoon when we were at rehearsal waiting for Sean and Danny to show up. It was "Don't You Want Me."

It was Willow.

We sat there, not moving for what felt like a very long time. The phone rang again, and he took it out of his pocket and silenced it. "Jesus, I am such an asshole," he said finally. He leaned his head back.

I was still wearing my skirt and underwear, but I felt completely naked. I scrambled off his lap, grabbed for a dark shadow on the armrest, and pulled my T-shirt on.

"I'm sorry," he said. Then he laughed bitterly. "Now I sound like fucking Sean."

"You don't have to be sorry," I said. "I'm the one who should be sorry."

I was staring at the back of the seat in front of me, tracing the seams with my eyes in the pale light that filtered through the window.

I glanced over at Declan, but he was looking straight ahead of him. "Great," he said finally. "Now we're both sorry." There was a silence, but I couldn't think of what to say to fill it. Finally, Declan pulled on the door handle and opened the door, putting one foot on the ground before turning to look at me. "So, look, are you going to be okay? Getting home, I mean?"

"Sure," I said immediately. "Yeah. I'll ... I'll be fine." I tried to smile at him, as if to show how unnecessary his concern really was.

He didn't say anything back, but he kept looking at me for a long time. His blue eyes were black in the darkness, and there was something in them that made me want to reach my hand out and touch his face. I forced myself not to, though, and after a minute he got out of the car, shut the door, and walked back into the hospital.

⚮ 22 ⚮

I almost forgot to put my bra on before going inside, but luckily at the last second I remembered I wasn't wearing it, and I pulled over in front of the house next door to Jason's, got out of the car, and dug around on the floor until I found it. It was one of my nicest bras—dark blue with a lacy border. This was exactly the bra you would put on if you thought you were going to have sex with someone in the back of your car. I got back into the driver's seat, pulled my arms out of my shirt, put on the bra, and slid the shirt back on over it.

As I parked in Jason's driveway, I realized I should make sure there was no evidence of what I'd just been doing. But it wasn't like Declan wore lipstick that he'd have left on my collar. Not that my shirt even had a collar. Did I smell like him? I lifted the bottom of my shirt up to my nose, but it just smelled like the detergent Jason's housekeeper used.

My lips felt chapped, and I touched my finger to them lightly. The pressure brought back kissing Declan, and my body gave an involuntary shiver. I forced myself to stop thinking about him and focus on what I had to do to make sure I looked normal, but just as I was about to turn the rearview mirror toward myself and check to make sure there wasn't lipstick smeared across my chin, the front door opened.

I stepped out onto the driveway. I'd assumed it would be Jason standing there, but it was Grace.

"Juliet?" she called.

"Yes," I answered. "It's me." I'd texted Jason that I'd be home late; then I'd pulled up in the driveway in my car. Who did she expect it would be?

I walked toward the house. Grace had stepped back inside, and when I followed her, I saw that Jason was standing in the entryway.

"Oh my God," said Grace, putting her hand to her mouth. "You—" She didn't finish the sentence, but Jason's face had an equally horrified expression.

How could she know? How could she know what I'd done?

My lipstick! It *was* smeared all over my face. But before I could turn to look at the hall mirror, Jason said, "What happened to your hair?"

"My—" I put my hand to my head and laughed with relief. Of course. My hair. I'd completely forgotten about cutting my hair. "I cut it."

"You *cut* it?" Jason repeated sarcastically. He stepped forward so he was between me and his mother and touched my hair like it was something he'd never touched before. The expression on his face made it clear he wasn't all that happy to be touching it now. "Is this black?"

"Yeah," I said. "Or . . . it's ebony."

Jason took a step back. "I don't get it," he said.

"What do you mean you don't get it?" I asked. "What is there to get?"

"Why would you do that to your hair?" he asked.

"Excuse me," said Grace, slipping out of the foyer. "Juliet, if you're hungry, I'll leave a plate out for you."

"I can't believe you would do that to your hair without talking to me," said Jason.

"What the hell, Jason?" I demanded. "I can't cut my hair without your permission? Do you, like, own my hair?"

"No, Juliet, I do not *own* your *hair*. I just thought we discussed major decisions. Like when the soccer team was going to shave their heads last year and you told me I couldn't do it and so I convinced the whole *fucking* team not to do it. Or is it just *my* hair that we co-own?" His arms were crossed tightly over his chest.

"We don't *co-own* anyone's hair, Jason. And I didn't tell you you *couldn't* shave your head. I told you you looked good with hair. The fact that you then turned that into some kind of interdiction against—"

"Who the fuck are you, Juliet?" Jason was shouting now,

angrier than I'd ever heard him. He pointed at me, his index finger practically in my face. "You're talking about not going to college. You're singing in this fucking band. You're dyeing your hair. Why are you pretending to be this person you're not?"

"I'm not *pretending* to be anyone," I shouted back, pushing his finger away. "I made a *joke* about not going to college—I'm sorry if college is, you know, too sacred to joke about. And I like singing in a band. I wanted to try a different hair color. It's a free country, Jason."

Jason stepped back, almost as if he was too angry to trust himself standing so close to me. "Well, I liked you the way you were before."

"Fine," I said, and I picked up my bag from the bench. "I'm glad you told me."

"Juliet, don't go." He grabbed for my arm. "You know I don't mean it like that."

I shook it free. "No, Jason. I really . . ." I was about to cry, but I forced back the tears. "I really think it's better if I go now."

"You can't go," said Jason, exasperated. "You live here. My mom will freak out. Just . . . just calm down, okay?"

But I couldn't calm down. I yanked open the door and stumbled along the gravel path to the driveway. As I pulled open the door of my car, Grace stepped out of the house.

"Juliet," she called. She stayed on the porch, as if I were a deer or some other skittish animal she didn't want to scare. "Juliet, come inside."

"I'm sorry, Grace. I can't stay here tonight." I hadn't realized I was crying until I heard how high and thin my voice was.

"Just come inside, Juliet. I can't have you leaving in the middle of the night like this."

"I need to go, Grace. I need to go home." As soon as I said the words, I knew they were true. Today had been too much. The hospital, Danny, Declan. I needed to sleep in my own bed.

"You can't go home," said Grace. "There's nobody there."

I hated that what she was saying was true. There really was nobody at my house. But that didn't mean *I* couldn't be there. I slipped around the door of the car. "It's okay, Grace," I said. "I'll be okay."

"Juliet—" She took a step toward me, and I thought she might try to stop me physically. I imagined driving across the lawn, tearing over Grace's perfect flower beds in order to get away from their house. But all she did was raise her hand in my direction, and I just shook my head, got into the car, shut the door, and drove away. As I passed the house, I saw Jason outlined in the doorway, and part of me wanted to try to explain everything to him so he wouldn't be mad at me and part of me wanted to keep driving so I would never have to see him again.

23

What was the matter with me? I was losing my mind. It was a good thing my mother was going to get released from Roaring Brook, because I needed her room there.

Who the fuck are you, Juliet? Jason had been so mad there'd been spit flying out of his mouth. *Who the fuck are you?*

Well, who the fuck *was* I? Practically having sex with Declan in the backseat of my car. Throwing a fit and storming out of Jason's house in front of his mom. Ignoring her when she told me not to go. Who was this person walking around with my face and my driver's license and nothing else about her that I recognized?

I was sure that Jason's dad was going to come after me. It was one thing to tell Grace and Jason to leave me alone, but I didn't think it would be so easy to shake off Mark Robinson.

Like most dads, he had something a little scary under all his niceness. I could imagine him telling me to get my ass in gear and hightail it back to the Robinson house and not taking no for an answer. And who could blame him? What sane adult would trust me to act responsibly?

I was certifiable.

With no awareness of how I'd made it from Jason's driveway to mine, I put the car in park and turned off the headlights. But I didn't get out of the car, just sat and looked at the front of my house. The solar-powered lights leading up to the front door were on, of course, because while my family might have imploded, the sun continued to shine. As I watched, a light in the guest bedroom went off, and my heart skipped a beat at the thought that a person was in the house before I realized that someone—my dad, probably—had set the timers, as if we were just on vacation and wanted to keep the house safe for the week or two we were away.

I pressed my forehead against the steering wheel. How had my life become such a reality show? Why had I run off like that? I should have just worked it out with Jason.

But the thought of turning the car around and driving back to Jason's house made it suddenly hard to breathe. What was going on? Why was it easier to make out with Declan than to talk to Jason?

I opened the car door and sucked in the chilly night air. The effort calmed me down, made it possible for me to think.

I was acting crazy. Grace was furious. Jason was furious. Mark was probably dealing with the two of them right now. Not to mention poor Bella, who we'd no doubt woken up with our screaming.

Standing there on the lawn of my empty but seemingly occupied house, it felt as if what had happened to my family was some kind of communicable disease, its chaos and unhappiness infecting everyone I came in contact with. I pictured the Robinsons conferencing in the foyer, trying to decide what to do about Jason's crazy girlfriend. Then I pictured Declan's face as he realized he'd been cheating on Willow with me.

What was wrong with me? How had I become so toxic?

I had to explain to Jason and his family that I was safe. It wasn't fair to leave them all wondering what was going on, Grace feeling responsible for me as if I were some stubborn, explosive teenager who she'd accidentally adopted.

But I couldn't deal with Jason and his perfect, perfect family. Maybe I *was* crazy, but they made me feel even crazier than I was.

Leaning back against my car, I took my phone out of my bag and hit his number on speed dial. He picked up on the first ring.

"Juliet? Is everything okay?"

The voice was so familiar it hurt. *I'm sorry,* I wanted to say. *I'm sorry that everyone but me seems to know how to keep it together. I'm sorry you can't be proud of me the way you used to be.*

But I knew that if I made a scene, I'd scare him and he'd send me back to Jason's. Instead, I took a deep breath and got myself under control.

"Hi, Dad," I said calmly. "I need your help."

"Okay," he said, not sounding at all angry that I'd called and woken him up at one o'clock in the morning. "Tell me what you need me to do."

I'd had to promise my dad I wouldn't "do anything" (i.e., try to kill myself), and in exchange for that, he agreed to tell the Robinsons that it was okay for me to spend the night at the house. When I hung up the phone, I walked across the lawn and up the front steps. It almost surprised me that after everything that had happened the key still slipped easily into the lock and opened the door.

I stepped into the foyer. The house was spotless. Like the gardener, the cleaning woman must have kept coming. I figured my dad was paying her, and I wondered if it was strange to him to be writing the same checks he'd been writing for years to keep a house running that he was never coming back to.

I wandered into the living room and then into the den, flipping on the lights as I went. When I was little, the room had housed all my toys, but as Oliver and I got older, it had become a space without a purpose. The TV in the basement was bigger, the sofa wasn't very comfortable, and it was too far from the kitchen to be convenient for studying. It was sort of a forgotten room, which might explain why on the bookcase next to the French doors leading out to the patio there were still family photos. These were from a series my parents had hired a professional photographer to shoot when I was two and Oliver was four. We were still in our old house, the small one where we'd lived before my dad had become a partner at his consulting firm. My mother wore a gray silk blouse and her hair was long and loose. In one of the pictures, she and my dad were sitting next to each other on the couch and my brother was sitting on my dad's lap holding a stuffed animal while I sat on my mom's lap, grabbing at the animal's tail. My parents were laughing, and the picture looked completely candid.

It was as if the people in the photos were all dead, and when I looked at them and tried to remember what it felt like to be part of that perfect, beautiful family, all that happened was that I felt more and more alone, as if I were the last surviving human after an earth-wide apocalypse. The feeling was so intense that when my phone rang, the noise startled me and I dropped it.

Even more shocking than the ringing was the person who was calling me.

I picked up.

"Oliver?" When was the last time my brother had called me? He texted me sometimes, sure. But he never called. And definitely not in the middle of the night.

"Hey," he said. "Dad texted me you were at the house. He asked me to call you if I was up."

"Really?" That my dad would suggest my brother call me felt like more evidence that he didn't know me very well.

"Is it weird?" I thought he meant his calling me, but then he added, "Being there alone?"

"It's . . . I don't know." I looked around the unused room, the pussy willows artfully arranged in the vase by the French doors, the stone tile in front of the fireplace. "It's how it always was. It's . . . you know. Perfect." I'd crossed the room, and now I looked back at the photographs on the mantel. "We were so happy, Oliver. What happened?" My eyes stung.

"Oh, Juliet . . ." He sounded impatient, and I was sure he was sorry he'd called. I expected him to snap at me and tell me to grow up, but instead he said, "I'm sorry. I know you feel that way, and I don't want to be an asshole, but I just don't think we were so happy."

I was the one who snapped. "How can you say that? You always say that!" I was crying now, but I didn't want Oliver to know. Crying felt like admitting defeat.

He sighed. "Look, do you want to talk about this or do you want to yell at me?"

I didn't know if I wanted to talk about it, but I didn't want him to hang up the phone and leave me alone in our empty, purposeless den. "I want to talk about it," I said quietly.

"Well . . ." There was an uncharacteristic pause, and

when he started talking, he spoke slowly, as if he were picking his words with care. "I guess I just don't get what was so happy about our family. Dad was always traveling for work or getting home from the city at midnight. . . . Mom was always, you know, *organizing* everything." When he said that, we both laughed. "It was weird. And even when they started counseling—"

I almost dropped the phone. "They were in *counseling?*"

"You knew that!"

"Um, no I didn't."

"What did you think they were doing on Tuesday nights?"

I knew exactly what my parents had done on Tuesdays. "They were having date night."

Oliver didn't say anything.

"Weren't they?"

He sighed again. Sometimes it felt like I'd been listening to my brother sigh at my stupidity since the womb. "Juliet, I'm sorry, but I just don't think they were very happy together."

"Do you think . . ." I had to swallow over the lump in my throat before I could ask the next question. "Do you think he was having an affair?" I remembered my lunch with my dad over the summer, how I'd had the same thought then but hadn't voiced it.

Oliver didn't answer right away. "I don't think so," he said finally. "But they weren't really . . . together. Mom was always playing tennis and wanting to redo stuff in the house. And then she'd talk about going back to work, but she wouldn't do it."

I was instantly on the defensive. "So you're saying it's her fault?"

"That's what I'm *not* saying," Oliver yelled, and it felt oddly good to hear my always-in-control brother lose his temper. "I'm trying to get you to see that it was no one thing or one person. It was everything. Dad was trying to make all this money. Mom was trying to have the perfect family. I was trying to be the perfect student. *You* were trying to be the perfect student. But was anyone happy? Apparently not."

I swiped at my nose with the hem of my skirt. "I feel like you're saying that everything I thought was true about my life was a lie."

"It wasn't a *lie*," Oliver said, calmer now. "It just wasn't what you thought it was."

I slid down against the cool plaster wall, suddenly too tired to keep talking. "I should go to sleep."

"Yeah," said Oliver. "Me too." But neither of us made a move to hang up. I leaned my head back, thinking about Oliver. Someday he'd be grown up. We both would. And one day we'd be old and our parents would be dead, and he'd be the only person who'd known me my whole life.

I couldn't figure out how to say what I was thinking without sounding like a cheesy ass. Finally I settled on, "I'm glad you called me," and then, scared that he'd tease me for my sincerity, I added quickly, "Even if all you managed to do was destroy my few remaining illusions about my childhood."

He chuckled. "Hey, what are big brothers for?" When I didn't answer right away, he said, "I'm glad I called too. Sleep well, Juliet."

"Sleep well, Ollie."

But when I went upstairs, I couldn't fall asleep. Every sound made me sure someone was breaking into the house, and after an hour there was so much adrenaline pumping through my system, I could have wrestled a wild animal to the ground with my bare hands. At three a.m., I got a text from Sinead. *danny in recovery going 2 be ok.* I put on my clothes, went downstairs, set the alarm code, and locked the door behind me.

The house was dark. I let myself in, disarming and then rearming the front door. I held my breath, but my coming in didn't seem to have woken anyone. I climbed the stairs silently, like a burglar. Jason's door was closed, but I didn't knock, just pushed it open as stealthily as I'd done everything else since pulling up in his driveway with my headlights off.

The room was cold. Jason loved fresh air, and while the windows in the rest of the house were shut and locked, his were wide open. His shades weren't pulled down all the way, and there was enough light that I could see him lying on his back, his hair tousled, the comforter bunched up around his knees because he untucked the sheets at the bottom so—as he put it—his feet could roam free.

I climbed into his bed, smelling the familiar combination of soap and shampoo and laundry detergent and wrapping my chilly body against his warm one.

"J?" he asked sleepily.

"Shhh," I said, kissing him.

"Where did you come from?" he asked, running his hand along my side.

"Shhh," I said again, kissing his neck. "I'm sorry."

"'T's okay," he said, the words muffled by his pillow. "I'm sorry too."

Later, after Jason had fallen asleep, I lay beside him, watching the shadows of the trees dance on the back of the shades. Deep inside me, something felt broken. Getting a perfect score on my SATs hadn't fixed it. Dyeing my hair hadn't fixed it. Talking to my brother hadn't fixed it. Sex with Jason hadn't fixed it.

And as I lay there, with Jason breathing quietly next to me, I thought that maybe college would fix it. Maybe next year, if I was a freshman at Harvard, I'd feel whole in some way I could only imagine now.

But even as I thought that, I couldn't help wondering if maybe some things, once they're broken, can never be made whole again.

24

Monday morning right before school, Jason and I sent our Harvard applications in at the same time. We celebrated with really disgusting chocolate buns at Jaybo's. As soon as we finished eating them, we both vowed never to eat another chocolate bun from Jaybo's, which was what we always did after we ate a Jaybo's chocolate bun. Even being nauseated felt good somehow—familiar and normal. Nothing like the crazy drama of Friday night.

"We're gonna get in, J," Jason said as we pulled into the parking lot at school. "I can feel it."

"Do not jinx it." I put my hand over his mouth.

He kissed my palm. "That's for luck," he said. He took his keys out of the ignition and turned to open the door.

"Wait," I said.

He swiveled his head back to look at me. "What?"

"I have to tell you something," I said. This weekend had been too insane—Declan, running away to my house, running back to Jason's. I was keeping too many secrets.

It was time to come clean. Maybe not about all of them. But at least about one of them.

He gestured at the clock on the dashboard; we had less than five minutes to get to class. "Can you tell me while we walk inside?"

My hands were in my lap, and I moved them together, nervously washing one with the other. It was now or never, and it couldn't be never. Before I could lose my nerve or let Jason convince me to wait, I opened my mouth and blurted the whole thing out at once. "My mom was taking pills and drinking even before my dad left. The doctors think she might not have tried to kill herself. She might have just . . . taken too much." I couldn't quite bring myself to say *OD'd*.

"Jesus." Jason let out a low whistle and put his hand on mine. "Did you just find this out?"

I shook my head. "Not exactly. I've known for a while. Since the night she went to the hospital, actually." I couldn't bring myself to meet his eyes, so I just kept staring at my lap, where our hands were joined.

"Wait, you've known for months?"

I nodded stiffly, still studying our hands. Jason had a Band-Aid on his thumb, and I had no idea how he'd gotten hurt or

259

when. We lived in the same house. Except for when we were asleep, we'd been together constantly for the past forty-eight hours. Yet somehow, I hadn't noticed him wearing a Band-Aid.

Suddenly trying to know another person felt like an impossible task.

"Why didn't you tell me?" His voice was soft. Surprised or hurt, I couldn't tell.

I didn't answer right away. Usually Jason offered answers when I was quiet, but this morning he just sat there. I tried to find the words to explain why I'd kept silent about my mom. "It just felt gross." I looked out the window. "And I thought you'd judge her. And me."

"Ouch."

I turned to face him. "Sorry. I'm sorry. I should have given you the benefit of the doubt." Now I leaned across the seat and put my arms around him. "I love you, J. And I'm sorry I've been acting so crazy lately." His shoulders, his lips, his hands. Everything about him was so familiar. My father and my brother and my mother had become strangers, but Jason hadn't. I didn't just love him. Maybe I didn't know how he'd hurt his finger, but I knew him. And he knew me. And we loved each other.

"Hey, easy. Easy. It's okay." He let me kiss him for a minute before he pulled away. "No more secrets, okay?"

For a second, as we looked at each other, I considered telling Jason what had happened with Declan. The possibility of letting everything I'd been keeping bottled up inside me escape, of there really being no more secrets between us, was almost too tempting to refuse. But I knew I couldn't. Jason would never forgive me, and the thought of Jason not forgiving me was more than I could bear.

Instead, I nodded. "No more secrets," I echoed.

He kissed me. "Come on," he said, "we're gonna be late."

We walked into the building holding hands, our fight a million miles away. The sad, empty feeling I'd had lying next to Jason Friday night was gone, and everything felt like maybe it was all really going to be okay.

The one thing that kept my morning from actually *being* okay was my dread of running into Declan. My only hope was that he was as eager to avoid me as I was to avoid him. I had reason for hoping that—he hadn't exactly not cared that Willow had called while we were making out. Clearly his loyalties lay with her. He'd just had a moment of insanity that had led him into my arms. I'd had one also. Well, two if you counted the night this summer. Two moments of insanity versus four years of true love.

Like it was even a contest.

On my way to calc second period, I turned the corner and almost ran smack into a guy I was sure for a second was Declan. He was tall and thin and he had dark hair, and in the instant between seeing him and realizing he wasn't Declan, I felt my heart slam against my rib cage so hard I couldn't catch my breath. Luckily I was alone—no way would I have been able to hide my panic from Sofia or Jason.

During math I decided to cut English even though I'd never cut a class in my life. I'd go to the nurse and tell her I was feeling sick. It wasn't a lie, either. The thought of walking into English class and facing Declan *did* make me feel sick. And there was no way I was going to be able to go to band practice later, that was for sure. I had to tell Sinead I wouldn't be singing with the Clovers anymore.

The thought of not singing with the band made me feel as if I were standing in a room in which someone had just turned the lights off. I remembered driving with Jason while I blasted Blondie, how powerful and kick-ass I'd felt while the music played. Well, I'd certainly fucked *that* up. The one thing in my life I really loved, the one thing I was doing just because I wanted to do it. And now I couldn't do it anymore. Sitting in the courtyard with Elise and Sofia and Margaret at morning break, it was all I could do to feign interest in the conversation when the only thing I wanted to do was put my head on my knees and bawl.

"Read it out loud," said Margaret.

After the Clovers' show was canceled, Lucas and Sofia had talked for what Sofia defined vaguely as "a really long time," and now she and Elise and Margaret were trying to figure out what the cryptic text he'd sent Sunday afternoon meant.

"'We should hang out,'" Elise read off the screen. She looked up at Sofia. "It means he wants to have sex with you."

"God, Elise, you are *such* a romantic," Margaret said. Next to her sat Sofia, who was buzzing with nervous energy, bouncing her knees like she sometimes did before a meet.

"Well, what do *you* think it means?" Elise turned to me. "That he wants to marry her?"

"Those are her options, Elise?" I asked. "There's no middle ground?"

A shadow fell over the bench we were sitting on. I looked up and found myself staring at Declan. All morning I'd been scanning the hallways for him, and now here he was without any warning, as if he'd materialized out of thin air.

Behind his sunglasses, he looked pale and tired. "Can I talk to you?"

My chest ached from my heart's anxious thumping, and I felt dizzy. But I managed to keep my voice normal. "Yeah," I said. "Sure." I was scared that Elise or Sofia or Margaret would immediately guess something was up between us. I forced myself not to turn around and see if they were exchanging a look as we walked away.

I followed Declan out of the courtyard and into the lobby, which was oddly deserted. He stopped at the door of the theater and pulled it open.

"I don't think we're supposed to be in there." I doubted I'd ever been this scared in my life. My voice sounded breathy and strange, and my lips shook; my mouth had to work hard to form the words I spoke.

"Probably not." He held the door open, and after a beat I walked through it.

It was hushed in the theater, the velvet seats that were part of the renovation the school did the summer before my freshman year absorbing every sound except that of my deafening heartbeat.

Declan sat on the arm of an aisle seat. It was dark, but there was an exit sign over the door that let me make out his silhouette. I felt painfully conscious of being in this dimly lit, silent space, alone with him.

"I broke up with Willow."

"*What?!* Why?" My pulse was so loud in my ears that for a second I thought I'd misheard him.

"Why?" he echoed, and now it was light enough that I could see his raised eyebrow. "Seriously?"

His face was so familiar to me.

When had it gotten so familiar?

"Declan," I said, trying to keep the terror from my voice, "I didn't mean for you to break up with Willow."

Instead of answering, Declan reached forward and took my hands in his. And it felt the way it always felt when Declan touched me—electrifying. "Jules, this is stupid." His voice was almost a whisper. "There's something here. It's not just about hooking up. Let's see what happens if we give it some room to breathe."

That was what it suddenly felt like I didn't have room to do—breathe. "Declan, I'm sorry. I'm going out with Jason." But I didn't pull my hand away.

He laughed. "I'm not an idiot, Jules. I know you have a boyfriend." Now his fingers were intertwined with mine.

"No, Declan, he's not just a boyfriend. He's—I'm . . . we've been going out for four years. I'm living with his family right now." I was whispering too, even though there was no one else in the theater.

"You are? I didn't know that." He pulled me toward him gently. "Why?"

Don't. Don't. I let my body sink against his, and it felt just like it had in the car. Right. It felt so right. "Declan, there are a lot of things you don't know about me." My voice was breathless.

"I know," he said into my neck. Without meaning to, I tilted my head slightly, as if to give him better access to my skin. "And I'd really like to learn what they are." His lips were so close that his words were kisses.

My mother's in a mental hospital. She might be addicted to prescription medication. Either that or she's suicidal. I'm having a nervous breakdown. I'm totally alienated from my entire nuclear family. The only stable thing in my life is my boyfriend.

My boyfriend.

I jerked away, pulling my hands and neck free of Declan's fingers and lips. It was painful, like tearing something out by the roots.

His hand hung in the air between us.

"I'm sorry," I said, breathing too heavily, almost panting.

"I've been a total bitch. I realize that. And I don't blame you for hating me. But I can't break up with Jason." I stepped into the aisle and turned to go, every inch of my skin itching to stay and let Declan touch me more.

"Juliet, that's crazy," Declan protested.

I didn't turn around. "No, Declan. *This* is crazy."

"Juliet!" There was the creak of the seat. Was he standing up?

"I have to go."

The warning bell hadn't even rung, but I blew through the door of the theater and across the lobby as if I were already late for class. I was prepared to ignore Declan if he called after me, but he didn't.

At lunch I told Elise and Sofia I had to take care of some band business, and I texted Sinead to meet me by the fountain near the main entrance. I found her sitting cross-legged on a low wall across the walkway from the main doors. She was wearing a gray sweater and a bright yellow skirt, and she looked as beautiful as if she were a model on break from a photo shoot. I hated how she looked—how she looked like a girl version of Declan.

"Hey," I said. "How's Danny?"

"Better." She slid her sunglasses onto the top of her head. "He had to have his spleen removed, though."

"My brother had to have his spleen removed. And he's fine

now." It was true. When he was in eighth grade, Oliver had had a bike accident and he'd needed emergency surgery.

"Really?" She looked unconvinced, as if I might be making the story up to comfort her. "I never heard of anyone having a spleen removed."

"Maybe it's an American thing." Up close, I could see the dark circles under her eyes, and I felt a pang of guilt for what I was about to do. She'd had a shitty weekend. She didn't need more bad news.

"Oh." She smiled. "Well, I feel better now. Anyway, the doctors said he's going to be home in a week or so. And he'll be playing the drums again by Christmas. So, you know, the new and improved Clovers will rise again." She didn't mention Sean by name, but I understood what she meant. Even if Danny was going to be okay, Sean was out of the band.

"Yeah, the band's kind of what I wanted to talk to you about." I ran my thumb over my lips nervously. "I can't be in the Clovers anymore, Sinead."

"What?" I'd never seen anyone's jaw drop before, but Sinead's mouth literally hung open briefly before she snapped it shut. "What are you talking about?"

I shook my head. "I just can't do it. I'm really busy. I'm going to get a Latin tutor, and if I don't get into Harvard I'm going to have to work on all of my other applications. It's just not a good time for me. And anyway, if Sean's not going to be in the band because of . . . everything, well"—I snapped my fingers and tried to sound enthusiastic—"there goes the Sean factor."

"I don't understand."

Why was she acting like my quitting the band was even worse than Danny's having his spleen removed? Guilt made me mad, and my voice was harsh. "I can't do it, Sinead." I took a step backward.

Her face was the picture of hurt bewilderment, as if I were a dog that had growled at her when she'd bent down to pet me. "I thought we were having so much fun."

"I just don't have time for fun right now," I said. "I'm sorry."

I didn't cut English. I was too scared Mr. Burton might not accept that I was at the nurse and would take points off my grade. I stood across the hall from the door to the room, and I waited until Declan went in. Then I took a deep breath and held it, like the next forty-five minutes were a deep body of water I had to cross. Jason was waiting for me in our usual spot, and I slid into the seat next to him without raising my eyes to look at anyone else in the room. As soon as I sat down, I wondered if Declan was right behind me. And then I reminded myself that it didn't matter, that Declan wasn't someone I had to think about anymore, and I took out my notebook and faced the front of the room.

25

When my mom stepped out of the car on Saturday morning, she had her hair up in a ponytail. The hair after the rubber band was blond; the hair closer to her head was dark brown streaked with gray. I realized that when my hair started to grow out, it would be the opposite of hers, dark at the ends and blond at the roots.

Aunt Kathy was carrying her suitcase, and Oliver was carrying her jacket. My mom walked carefully, almost as if she had hurt some part of her body and was babying it, and when she saw me standing at the front door, she stopped, like she couldn't take another step.

"Oh my God, Juliet. I . . . for a second I didn't recognize you. Your hair."

"I know," I said, adding, "I dyed it," as if she might have

thought my hair had spontaneously changed color.

She studied me, and for a second I thought she might start crying, but she just said, "Well . . ." Then she crossed the lawn and hugged me.

I was surprised by the force of her hug. I'd expected a gentle embrace with maybe a pat on the back, but her arms held me fiercely. "It's so good to see you, honey," she said.

"It's good to see you, too," I said.

She pulled away and she looked at me for a long minute. I was scared she was going to say something about how I hadn't visited her again after that first time, but she just squeezed my fingers tightly. Her eyes were shiny, but she didn't cry.

I followed her into the house. We were almost like a parade. My mom, then me, then Aunt Kathy. Oliver took up the rear.

I'd bought some flowers and arranged them on the kitchen table, and my mom noticed them right away. "How pretty," she said. "Thank you, Juliet."

She sat down at the table and looked around. I wanted to ask her what she was looking at, but I was afraid she'd say something depressing like *What a waste my life has been*, so I just asked if anyone wanted some tea.

"That would be great," said Aunt Kathy, and we practically fell over each other trying to get the mugs and tea down from the cabinet. Oliver sat at the table with my mom. Neither of them said anything, and the silence was starting to make me uneasy.

"It's so warm," said Kathy. "Not like November at all."

"I can't believe how close Thanksgiving is," I said, and I immediately regretted saying it. Surely Thanksgiving was the last thing my mother wanted to think about.

"If you come to Portland, I'll make pumpkin pie," said Aunt Kathy quickly. "I finally found that recipe of Mom's."

"Did you?" asked my mom. "I love that pumpkin pie." She smiled at me as I put a cup of tea in front of her. "Thank you." She gave my hand another squeeze. She seemed about to say something else, but she just sipped her tea.

"I'm glad you're home," I said abruptly. As soon as I said it, I wasn't actually sure if it was true.

"Thanks," she said, smiling at me. "I'm glad I'm home too."

It was weird to go to sleep in my bed, wake up in my bed, and know I was going to sleep in my bed again that night and the next night and the night after that. Even weirder was having me, my mom, and my brother in the house with Aunt Kathy there instead of my dad. We talked about how Oliver's classes were going. We talked about how soon I'd be hearing from colleges and how crazy it was that the kids who had been in Kathy's class the first year she taught were now old enough to have kids themselves.

But we didn't talk about my dad and we didn't talk about what had happened with my mom, not even when we were driving home from the airport alone after we dropped Aunt

Kathy off. I waited for my mom to bring up that night, and maybe she was waiting for me to bring it up, but in the end we just went for dinner at the Thai restaurant near our house. I got a Sprite and my mom ordered a Diet Coke instead of a glass of wine and we didn't talk about that, either. It was strange how we could talk so much and say so little, and as the weeks passed and we continued to talk and talk and say absolutely nothing, I wondered if something had changed or if this was how things had always been between us and I'd just never noticed.

26

Even though the Harvard website said that admissions decisions would be emailed at five p.m. eastern standard time, on December 15, Jason and I both cut practice that day, went back to his house, and at 3:27 started checking our email every five minutes.

"This is stupid," I said at 4:10. "I feel like they're sitting at the admissions office watching us check our email and laughing."

Jason was staring at his phone as if it might suddenly call him and tell him he'd been admitted to Harvard. "Just as long as they're not sitting there and deciding to reject us because we won't stop checking."

I laughed. "How funny would that be? If, after all the essays and all the tests and all the tours, they decided based on who waited to check their email until five o'clock."

"Hilarious," said Jason, hitting the refresh button. "I can't stop laughing."

"What if one of us gets in and the other doesn't?" I draped my legs over his and lay back on the soft cushion of the sofa.

"If I get in and you don't, I'm not going." He hit refresh.

"That is such a lie!" I kicked him.

"Ouch!" He pushed my legs off his lap. "Anyway, that's not how it's going to happen. I'm going to be the one who gets rejected. You're a *third-generation* legacy, J."

"So, what, in September I couldn't drop Latin; now I'm guaranteed a spot?"

He hit refresh. "Something like that."

I folded my legs under me and stared at the ceiling. "What if we both got in and both deferred? We could spend next year working our way around Europe."

"No working papers," he said, taking his eyes off the screen of his phone long enough to look at my phone. "Would you check your email already? Maybe they're going alphabetically."

I checked. Nothing. I closed the window. "What about China? We could teach English in China."

Jason hit refresh. "We don't speak Chinese."

I closed my eyes, enjoying the fantasy. No classes. No homework. No finals. "Can't you see us, two accepted Harvard students, one with perfect SAT scores, offering tutoring to—"

"Holy shit!" he screamed.

I sat up and stared at him. "Holy shit?"

He turned to me. "I got in!"

"Oh my God!" I screamed. I threw my arms around him. "You got in! You got in!"

"Check. Check." He gestured frantically for me to get my phone, and I scrambled for it, my hands shaking so much I couldn't get my email to open.

And then it opened.

And there it was. *Dear Juliet. Congratulations! I am delighted to welcome you to the Harvard class of . . .*

I sat, not moving, staring at the screen. "It says . . . it says I got in." I waited for the joy that had flooded me when I got my SAT scores to wash over me again, but all I felt as I looked at the screen was numb.

"Hallelujah!" Jason cried, and he picked me up and twirled me around. "We did it! We did it! We fucking rock!"

I kissed Jason and I let him dance me across the room and I hugged Grace and Mark when they came downstairs to congratulate us.

But the whole time, I had the strangest feeling that all of this was happening to someone else.

I called my dad to tell him my news, and he said if you'd told him when he was a boy that one of his children would go to Yale and the other would go to Harvard, he wouldn't have believed it. I think he was even crying a little. "I'm so proud of you, Juliet," he said. And he kept saying it. "I'm so incredibly proud of you." That night, we went out for dinner—Jason, his parents, Bella, me, and my mom. The Robinsons were laughing and making Harvard jokes. They weren't very funny, and I'd heard most of them before, but I laughed anyway. My mom was quiet. She'd gotten her hair highlighted, and she was wearing a pretty blue silk dress, so she looked more like she used to look before. But when I thought of my mother going out for dinner in the past, I remembered her being . . . shiny. Her skin glowed; her eyes sparkled. She had been glittery and alive, and she would laugh a lot and touch the people she was sitting next to, and those people would laugh and sparkle too. If my parents had friends over and I was home, I'd always hear my mom at the center of the conversation, but tonight she wasn't saying much, just toying with her food and smiling whenever someone said something she was supposed to smile at. We were sitting on opposite sides of the table, and she seemed vulnerable to me somehow. I wished I were sitting next to her.

"And here we go," said Mark as Grace pulled out a bag from under her chair. She reached into it and took out two boxes wrapped in red with white ribbon.

Harvard's colors.

"Nice touch," said Jason. He was smiling. He'd been smiling for hours.

"I wrapped them," Bella said. She was wearing a Harvard T-shirt.

Jason ripped open the paper and took the Harvard baseball cap out of the box, popping it on his head and turning to me for approval. I nodded.

"Looks good," I said.

"Open yours," said Jason. He turned to his parents. "What would you have done if I'd been rejected?" As soon as he asked the question, he laughed at the absurdity of it.

"Burned all of it," his dad said, laughing also. "Immediately. In the dead of night."

Everyone laughed. I opened up my box. In it was a notebook with the Harvard crest on it and a red scarf with a white *H* at each end.

"Thank you," I said, looking up at Jason's parents. Grace and Mark were smiling widely at me.

"It was our pleasure," said Grace.

"Just think," said Jason. "Next fall, you'll be taking notes in your Harvard class in your Harvard notebook." He put his arm around me. "While sitting next to your Harvard boyfriend."

More laughter.

"I still remember my first class at Harvard," said my mom, and everyone turned to look at her. "Freshman English with Professor Darling. If you got something wrong, he'd say"—she made her voice deep—"'Has Harvard no standards for admission at all anymore?'" My mom started laughing.

The Robinsons chuckled, but when my mother kept laughing, I could tell everyone was getting uneasy. I was about to ask if she wanted to go to the ladies' room with me when she dabbed at the corner of her eye with her napkin. "Sorry," she said. "It was just . . . a funny memory. I guess you had to be there." She looked around the table a little nervously, then sipped her seltzer with cranberry juice.

"Can you believe these two are old enough to go to college?" asked Grace, fiddling with her diamond stud earring. "It feels like you kids were born yesterday."

Grace was an excellent hostess. She meant to be polite, but her changing the subject made me feel as if my mother's memory were something dirty that had to be whisked away as quickly as possible.

Across the table, my mother sat, watching her hands toy with the blue plastic straw that had come with her drink. I tried to catch her eye to let her know what she'd said was okay, but she didn't look at me, so I couldn't.

Later that night, I was finishing up my English reading when my mom knocked. "Yeah?"

She pushed my door open hesitantly. "May I come in?"

"Of course." I spun my desk chair around. She came and sat on the edge of my bed, like she wasn't sure if it was okay for her to be sitting there.

"I'm sorry," she said. "If my being there embarrassed you."

"What?" I felt awful. "Is that what you thought?"

"I'm not so great with people these days. I feel very"—she touched a small throw pillow on the end of my bed lightly—"exposed."

"Grace and Mark won't judge you," I said quickly.

She sighed. "Yes. They will."

"Okay," I admitted, "they will."

My mom gave me a small smile. "Well. I'm glad you let me come. I'm so happy for you, Juliet. I know how hard you've worked for this. You should be very proud of yourself." It was funny how my dad was proud of my acceptance while my mom said I should be proud of it. Given everything she'd done for me for the first three years of high school, she was the one who deserved to be proud.

"You helped a lot," I said.

She shook her head. "I'd say I've been more of a hindrance than a help."

Remembering how I'd thought that exact thing while she was away made me feel guilty. "Mom, how can you say that? Who organized my life for me for years? Who drove me to all my swim meets before I could drive myself? Who packed the lunch bags for everyone?" I waved an imaginary Ziploc in the air, singing, "Come and get it."

She still looked sad. "Who indeed?" she asked quietly. Abruptly she got to her feet. "I should let you do your work. Good night, sweetheart."

"Good night."

I didn't like how my mom had said *Who indeed?* like she really didn't know. I wasn't sure what to do, and after a minute I got up and walked out into the hallway. My mom's door was partway open. I took a few steps toward it. She was talking on the phone. For a minute or so, all I heard was the low murmur of her voice. Then silence. Then she said, "Exactly."

I tiptoed back to my room, embarrassed for having been eavesdropping. But why shouldn't I eavesdrop? How else was I supposed to know if my mother was happily chatting on the phone or was sitting in her bathroom holding a razor to her wrist?

Did you mean to do it, Mom? That's all I wanted to know. *Did you mean to do it?*

It was the one question I needed the answer to and the one question I couldn't ask.

I closed my door, then sat at my desk and stared at my open copy of *The Canterbury Tales*. I really hated the book. Mr. Burton kept saying how funny it was, but I didn't think it was funny at all. Half the class wasn't even reading it; they were just using SparkNotes. Even Jason, who pretty much never cut corners, had said that if he got into Harvard early, he was never reading another sentence of Chaucer again.

I could just close the book, I thought. *I could just close it.*

And do what? Spy on my mother all night long?

I thought about my fantasy of deferring admission. Just a year to spend doing . . . what, exactly? With no classes and no homework and no finals, what would I *possibly* do with myself?

I went back to reading Chaucer.

ᷔᷓ 27 ᷒ᷕ

The first week of Christmas vacation, I met with my new Latin tutor twice. Jason had convinced me to stick with Latin just through the American Latin Exam, which was in January, and I figured I might as well. Plus the exam, which was given in a different place every year, was being given this year at Harvard, and Jason declared that it was a sign from God that we were meant to go. Jason believed in God about as much as I did, which is to say not at all, but I could tell he wanted us to go up there together, so I said okay. He was right—it was stupid to have worked so hard on Latin for years only to drop it now.

It was weird to be meeting with a tutor again. The guy— his name was Adam—even looked like Glen, and he and I sat in the exact same seats Glen and I had sat in when I was working on my SATs. Adam worked for the same company Glen worked for, and he broke things down just the way Glen had, and a couple of times during our sessions, I had the strangest feeling that time was rolling backward and I'd wake up Saturday morning and have to take the SAT again. Still, after meeting only two times, I could feel myself getting better at Latin the same way I'd gotten better at SAT reading passages and math problems. These guys really knew what they were doing; if they'd had a marriage counseling arm of their tutoring business, maybe my parents would have stayed together.

For Christmas, my mom and my brother and I met Aunt Kathy and her family at my nana and papa's house in Connecticut. My mom always talked about how her father had built the house, which was enormous and right on a private lake, and for years I'd thought she was being literal, that my grandfather had laid the foundation himself and put up the brick walls, roofed it, put in the kitchen sinks. I don't know when I realized he'd built it in the sense of bought the land and hired an architect and builders. My confusion wasn't that weird considering that when I was little, my grandfather had been enormous, literally and figuratively—he was even taller than my dad, and he had a loud voice that scared me. But when I was in seventh grade, he had a heart attack and open heart surgery, and ever since then he'd been a little quieter and slower and even smaller, as if the experience had literally shrunk him.

It was a hard visit for my mom, I could tell. Whatever my aunt had said to keep her parents away from my mom while she was in the hospital had made them nervous around her. It didn't help that nobody was drinking, which was pretty noticeable since my grandparents were big on cocktail hour. Every other visit with Nana and Papa, we spent our evenings sitting around the huge living room in front of the fire eating nuts and having drinks. Even little kids like Andrew and William got served a tiny glass of this very sweet drink called Cherry Kijafa, and by the time I was a freshman in high school, it was assumed I'd have "my" drink (which was always a port, one of the only alcohols that didn't taste disgusting to me).

Nobody said anything about there being no cocktail hour this year; we just didn't have it. I would have liked to ask my mom if she was glad nobody was drinking or if she felt guilty, as if she was somehow spoiling everyone's fun, but since we hadn't acknowledged the change, I didn't know how to bring it up. We also didn't talk about my parents' separation or my mother's stint in the mental hospital. We talked about my getting into Harvard a lot. My grandfather kept telling William and Andrew that soon *they'd* go to Harvard, and even though my aunt and my uncle exchanged a couple of looks, nobody told my grandfather to drop it.

On Christmas Eve day, my grandfather went for a walk with my mom while my aunt and I stayed back and helped my grandmother cook. I saw them standing on the lawn about an hour later, my mom shaking her head while my grandfather talked. When he came in, she stayed outside, and I went to find her.

She was sitting on the swing on the back porch, looking out at the lake. It was cold, but not freezing, and I sat next to her even though I didn't have my coat on.

"Hi," I said. "I think we're having dinner soon."

"I guess I should get dressed," she said. At my grandparents' house, we always dressed for dinner.

"Screw it," I said. "It's stupid to get dressed up just to eat."

My mom leaned her head back against the top of the swing. "I've always hated it and I've always done it. I even tried to make you kids do it when you were little. Do you remember?"

I shook my head. "I just remember doing it here."

"Well, we stopped when you were about four. It was a lot of trouble." She lifted her head and stared out across the lake, but I had the feeling she wasn't seeing what was there so much as she was looking at the past. "It turns out making things look nice is a lot of trouble."

"I'm sorry," I said abruptly.

"What are you sorry for?" she asked. She turned to face me, but there was something vacant about her look, almost like she wasn't seeing me. It reminded me of how she'd looked at me that day at the hospital.

"I'm sorry that . . ." I didn't know how to explain everything

284

I was sorry for. I was sorry that when she talked about the past she looked so sad, and I was sorry that being with her family was hard for her, and I was sorry that she'd thought she had to make us get dressed for dinner when we were little even though she hated doing it.

But I was embarrassed to say all of that, so instead I just said, "I'm sorry that we have to change when we're so comfortable in our jeans."

She shrugged and got to her feet. "I'm used to it."

In the distance, I could hear my grandmother. "Barbara? Juliet?"

"Let's go change," she said.

I stayed sitting. "We should just wear what we're wearing. What are they going to do, refuse to serve us?"

She smiled, but it was a sad, tight smile. "Who knows?" She held out her hand to me, and I followed her into the house.

When vacation ended, it was actually a relief to be back in the grind of school. Thursday, Sofia came and found me in a corner of the library, where I was frantically cramming for a Latin test.

"Dude, I'm getting Battle of the Bands tickets right now for Elise, Margaret, George"—she hesitated for a second— "and Lucas." Over Christmas break, she and Lucas had started going out. Or kind of going out. Going out enough that she was getting him a ticket for Battle of the Bands but not enough that she was ready to call him her boyfriend. "Did you and Jason already get tickets or should I get tickets for you?"

"What?" I lifted my head from my textbook, deep in my Latin haze. Outside there was a dusting of snow on the ground. When had it snowed?

Sofia rolled her eyes at me, mimed getting punched in the chin, then moved her hands rapidly in front of her.

"You're running?" I guessed. She shook her head and moved her hands even more frantically. "You're having a seizure? You have to go to the bathroom—"

"No!" she finally cried in frustration. "Battle of the *Bands*. Get it?" She mimed the punch and then the hand thing again. "Battle. I'm getting hit in the face. Bands. I'm drumming."

"Oh! That's what you were doing." I nodded my comprehension.

"So, did you already get tickets?"

When I'd been in the Clovers, we'd talked about the Battle of the Bands. It was at the end of February. Sinead was going to skip her music class that week, and she and I were going to sing "I Got You Babe." Was there even a band anymore? Danny had probably recovered. But Sinead spent her weekends in Boston getting voice lessons and Sean was . . . I didn't like to think about where Sean was. And I was studying for Latin. Making music in the Brennans' basement felt like it had happened in another lifetime, to another person, a different Juliet. And as with all things related to Declan, I told myself that maybe it had.

"What are you doing, anyway?" asked Sofia. "Are you studying?"

"I've got a big Latin test next period. I'm kind of freaking out."

She stared at me. "Juliet, you got into Harvard."

"Really? Wow!"

She didn't respond.

"What?" I asked finally.

"You *got into college already.*"

"I *know,*" I said. I gave a brief laugh. "Did you, like, think I didn't know that?"

"Juliet, look at me." She sat down next to me, then held her hands wide to show there was nothing in them. "Am I studying? No I am not. Am I doing homework? No I am not. And *why* not, you ask? Because I am a second-semester senior who got into Stanford early, and second-semester seniors who have been accepted by the college of their choice do not do homework."

I shrugged. "It's just that the American Latin Test is coming up, and the whole class is going, and, you know, I want to do well."

"Okay," she said, but she was wearing a face.

"What?" I demanded.

"What what?" asked Sofia. "I just said okay."

I gave her a long look. "It's not what you said; it's *how* you said it." I pointed at her. "The face."

"You're being paranoid," she said.

"I am so not being paranoid. You made a face. What is your point?"

"My point?"

"The point of the face."

"The point of the face is . . ." She paused, then said, "For someone who got into Harvard early action, you sure seem pretty stressed out all the time." She stood up. "And that's all, folks. I'm going to go buy the tickets. If Jason already got you one, you can scalp it."

I thought about calling her back and asking her what she meant by *all the time*, but then I caught a glimpse of the clock out of the corner of my eye and I realized I had to focus on the Latin.

∽ 28 ∾

If you've never been there, Harvard looks exactly the way a college campus should look. Old brick and stone buildings. Geometric quads dotted with patches of melting gray snow. Spring break of junior year, I'd toured it with my mom, who'd kept pointing out things that had changed since she'd been a student. The school was a part of her; she'd clearly felt a right to be walking its lawns and paths. I'd never been jealous of an adult before, but as I followed the enthusiastic tour guide and tried not to get my hopes up, I felt jealous of my mom. She didn't have to deal with applying to college. She didn't have to stand in the bookstore looking at the T-shirts and the note-books and the mugs and the bumper stickers and wondering if she'd ever have the right to wear and drink from them, to put them on her car or the window of her bedroom. She did. I'd walked out of the bookstore empty-handed, positive that if I ever got into Harvard, I'd never wish for anything else in my life.

And now I had gotten in. And here I was with Jason, walking the very paths and quads we'd be walking as actual Harvard students in just over seven months. He kept putting his arm around me and squeezing my shoulders.

"That's us next year," said Jason, nodding in the direction of a small cluster of people talking in the lee of a building. The school was still on January break, and I wondered if the people he was pointing to were even undergrads.

"Which one of us is the smoker?" I asked, as one of them extracted a pack of cigarettes from his bag and lit up.

"Okay, so maybe that's not us." He laughed and kissed my ear, giddy with everything, still drunk on his acceptance letter.

Ms. Croft maneuvered all of us up the steps of a small stone building into which a sea of kids was flowing. We joined the current and followed it along a wide corridor that ended in a lobby, along one wall of which was a row of tables in front of three sets of open pale wooden doors that led into a lecture hall. Ms. Croft got on the line marked MID-ATLANTIC STATES while the rest of us huddled by the window, looking around at the competition.

The American Latin Test is given once a year, and it's only open to seniors who are currently studying Latin. Unlike the AP Latin Test, it doesn't focus on a certain text. Instead, it's the whole body of what you've learned. Each day we'd been back from vacation, Ms. Croft had given us a quiz that was meant to preview the material that was likely to be on the exam. There was a small college scholarship given to anyone who scored above the ninetieth percentile, but as far as I knew, nobody in our class needed the two-thousand-dollar break in tuition. It was more about the prestige.

Ms. Croft waved us over and gave each of us a badge. I hadn't thought I cared that much about the test, but as I tried to pin mine on, I realized my hands were shaking.

You weren't allowed to have any food or even water bottles in the exam room, and you weren't allowed to leave once the test started, not even to go to the bathroom. Ella Williams and I went to go pee, and as soon as we walked out of the bathroom, I immediately needed to pee again. I stood with our group, letting Jason hold my hand. He was rubbing his thumb over my knuckles in an irritating way, and between that and thinking I needed to pee, I was starting to feel itchy and impatient. When they called for people to start going inside, I slipped my hand out of Jason's and walked ahead of him.

The lights in the lecture hall were bright, and I could feel a slight ache at the back of my eyes. I slid into a seat at the end of a row, and Jason sat next to me. There must have been a thousand people in the room, but even though the test hadn't started, it was hushed. There was the squeak of people sliding into seats and lowering the small desks attached to them. People coughed, and at one point someone called out to a friend.

Otherwise, it was basically silent.

An older Asian woman stepped up to a microphone at the front of the room. "Welcome to the American Latin Exam. If you haven't been taking Latin this year, you're probably in the wrong place." Nervous giggles. She continued. "In a minute, the proctors will begin handing out the exams. When you get your envelope, please do not unseal it until you are told to do so. Once you have begun, you will have ninety minutes to complete the exam. When you are done, you will reseal the envelope, following the instructions. If you have any questions, please raise your hand and a proctor will assist you. As you have been told, you may not leave the room for any reason during the exam or you will not be allowed to return."

The proctors started walking down the aisle, handing out a pile of envelopes to the person at the end of each row. When mine came to me, I rubbed my finger over the stiff brown paper. Jason reached over to my desk and put his hand on mine.

"You're totally going to beat ninety percent," he whispered. He slipped his pinky into mine. "J power."

"You may begin," said the woman, and the rustle of hundreds of envelopes being opened filled the room.

The first question was an easy one. I answered it, but then I found my mind wandering as I thought about all the other Latin tests I'd ever had to take. I remembered how much I'd liked learning common Latin expressions, translating *e pluribus unum* and *et cetera* for my parents. I moved on to the second question. To my left, I could see Jason's head bent over his test.

I couldn't see his face, but I knew he was biting his top lip the way he always did when he focused on something.

I shifted in my seat. How many Latin tests had I taken in my life? Maybe ten a year starting in seventh grade. So that was fifty, plus five so far this year. Fifty-five. Fifty-five times forty-five minutes per test was . . . I did the math on my test sheet. Two thousand four hundred and seventy-five minutes of Latin tests. And how many more was I going to have to take? Well, this one, clearly. The AP. I started counting the number of quizzes Ms. Croft was likely to give before graduation. Probably about one per week. How many weeks were left in the year? I counted on my fingers.

Jason glanced over and saw me counting. He wrinkled his forehead like, *What?* and I smiled at him and shook my head, dropped my hand, and put my eyes on my paper.

If your main verb is pluperfect, what tense (or tenses) of the subjunctive can come after it?
A. present
B. imperfect
C. perfect
D. all of the above
E. none of the above

I read it through, then read it again. And again. The third time I read it, I realized something.

I didn't want to answer it.

I didn't want to answer it. I didn't want to answer it. I never wanted to answer another question on another fucking Latin exam. I knew as much Latin as I wanted to know. I didn't want to take the AP. I didn't want to take any of Ms. Croft's quizzes. I didn't want to take the next Latin test she would give.

I didn't even want to take *this* Latin test.

I imagined what Jason would say if I told him how I felt.

He'd point out that Harvard could always rescind my acceptance if my grades dropped second semester.

He'd say that I might not like Harvard, that I might want to transfer to a different college after my freshman year, which would mean my second-semester transcript for senior year of high school would suddenly matter.

He'd tell me to stick with it in case there was a class I wanted to take at Harvard that required me to have taken the *Aeneid* AP.

And that's when I knew.

That's when I knew the truth.

There would *always* be a reason not to quit Latin. Or not to quit something. There'd be graduate school and a job and a career and promotions. In a horrifying waking nightmare, I saw Jason and my parents and all my future classmates and colleagues and mentors and bosses telling me to keep doing something I hated doing because someday I would be glad to have done it.

I got to my feet. Jason jerked his head up. "J?" he whispered.

Every head in the immediate vicinity turned toward us.

"I'm okay," I whispered back.

"What are you doing?" he whispered, and even though he was trying to be nice, I could tell he was annoyed.

"I have to go," I said.

"*What?*"

"Shhh," someone whispered.

Jason ignored him. "J, if you leave, you can't come back."

"I know," I said. "I don't want to come back."

"J, what are you—"

"Quiet, please!" said a proctor, standing at the end of the row.

"Good luck," I whispered to Jason, and I slid in front of him and out past twelve pairs of annoyed knees and then up the carpeted steps and through the lobby and down the corridor. I told Ms. Croft I was leaving, got my cell phone from her, and stepped out, all alone, into the chilly Cambridge afternoon.

❧ 29 ❧

Remembering what I'd come home and found that night in August, I still felt a flicker of anxiety each time I pushed open the door to my house, but when I got home from Boston my mom's car wasn't in the garage, and there was a note for me on the counter. *J—if you get back, and I'm not home, I'm at therapy and then getting some stuff for dinner. Please text me if Jason's joining—Mom.*

I went to my room. There was clean laundry folded on my bed, and when I went to put it away, I saw that my drawers were totally disorganized. Rather than think about how I'd just bailed on an exam I'd been preparing for for months, or how mad Ms. Croft had been when I'd told her I was taking the train home by myself instead of waiting for the group, I took everything out of the top one and started putting it back, socks on one side of the drawer, underwear on the other, bras in the middle. I threw out a bunch of stretched-out bras I never wore anymore, and I folded my underwear in thirds.

I was so intent on what I was doing that I didn't even know my mother was home until she said hello from the doorway of my bedroom.

"Oh!" I dropped the pair of socks I was rolling. "You startled me."

"Sorry." She leaned against the open door. "How'd the test go? I didn't expect you home until much later."

"Yeah. I kind of . . . walked out." I studied the socks in my hand.

"Really?" asked my mom. She didn't sound mad, more kind of surprised. I looked up at her.

"Really," I said.

"Huh." She twirled some hair between her fingers, and I realized she'd gotten it cut.

"You got your hair cut," I said.

"Oh, yeah." My mom put her hands to her head shyly. "Do you like it?"

I did, actually. She'd colored it, too, and it was darker, closer to her natural color instead of the blond that hadn't been natural since she was my age. "It looks great."

"Thanks." She slipped her hands into the pockets of her jeans. "So . . . why'd you leave the exam?"

"I don't know," I said, picking up another pair of socks.

She cocked her head at me. "You don't know or you don't want to say?"

"I don't . . ." I folded up the socks and picked up another pair. They were white, and they looked identical, but one had a pink stripe along the toe and the other didn't. Great. Just great. How was I going to find the other white sock with a pink stripe?

"Juliet?"

I threw the two socks onto the pile. "Look, I don't know what I can say to you, Mom. I don't want you to be upset with me. I don't want you to be unhappy. I'm scared of what will happen if you're unhappy."

She came in the room and sat on the floor next to me. "I can understand that."

"It's just . . . I don't understand what happened, Mom. One second you were fine and the next you . . . weren't. And then Dad says you were *never* fine, only now it seems like you *are* fine. I don't know what's going on. I don't know what I'm supposed to think."

"We've never talked about what happened," she said. But she didn't say anything else.

"Did you try to kill yourself?" I kept my eyes on the pile of socks.

She spoke quietly. Slowly. "I don't know exactly what happened that night. I know I was so sad and I was so tired and I just wanted to sleep and sleep and the medication wasn't working and I kept thinking, 'I'll take a little bit more; I'll take a little bit more,' and . . . it felt like nothing was taking away that feeling. That feeling of heaviness." She sniffed. "I'm so sorry, Juliet. I'm so incredibly sorry about what happened. And I'm sorry"—her voice caught, and she swallowed—"I'm sorry I didn't bring it up earlier. I just thought you must be so mad. You must be so mad at me. How could you ever forgive me and"—she swiped at her nose with the back of her hand, but she didn't stop talking—"how could I ever even *ask* you to forgive me? What I did to you was so awful that there's no excuse. I don't want to excuse it. But I want to . . . explain it, maybe, if there is such a thing as an explanation for something like that."

I started crying too. "I think I'm really mad at you."

"I know." She wiped my cheek with her sleeve. "I know you are, honey. And that's okay. I think I'm mad at me too."

Now I was crying really hard. My mom put her arm around me. "Maybe you want to see someone and talk about it."

"I can't see a doctor named Elizabeth Bennet," I said between sobs.

"How about if we find someone named Anna Karenina?" We both laughed, and then there was a silence into which my mom asked, "What happened today?"

"I just feel like I can't *breathe*," I wailed. "I don't want to take Latin anymore. And I don't want to keep worrying about the future. And I don't think I want to go to Harvard next year."

Admitting that scared me as much as almost anything that had happened to me all year. "And I know I'm disappointing you and Dad and everyone, but I feel like if I keep doing what I'm doing, I'm just going to be unhappy forever." The picture of my future unfurling ahead of me as a series of hurdles I had to jump came back to me, and I sat there and sobbed.

My mom rocked me gently back and forth. "Oh, honey," she said. "Oh, honey." It felt good to have her rock me like that. I felt myself relaxing into the rhythm of it, my body sliding forward and back in a movement it seemed to remember from when I was a baby.

She didn't say anything else. It wasn't like my mom not to offer a solution to a problem and not to tell me everything was going to be okay, but she didn't tell me what she thought I should do or not do. Instead, we just sat like that for a long time, her rocking me back and forth and calling me honey.

It wasn't perfect. But it was really nice.

 30

I still had keys, but I didn't use them. It felt wrong somehow. Instead, I rang the bell.

I didn't live here anymore.

Jason answered. He was wearing the same clothes he'd been wearing at the exam. It seemed impossible that it was still the same day I'd left him in Boston.

He didn't say a word or try to kiss or touch me, just stepped aside to let me into the house. We stood in the foyer.

"I think we need to talk," I said.

"Clearly," he said. Then he turned and started walking up the stairs. I followed.

When we got to his room, he sat down at his desk. Neither of us said anything, and I looked around the room, realizing as I did that I was trying to memorize it.

I took a deep breath. "First of all, I want to say that I'm really sorry for how I've been acting lately. I know you've tried to help me and I've been kind of . . . difficult." I smiled on *difficult*, but he didn't smile back.

I wasn't sure what I was going to say next, but luckily, Jason jumped in. "I don't get you anymore, Juliet. This should be, like, the happiest time ever. We've got everything we worked for. For fuck's sake, we got into Harvard. *Harvard*. You know how many people would kill to be in our situation?"

"I know," I said. My voice sounded strange to me, almost like I was about to cry even though I wasn't.

"And all you do is just mope around like somebody died." He realized what he'd just said and quickly added, "I *know* what happened with your mom is awful. I'm not, you know, saying you should just *get over it* or anything. But everyone's doing okay. Your mom. Your brother. It's like you're the only one who's not okay."

I nodded my head almost violently. "I know. I know they're all doing okay. But I'm *not*. I need to take a breath, Jason. I can't keep doing all this shit I've been doing just because I'm supposed to be doing it."

"J," he said, and he took a step toward me. "J, what's wrong? I feel like I don't know you anymore."

"I think you're right," I said, not moving to meet him. "You don't know me anymore."

"What?" Suddenly he sounded suspicious. "J, what's going on?"

I imagined telling Jason about Declan, how if I did, everything would fall into place for him. He'd think this was all because I'd fooled around with someone else, and there would be no way I could explain that it wasn't that. This wasn't about Declan. Declan was just a small part of a much, much larger and more bewildering whole.

I took a deep breath and got my shaking voice under control. "I'm not who I used to be, J. I'm different. Everything that happened to me this summer, it made me different. Or maybe I was always different and I just didn't know it. The point is, I don't *want* to be who I used to be. I don't want to be just . . . doing things to get As and make other people happy. *I* want to be happy."

"Then be happy," said Jason.

"I'm trying," I said, and now I couldn't stop myself from crying. "I'm not going to Harvard next year. I'm going to defer." I hadn't known for sure until the words were out of my mouth that I was going to say them, but as soon as I heard them, I knew they were true.

Jason stumbled away from me. The backs of his legs hit the chair, and he fell into it. "This is crazy."

"Maybe," I said. "But this is who I am right now."

"What do you *want*, Juliet?" He leaned forward. "What the hell do you want? Do you even know?"

"I want to be happy."

"Well, let me tell you something." He pointed his finger at me to emphasize his point. "If getting into Harvard early action doesn't make you happy, nothing will."

I threw my hands up in the air. "Can you seriously not see how fucked up that is, Jason? Can you seriously not see anything beyond Harvard and the American Latin Exam and just . . . being the best at everything?"

"You make it sound like there's something wrong with being the best at everything. But there isn't. And you may not remember this, but once upon a time, *you* wanted to be the best at everything also."

"I know I did."

We stared at each other, neither of us saying anything.

Jason finally broke the silence. "I feel like we don't want the same things anymore."

And even though he wasn't saying anything that I didn't already know, I started to sob. Neither of us moved. Jason sat on his desk chair, and I stood a few feet away, just bawling.

"I think you're making a huge mistake," said Jason. His voice shook, and when I looked at him, I saw that he was crying.

He's right, I thought. *I am crazy and I'm making a terrible mistake.*

But even if the rest of my life's happiness depended on it, I couldn't change my mind. I couldn't go to Harvard next year. I couldn't want the things Jason wanted, the things I'd once wanted also.

And if I couldn't want what he wanted, I had to let him go.

"I'm sorry," I sobbed. "I'm really sorry, Jason."

"You should leave," he said. He turned his chair around, and he put his elbows on the desk. "I want you to leave."

As I walked down the stairs, I thought about how this house had only been my home for a few months but Jason had been my home for four years. And then I thought that it wasn't fair that at seventeen you could make choices that you might regret for the rest of your life because you really had no idea what you were doing and the stakes were just too high.

I put the keys on the table in the front hallway. And then I walked through the front door, got into my car, and pulled out of Jason's driveway for the last time.

❦ 31 ❦

"I can't do this."

"Yes you can."

Sofia and I were standing at the edge of the senior parking lot, twenty yards from the door of school. We'd been there for ten minutes. In another minute, we were going to be late for first period.

"No, I really can't."

It was just after eight a.m. on Monday morning. All weekend, I'd been dreading this moment. It was bad enough being at home knowing Jason and I weren't together anymore. Being at school without him was unthinkable.

It was also happening.

Sofia put her arm around me, and at first I thought she was just being reassuring, but then I felt the not-so-gentle pressure across my back.

"You're about as subtle as a Mack truck."

"You don't need subtle right now, my friend. You need to get to first period."

I let her push me forward, open the door, and guide me through it. The hallways were almost empty, a sign that I was actually going to be late to history for the first time all year. Sofia was going to be even later than I was because apparently she'd decided to escort me to history class before going to science, which was on the other side of the building.

She patted me on my cheek. "I'll meet you at your locker before English, okay?" Today was a B day, so English was the first class I would have with Jason. Or *without* Jason.

I leaned against the cool metal of the lockers. "Let's cut English today."

"*And* Latin?" asked Sofia. "*And* science? What are you going to do, get homeschooled because you broke up with your boyfriend?"

"Okay," I said.

"Ha-ha," said Sofia. "I'll see you in forty-two minutes."

Seeing Jason in person was actually the least dramatic part of my morning. I got to English before he did and sat toward the back, and he came in about a minute later and sat in his usual seat. When he saw me, he hesitated, then nodded. I nodded back, thinking, *I'm going to throw up. I am seriously going to puke all over Mr. Burton's classroom.*

But then I didn't. We had class. The bell rang. Jason left. I left.

The earth continued its rotation around the sun, and I realized walking down the hallway with Sofia that I'd been so freaked out about seeing Jason I hadn't even noticed if Declan was in class or not.

I didn't see Jason at morning break, but it was there that I learned that my personal life had rocked the senior class so hard you'd have thought there'd been an armed attack on the school. Elise and Margaret huddled next to me, stroking my hair and shoulders.

"Are you okay?" asked Elise. "Oh my God, I can't believe it. I feel like my parents are getting divorced or something."

"That is seriously insane, Elise," said Sofia. "Jason and Juliet are not your parents."

"Even your names sound good together. You guys are so much more of a better couple than me and George. *We're* the ones who should have broken up."

Margaret rolled her eyes. "Then do it already, why don't you?"

"Oh yeah," said Elise. "I'm going to go out with George for three years and then break up with him five months before prom."

"But who's counting?" said Sofia.

Elise pressed her knuckles to her lips and stared at me. "Oh my God. Prom."

"Hello!" Sofia cried. "You're supposed to be helping her, remember?"

"Sorry," said Elise immediately. And because she was Elise, she started organizing. "Okay, Friday night, my house. Girls only. Incredibly stupid rom-com. Ice cream."

"Guys, I really think I'm okay. Really." I looked around my circle of friends. "You have to believe me. I'm no longer into saying I'm okay when I'm not." I gave a little laugh. "That's kind of what got me here in the first place."

"Just tell me this," said Elise, briefly considering what I'd just said. "Who broke up with who? Because if you broke up with him, I'll believe you're fine, but if he broke up with you, rom-com and ice cream."

I thought about how I'd hammered that question home with my parents. *Whose choice was it? Whose fault was it?* Not that my four-year relationship was the same thing as my parents' twenty-year marriage, but for the first time, I got an inkling of what my dad meant when he talked about their splitting up. He was right: People could want different things. It was possible to love somebody but to grow away from that person.

Sometimes, it was nobody's fault.

"It was a mutual decision, Elise," I assured her.

"Oh, please," she said, but the bell rang before I could convince her, and really, I didn't need to anyway.

. . .

I called Harvard when I got home from school. The woman in the admissions office gave me the name of the dean I had to write to if I wanted to defer my admission, and she told me to explain in my letter why I wanted to take the year off.

"The problem is, I don't *know* why. I want to not go to Harvard next year. I don't exactly know that I want to *do* anything else." Outside it was snowing. Inside, my mother and I were cleaning up from dinner. There was music playing quietly, and the house didn't feel lonely. It felt cozy.

"Maybe Dr. Bennet can help you figure out what you want," said my mom. She passed me a scraped plate, and I put it in the dishwasher. That morning, before going to school, I'd agreed to think about seeing Dr. Bennet, since it seemed stupid to say I wouldn't see someone because of her name. When I got home from school, I'd decided I would *definitely* see her because (and this was embarrassing, but it was also the truth) my mom had spoken to her that morning and Dr. Bennet had said she wouldn't have any openings in her schedule until March at the earliest.

March was more than a month away, but I'd told my mom to call her back and say I'd take her next available opening.

Because even when it came to therapists, I wasn't interested in one who wasn't highly selective.

32

I wanted to tell my dad in person about breaking up with Jason and deferring Harvard, so I called him and said I wanted us to have dinner. We agreed I'd meet him in Manhattan Thursday night, and he texted me an address. I'd assumed it was a restaurant, but when I got there, it turned out to be an apartment building, all glass and steel, nothing like our brick colonial in Milltown. The doorman asked who I was there to see, and I said, "Richard Newman," and then I added, "My dad" and I asked what floor to go to. If it was odd to him that Mr. Newman had a daughter who didn't know where he lived, the doorman didn't show it. He just gave me the apartment number and waved me up.

"I didn't know you were so into modern stuff," I said as we sat at the white table on the white chairs, eating the Chinese food

311

he'd ordered from a place across the street. It was strange to see how my father had chosen to furnish his own space. Everything in our house on Long Island had been carefully chosen, furniture you could imagine handing down to your children through the ages. This was all Ikea or Ikea-esque.

He looked around as if he'd never really noticed the furniture. "I just grabbed a bunch of stuff. I've never furnished an apartment before. Well, in college I lived with some friends the summer after junior year. I found a sofa on the street and we used that. So I guess, you know, I had some experience." He held a container in my direction. "Dumpling?"

"No thanks." I watched him serve himself a dumpling, then drip some sauce over his plate. And into the silence I blurted out, "I don't know you very well."

"What?" My dad put down the container. "What do you mean?"

"Like I didn't know that about you—that you'd lived with friends the summer after your junior year of college."

"That's not exactly crucial information, Juliet." He shrugged. "But anyway, now you know."

I toyed with the edge of my napkin so I could say the next sentence without meeting his eyes. "And you don't know me very well."

"Why would you say that?" he asked, hurt.

"I mean . . ." I took a deep breath. "I'm more than my SAT scores and my grade point average." I finally made myself raise my eyes and look at him.

My dad stared back at me like I'd punched him. "Do you think I don't know that?"

Suddenly I felt defensive. "It's what you always ask me about. It's what you're always telling me you're proud of. I just . . . it seems like that's all you care about."

"Juliet," he said quietly. "You have to know—"

"I'm not going to Harvard in the fall." I crossed my arms and stared at him, hard, across the table. I'd planned on building up to it slowly, but hurling it at him like that was unexpectedly satisfying.

"*What?*" If I'd meant to shock him, I'd succeeded. He sat there, staring at me, his eyes wide behind his glasses.

"You heard me. I'm deferring admission." I squeezed my biceps with my hands, willing my arms to stop shaking.

He shook his head slowly. "I have to admit I can't believe you're saying this."

"Well"—I gave a little laugh—"believe it."

My dad shrugged. "Okay," he said. "I believe it."

"That's *it?*" Now I was the one who couldn't believe what I was hearing. "That's all you're going to say?"

He took a sip of his water and put it down on the table, turning it slowly as he spoke. "I guess I'm surprised that you want to take time off. You've always seemed so driven to me. Sure of what you want. You're more like your mom in that way. I took forever to commit to college. And even when I went, I kept dropping out. Remember, I didn't graduate until I was almost twenty-five."

"But you always told me not to do that!" I cried. "You told me not to waste my time the way you did."

My dad frowned and looked up at the ceiling. "I don't think I said that." He shook his head slowly, as if he was struggling to remember. "I really don't think I would have said that. Maybe I said it was great that you were so driven. I've always admired that about you. And your brother. But I don't think I put pressure on you to know what you want to do."

"Are you *kidding* me?!" I was practically screaming. "Every time I got an A, you told me how proud you were of me."

"I *was* proud of you."

I pointed my finger threateningly at him. "That was all you ever cared about."

"No it wasn't," said my dad, and now he sounded angry. "I'm proud of everything you do. I was proud when you got that internship with Children United—"

"Because it was so prestigious!"

"Because you *wanted* it so much!" my father yelled back.

"I just want you to love me for who I am!" I wailed.

"Juliet, how can you say that?" My dad looked like he was about to cry. "Do you really think I only love you because you get straight As and fancy internships?"

"I'm not an *idiot*, Dad," I snapped. "I know you'd love me if I didn't get straight As and fancy internships. But you love me *more* when I do get them."

He started shaking his head, slowly at first, then more violently. "That is not true," he said. And then he said it again. "That is not true. Juliet, I love you no matter what you do. I'd love you if you *killed* a person."

"But that would never happen!" I shouted in frustration. "It's easy to say because it would never happen."

My dad slid his chair back and came around to the side of the table where I was sitting. He knelt down by my chair. "Juliet, I love you. I love that you are so determined and hardworking and I love that you go for what you want. And if what you want is to not go to college next year, then I love you for pursuing that."

For a minute, we were both quiet.

"I miss you, Daddy," I said finally, staring at the tabletop. My throat felt tight, and my eyes stung. "I miss not having to think about our relationship."

He reached forward and tucked the hair that covered my face behind my ear. "I miss that too." He hesitated before he continued. "But maybe—maybe it's better to have to think about something. Maybe it's hard but it's better."

I wanted to believe him, but I didn't. Not completely. Not yet.

"Are you okay?" he asked.

I nodded.

"Are we okay?"

I nodded again.

"Are you ever going to say anything?" He'd bent forward so he could see my face, and now he was staring at me with his eyes humorously wide.

I was tired of talking about all of this. I wanted to say something that was clear and true and that I wouldn't have to explain once I'd said it. I took a deep breath. "I want a dumpling."

My dad hesitated, like maybe he wanted to force me to continue our conversation. But all he said was, "Well, let's get you a dumpling, then." Then he walked back around the table and sat down. He held the container of dumplings toward me. I took one out and put it on my plate. He passed me the dumpling sauce. We sat there, eating but not talking, for several minutes.

And it was really okay.

33

The Battle of the Bands was completely sold out, and the lobby was packed. Since Jason and I had broken up, Elise had been obsessed with Friday nights being girls' night, so I was there with Elise, Margaret, and Sofia but without George and Lucas. Lucas had wanted to come with us, and I'd said that was fine, but Elise had acted like Sofia had violated some ancient code of sisterhood, and so Sofia had told Lucas maybe they could do something after the show.

"Thanks a lot," she'd said after she'd texted him.

"Don't blame me. You're the one who's listening to Elise."

She rolled her eyes and put her phone back in her bag. "Eighteen years old and still succumbing to peer pressure. When will it end?"

· · ·

The lobby was crowded. There were band posters up everywhere, and I stared for a minute at the Clovers'. It was a new photo; Danny's drums were set up on a fire escape and Declan was on the ladder above him while Sinead smiled out an apartment window, wearing a dress with a scooped neck and watering a pot of flowers. Sitting on the fire escape next to Declan was a kid I didn't know, but I'd heard he was the new bass player. Seeing him in the photo where Sean should have been made me miss Sean in a weird way. But maybe I wasn't missing Sean so much as I was missing the band I'd been in. I pulled my eyes away from the poster, sadder to see the smiling new Clovers than I would have expected.

Across the lobby from where I stood were the carpeted platforms of the senior lounge. Technically it was only for seniors—the other three grades were supposed to hang out in the student center around the corner—but nobody really minded unless underclassmen sat on the top platform, which was definitely seniors-only territory. Right now, for example, Jason and George were on the highest square, looking out over the crowd like two kings surveying their subjects. George had on a pair of jeans and a Hawaiian shirt, and Jason was wearing a pair of cargo pants and a blue sweater his mom had given him for Christmas two years ago. He'd been wearing it the day I'd gotten home from Connecticut after being at my grandparents'.

How bizarre that you could know someone so well and love him so much and then not have him in your life anymore.

Jason's eyes circled around the lobby and finally they came to rest on me. I kept looking at him, but either he didn't see or he pretended not to see, and he went back to talking to George. I had a sudden flash forward to two years from now. We'd be at Harvard. He'd be a sophomore and I'd be a freshman, and we'd pass each other on the quad, both of us rushing to a class. We'd say hello. Maybe chat for a second. And then one of us would have to go, and after we'd separated, the friend he was walking with would say, "Who was that?" and Jason would say, "Just a girl I used to go out with."

The thought of his saying that made me feel strange, almost as if I were disappearing, and I turned to Sofia. "I need to get some air."

"Seriously?" she asked. "They're about to open the doors."

"I'll meet you inside."

"You want me to come with?"

"I'm okay."

She gave me a look but she let me go. I pushed through the crowded lobby, the voices and the laughter and the heat of the bodies overwhelming me.

Outside, the night shimmered with cold. A car pulled into the traffic circle at the front of the building, and a bunch of kids piled out of a minivan. I heard the mom yell, "Text me when it's over," and the kid who'd gotten out of the passenger seat yelled back, "I will," and then he hustled to catch up to his friends.

As I watched them walk into the building, I thought, *I bet this is their first Battle of the Bands.*

And then I thought, *This is my last Battle of the Bands.*

I hopped onto the low brick wall and looked up at the sky, the planets and stars overhead glistening in the freezing air. It was stupid to think about running into Jason on the Harvard quad in two years. Maybe after all this I wouldn't even go to Harvard. Maybe I'd move to China. Or to Europe. Maybe I'd never go to college. Maybe I'd stay in Milltown and see Elizabeth Bennet once a week until I knew enough about what I wanted to write it down on a piece of paper.

Anything could happen. And maybe that was okay too.

Behind me I heard voices, and then Lucas and this guy Justin Frank walked by. I thought maybe Lucas would ask me where Sofia was, but he and Justin just nodded at me and kept walking. I nodded back at them but didn't say anything. Then I went back to staring at the stars.

"Hey!"

I turned around. Emerging from the shadows was Declan. He was carrying a guitar case and wearing his black suit and his white shirt. I thought about how much had happened since I'd first seen him in it at the Milltown Country Club. It was crazy that he'd been there the night everything with my mother had started.

"Hey," I said back.

He glanced up at the sky. "See anything suspicious?"

"Nope. Everything looks pretty solid up there."

"That's a relief." He switched his guitar case to the other hand. "I had the strangest dream last night. It was the Battle of the Bands, and you were there, and you and Sinead sang 'I Got You Babe.' And we won."

"That is a strange dream," I agreed. "I'm supposed to start seeing a therapist in March. Maybe I'll see if she can analyze it for you."

"Are you going to see her because when you refused to go out with me you realized you must be going crazy?"

I burst out laughing.

"Ouch! Laughed at." He shook his head. "That's harsh, Jules."

We stood there, not saying anything, and then I hopped off the wall. "I should go inside. They're starting soon."

"They can't start without this." Declan indicated his guitar. "Or this." He pointed at himself.

"Who's to say?" I gestured toward the lobby with my thumb. "Maybe Sinead's inside getting a new lead guitarist as we speak."

"Maybe she is," Declan acknowledged. "And maybe I'm out here talking to our secret weapon. The girl who's going to win us the Battle of the Bands tonight."

"What are you going to do, call me up onstage in front of everyone and make me sing?" I rolled my eyes at the implausibility of it.

But Declan didn't crack a smile. "I might."

"Oh, please." I stared at him. He didn't say anything. "You're serious."

"Totally."

I crossed my arms over my chest. "So, what are you saying? That you're going to force me to sing 'I Got You Babe'?"

"I'm not going to *force* you," said Declan, his voice calm. "I'm simply going to call your name in front of a thousand people. If you choose to ignore me, that's your right."

My voice was calm as well. "And what if I choose not to go to the show at all?" I scooted back up onto the wall. "What if I just sit here all night? Or get in my car and drive home?"

Declan shrugged. "If that's your choice, that's your choice."

His calm was starting to irritate me. "So my choice is between going inside and singing with the Clovers or making you all look like assholes because you call me up as your special guest and I'm not even there?"

"Au contraire." Declan tapped my knee lightly with the narrow end of his guitar case. "Your choice is between going in and not going in. Whether or not we are judged to be assholes for calling up an absentee special guest is entirely up to the audience. And now, I must go." He tilted his head at me in a formal gesture of farewell and started to head into the building.

"Don't do it, Declan."

He spun around. "People make choices, Jules. That's what life is. Making choices and living with them. So if you want to choose to go home instead of being the special guest of the greatest band Milltown has ever seen, so be it. And if you want to take a chance on being a rock star . . . well, it's up to you." He spun back and continued into the building.

"I'm not coming in, Declan. I mean it."

But he'd already disappeared inside the building.

The lobby lights flicked once to indicate that the show was starting. I stayed where I was as the music—something heavy metalish—filtered out the doors. I didn't go inside through the whole set, or through the next band, which played a One Direction song I recognized followed by two other songs I didn't know.

And then, in the still night air, I heard Sinead's voice. "We're the Clovers." The audience exploded, and the band went right into "One Way or Another."

I imagined the song ending, imagined Declan scanning the audience. "We'd like to invite a special guest to come join us for this next number. Jules? Are you out there?" I imagined the spotlight finding me. Me making my way up to the front of the auditorium. Declan helping me up onstage. Handing me over to the mic. Sinead counting off and the music starting.

Then I imagined not being there when Declan called my name, the circle of light illuminating the empty seat I wasn't sitting in.

"One Way or Another" was almost over. It was time to make a decision.

Stay? Go?

I slid off the wall and started walking.

Even as I took my first step, I wasn't sure if I was walking toward the lobby or away from it.

I took another step. Then another. Then a fourth. The unseen audience burst into applause. Their cheers and whistles grew louder as I opened the outer door to the lobby, and by the time I was halfway to the auditorium, they were deafening.

"We'd like to . . . ," Declan began, but the audience was screaming too loudly for him to continue. He laughed into the mic. "We'd like to invite . . ." The audience started clapping and cheering, and he laughed again. "Guys, give me a chance here." The whole audience laughed with him and then grew quiet. "We'd like to invite a very special guest up here tonight. I hope you'll all join me . . ."

Everyone started clapping again, and I quickly crossed the last few feet between me and the door to the auditorium.

I wanted to be in the auditorium when he called my name.

I wanted to choose what would happen next.

Acknowledgments

Rachel Cohn, Rebecca Friedman, Emily Jenkins, Benjamin Gantcher, Bernie Kaplan, Jennifer Klonsky (and the entire Harper family including Catherine Wallace, Christina Colangelo, Kara Brammer, Patty Rosati, Molly Motch, Sandee Roston, Gina Rizzo, Melinda Weigel, Alison Donalty, Alison Klapthor, Sarah Creech, Kate Jackson, Susan Katz, and the entire sales team), Helen Perelman, JillEllyn Riley, Robyn Schneider, the Saint Ann's faculty and staff . . . how do I love and owe thee? I cannot count the ways.